CURSE OF THE KITSUNE

by

Phil Kline

PROLOGUE

Kitsune (Kee-tsu-nay') are mythological foxes that live in the
hills of Japan.

Two gray foxes scurry down the slope of Mount Fuji,
darting from one bush to another. At dusk they trot down a dirt
road toward the thatched-roofed huts of Fuji Yoshida, between
Mount Fuji and Yokohama. An old man smokes a cigarette and
watches with little interest as the two enter a grove of stunted
pines at the edge of the village.

Minutes later, two beautiful women wearing short
skirts walk out of the pine grove. One appears to be in her mid-
teens, and the other, an older sister. The man gapes at them,
cups his hands in front of his mouth, and yells, "Kitsune." He

hurls his cigarette to the ground, stomps on it, and scurries into his house--he bangs the door shut and latches it. The sounds of other doors being slammed pierce the night.

The petite women pay no attention to the ruckus they've caused in the village. As they stroll down the deserted street, the shorter of the two says, "Yokohama won't be the same without Yoshi."

Emiko looks straight ahead. "We don't need her."

"But she was fun, and now she's gone."

"I know, but when that half-breed daughter of hers enrolled in an American college, Yoshi wanted to go with her."

"Why? Megumi's worthless. She's almost as old as we are, and not once has she gotten a man into the sack."

"True, but Yoshi thinks she can get her hooked up with an American. She wants a human grandchild."

They arrive at the stairs to the railway station. Halfway up, Kyoko stops. She turns to Emiko and grins. "You know what we ought to do?"

"I know what you're thinking. No--we're not going to America." They vanish and the sound of their voices is replaced by the slap of sandals against the deserted platform as they hurry to board the train to Yokohama.

CHAPTER 1

While staring over the pond behind his home in Michigan, Harvey Long downed his glass of merlot, took a deep breath, and set the empty glass on the deck rail. He shook his head. "I'm in trouble if I believe she was that beautiful." Then he nodded. "Yes, it has to be my imagination. Just loneliness catching up with me." Almost forty, he couldn't remember the last time he had talked to himself. He took an extended drink from the bottle and held it at his side.

His thoughts took a wild swing when a tiny Asian woman startled him by stepping through the door onto the deck. He set the bottle down and jumped up from his chair. "What are you doing in my house?"

The woman bowed, then as she stood erect, her gaze traveled from his face, down his long frame to his feet, and back again. "I'm so happy to meet you, Professor Long." She pursed her lips and leaned one way, then the other, studying him from both sides. She switched her gaze to his face. "You haven't been ill, have you?"

Harvey glared at her. "Who are you, and what are you doing in my house?"

The woman seemed not to hear him. "I must admit, I do like the lean look. I guess it's what women seek in a man these days. And you're better looking than I expected, quite handsome even by Japanese standards."

3

Harvey leaned against the rail and studied the intruder he guessed to be in her early thirties. "I'm so glad I meet with your approval, but I still want to know what you're doing here." He felt ill at ease looking down at her from two feet up, so he sat, leaving their heads at the same level. He looked into amber eyes that glistened. "Who are you?"

"My name is Yoshiko, but my friends call me Yoshi. You may call me Yoshi as long as you're going to be the father of my grandchildren."

From the door to the house, came a voice. "Really, Daddy?" A young blonde, who resembled a college cheerleader on her day off, walked onto the deck, wearing low-rider jeans and a short linen top that let her belly show.

Harvey heaved a sigh of relief. "Oh, Rosie, I didn't realize she was with you."

Rosie sauntered across the deck, leaned against the rail, and studied Yoshi. She turned toward her father. "I never saw her in my life, but it seems you know her daughter quite well."

He glared at Rosie, then turned back to Yoshi. "Tell me who you are and what you're doing in my house."

Yoshi moved in front of the glider next to his chair but remained standing. "I am Kitsune, often called Enchanted Kitsune. They have elves in Europe, and in Ireland, leprechauns, but their powers pale in comparison to ours." She put her hands on her hips and stuck out her chin. "We were around ages before those you call mortal, and we have a mission in life for which we are famous. We perform with vigor and accomplish it exceedingly well."

"Just what is the mission you do so well?"

She cradled her chin in her hand, looked around up in the sky, then at Harvey. "My specialty is guessing people's heights. I'd say you're about six feet four."

"Don't try to convince me you're famous for that."

4

"You're right. Let me think about it for a moment."

"Why do you have to think about it? I asked you a simple question, and I deserve a straight answer. What is the mission Kitsune do for which you are famous?"

She hoisted her tiny body onto the glider and turned toward him with a finger covering her upper lip. She tapped on the arm of the glider with the fingers of her other hand. "For now, let's just say I have magical powers, somewhat limited, but magical nevertheless."

Harvey nodded over and over. "Okay, I can accept that. And I expect, if you had a daughter, she'd have them too."

Rosie's eyes shined, and her mouth opened wide as she pointed at her dad. "Aha."

Yoshi glanced at Rosie and back at Harvey. "Megumi's beautiful, isn't she? But she's only half-Kitsune. In the year 1853, when I was just two hundred years old, I had the good fortune to meet a sailor from an American ship that visited my homeland."

After a pause, Harvey raised a finger. "That would have been Commodore Perry."

"It was not the Commodore who made out with me, but one of his crew, a redheaded gentleman from the city of Detroit." She sighed.

"Your last name must be Sakuma."

"I have only one name. I didn't learn Megumi's father's name, but since we met in the port of Sakuma, I gave her that last name. She grew tall because of her father's genes--five feet-three." Yoshi wiped at a tear with a tiny finger. "He died three months after we met, so she never had a chance to know him."

Rosie pointed at her dad, then at the wine bottle standing next to the rail. "So Yoshi's daughter's the reason you went through half-a-bottle of wine on a Wednesday afternoon."

Yoshi opened her eyes wide and smiled at Harvey.

5

"You drink wine?"

"Even without magical powers, you should know that." Yoshi's smile changed to a fake grin.

Rosie turned to go into the house. "I'll be right back with another bottle."

Yoshi raised a hand. "No need to bother." She reached into the pack tied across the front of her kimono, lifted out a bottle, and held it up. "I have sake."

"I'll get glasses," Rosie said.

Yoshi reached into the pack again. "I have some." She pulled out two white-wine glasses and set them on the rail. She pulled out a corkscrew and extracted the cork, poured sake into the glasses, and held the bottle up toward Harvey. He waved his hand to reject the offer.

Yoshi raised her glass. "To my future grandchildren."

Rosie raised hers. "To my future brothers and sisters."

Harvey stared at his daughter, amazed at her acceptance of this stranger who claimed to be some sort of a witch. Then he held both palms up to the two smiling faces. "You two talk as if I have no say in this."

Rosie winked at him. "Sure, you have to participate unless you expect a virgin birth."

Harvey wrinkled up his face. "What sort of lewd daughter have I fathered?"

"By the way, Daddy, where did you meet this hundred-and-fifty-five-year-old witch who will sleep in your bed?"

"She's not a witch. She's a student of mine, and she won't be sleeping in my bed."

"Your father's right," Yoshi said. "Megumi's only half-Kitsune, so she doesn't have all the magical skills of full Kitsune, and she won't sleep much. She takes more after me than her father in the practice of amorous skills."

Rosie flashed a huge smile. "Exciting."

Harvey rolled his eyes. "What's with you, Rosie? You fall off your rocker?"

"From what I'm hearing, she sounds like the woman you've been waiting for."

"I've not been waiting for anyone."

"You have too--you just didn't realize it. When do I get to meet her, Daddy?"

"At nine," Yoshi said, then bit her lower lip.

Harvey sighed and surveyed the cloudless sky over the pond.

Rosie giggled. "I can't wait."

He pounded a fist on the chair arm. "You're right. You're not going to wait. You'll be on your way to the university." He pointed at Yoshi. "And take her with you. Megumi's aggressive enough by herself. I don't want you two egging her on."

Rosie moved from the rail. "Oh--that reminds me. Eggs. I'd better fix you some. We have only two hours to get some nutritious food in you."

Yoshi stood. "I'll help."

"Both of you stop it right now," Harvey yelled.

Yoshi sat back on the glider, and Rosie leaned against the rail again.

Harvey glared at Yoshi. "It may have been a lot of fun for you and my daughter to plan my surrender to a hundred-and-fifty-year-old-half-witch, but--"

"Hundred-and-fifty-five," Yoshi said.

"Whatever. I will not be a participant in this plan of yours." He pointed at her. "If I'm going to be seduced, I'll pick my own seducer--and it certainly won't be a student."

Yoshi pointed back at Harvey. "It was not my plan. It was Megumi's, although I'm in complete agreement with it now that I've met you."

"You mean now that you've conducted your inspection, don't you?"

Rosie put her hands on her hips and glared at her father. "I don't see what harm there can be in a little innocent sex to get back in practice."

Yoshi stood and walked over next to Rosie. "Hold it. I wouldn't call it innocent or practice. This is the real thing. He'll be in the finals, and knowing Megumi, I'd recommend half-a-dozen eggs."

Rosie grinned at her father. "Over easy?"

"Leave them in the fridge and stop it, or I'll run you both out of here."

Harvey stared at the two women as they walked to the other end of the deck and whispered between themselves. After a bit of hushed conversation, they returned and faced him. Rosie poked a finger at her dad as if she were going to shoot him with it. "Okay, buddy, you asked for it. You're on your own, and good luck." The women nodded at each other and marched into the house.

Harvey checked his watch; a quarter after seven.

The sliding door opened, and Rosie stuck her head out. "You wouldn't consider two eggs, bacon, and a glass of orange juice, would you?"

"Git." He glanced at his watch again.

Rosie retreated into the house. Five minutes later when she returned to the deck alone, Harvey sat in the same chair, staring at his watch. Rosie tapped her wrist. "A watched watch doesn't change."

He looked up at her. "Where's your friend, Yoshi?"

"She came to see you, not me, and you asked her to leave; remember?"

"My memory says she was to leave with you."

Rosie backed up to the railing, put her hands on it, and

boosted herself up. "My memory tells me her daughter has your heart turning flip-flops."

"Get off there and go back to school before you fall off and break your neck."

"Not until you tell me about Megumi."

Harvey averted his gaze. "Just forget the whole thing. What's new in your life?"

Rosie jumped down and stood in front of him.

"Evidently, not as much as in yours."

"She's just someone in my marketing class--a bit unusual."

"So you don't want to tell me about this student of yours who interests you."

"She doesn't interest me. She's an interesting person."

"You're not afraid of her being a witch, are you?"

He smiled for the first time in a while. "You know I don't believe in witches."

"What about Yoshi?"

"I didn't see any magic there--just a woman who yearns to be a grandmother. She said herself, her powers were limited."

Rosie reached out to him. "I know your problem--you can't look at another woman without feeling unfaithful to Mom." He closed his eyes and shook his head.

She leaned over and kissed her dad on the cheek, then went to her knees and wrapped her arms around him. "She's been gone for years. I miss her too, but I'm alive. And you're alive, not as much as before, but still somewhat. I love you very much, but I like you most when you're really, really alive like you used to be. Back then we lined up in anticipation of your coming home. When you let Jason win as you wrestled across the room, I shivered, knowing I'd be next to swing around in a whirling dervish. That was so much fun for us and for Mom too, as she waited patiently for a romantic dance and a mushy kiss. I'll always remember those days."

They held each other for a moment before she stood. He held her hands and let them slide away as she backed off. He blew her a kiss, and she caught it. She blew him one as she left.

Harvey sat on a leather sofa in quiet thought of Rosie's memories. Eventually, he looked up and saw the living room clock showed nine-fifteen. He walked to the window and peered into the darkness. The street was bare. He started to slide a chair in front of the window but pushed it back where it had been, opened the hall closet door, grabbed his cornet, and walked to the deck. He sat on a chair and played with his eyes closed, creating a bluesie sound out of the intro to "Stardust." The fragile notes carried into the night sky.

He put the cornet on his lap and sang the refrain to himself as he gazed over the pines on the other side of the pond. He closed his eyes. "You left me, Ami, and now you're just a melody that continues to haunt me." Quiet enveloped Harvey Long, and he stared at the pond that was as still as the evening. Even the frogs had taken the night off.

Harvey was nineteen when he met Ami; young, vibrant, and alive. Until then he had been the serious one of his gang, who concentrated on school and what he was going to do with his life. Ami changed that. They were married two months after they met and concentrated on dancing through life. They weren't watchers--they were doers. Their motto was, "Get in trouble for the things you do, not the things you don't do." Rosie was born nine months and a day after their first date, and Jason ten months later. Ami died, and Harvey's life disappeared with hers. He was left with two teens and memories.

He sang the last line of the song, then pulled himself out of the chair and shoved the cornet to the back of the shelf in the closet. After one more glance through the front window, he went to bed, knowing that tomorrow he'd discover Megumi Sakuma was just an ordinary student, and he could get back to living a life free of unnecessary turmoil.

CHAPTER 2

Harvey entered the office of Virgil Pigeon, Dean of the Marketing Department at Lansing Community College. Sophie, the dean's new secretary, left her chair and wiggled up close to him. "Hello, Mr. Long," she said in a sugar-sprinkled tone. "What can I do for you this lovely day?"

He stepped back and glanced around the office. "I left my briefcase in the classroom yesterday and thought Maintenance may have brought it here."

Sophie cocked her head and added another spoon of sugar to the smile. "I love your hair. The streaks of gray against the black give you such a distinguished look."

Harvey didn't like being reminded his gray streaks had appeared almost instantly. His thought pattern was interrupted when the dean's inner office door opened, and Mr. Pigeon waddled out. "I thought I recognized that voice," Pigeon said.

Sophie grabbed the briefcase from beside her desk, handed it to Harvey, and hurried back to her chair.

Pigeon smirked at Harvey. "Join the crowd. Forgetfulness is a problem you'd better get used to. That's what I've heard." He gave a two-bit laugh.

Harvey put on his plastic smile. "Thanks for the reminder, sir."

After the dean left the office, Harvey opened his briefcase and checked his Marketing 110 class roster. He stepped to Sophie's desk. "Thanks for helping me locate my briefcase. Something else you can do for me. A woman attended my Marketing 110 class yesterday, but her name isn't on the roster. Can you get me an up-to-date class list?"

"I can do better than that. Our instructor computer can give you all the latest adds and drops." She led him to an adjoining room that contained a coffee pot, a table and chairs, a magazine rack, and a computer. Harvey sat at the computer and brought up the roster for his class but immediately yanked his hands off the keyboard and sat back in the chair. The name Megumi Sakuma showed in brilliant orange, flashing on and off. He surveyed the room to see if anybody else saw the screen-- nobody was there.

He clicked on a florescent green print-sign. A band played "Stars And Stripes Forever," and a message appeared: *Check the magazine rack behind you.* He inched his head around and saw a magazine rack filled with *Time, Newsweek, People, Cosmopolitan,* and a dozen other periodicals. Megumi's picture smiled at him from all of their covers. He blinked his eyes. The music stopped, and the magazine covers reverted to pictures of politicians and movie stars. A printer pumped out a class roster with the name Megumi Sakuma in black type the same as every other student's.

In his classroom, Harvey breathed a sigh of relief when he saw Megumi was not in the room. The tightness disappeared from his chest, and he relaxed leaning against the edge of the table, so he wouldn't tower over his twenty-five students. He had just introduced the subject of selling yourself when a clack, clack resounded from the hallway. In unison he and his students switched their attention from selling yourself to the noise outside the door.

Harvey gasped as a young woman, with a streak of red

in her hair and the hint of Asia in flashing eyes, peeked around the corner. Japanese Zouri sandals clacked as Megumi took baby-steps in front of Harvey. She bowed, keeping her eyes focused on him. "Excuse me," she said and continued her noisy steps across the room to a seat on Harvey's right. She crossed shapely legs to reveal much of them beneath a denim skirt and removed a pen from her toy dachshund pencil case. She smiled, and her upper lip raised to showcase white teeth.

"We're talking about selling yourself," Harvey said to Megumi, then faced the class and read material he had already covered. He glanced to the right, and Megumi's legs filled his vision. Like a flock of birds turning as one, his students shifted their gaze from him to Megumi and back. A young woman in the first row nudged her neighbor and nodded toward Megumi. They giggled.

"First we'll talk about selling yourself," Harvey said for the third time. After managing to get back on track with the lecture, his thought pattern was cut short when Megumi raised a hand in the middle of one of his sentences. He ignored her and continued talking, but she jiggled her hand. "Yes, Miss Sakuma," he said.

"Is beautiful day. When I walk between buildings, I notice picnic tables in shade next to fountain. Would be nice to have class outside in fresh air."

Harvey glanced out the window. "Maybe another time. Michigan weather is so unpredictable, it may rain before class is over."

"Then could move to deli across street."

"We'll talk about it later." He refused to look in her direction for the rest of the session. When class was over, the students chattered as they left the room. Megumi walked up and stood close to him, cocked her head to the side, and peered into his eyes. "I have questions about assignment. You have time to help Japanese girl who has problem with English?"

"I heard you weren't Japanese. . . . No. The next class is waiting to use the room."

"Could go to lounge across hall from main office."

"Ten minutes."

A smile made her face shine and her eyes glisten. As they walked to the lounge, students milling in the hall turned their heads at the sound of her Zouris. He sat on a sofa, and she sat next to him, so close a knee touched his. His mind raced. He moved his knee away but felt drawn to look at her. Sculptured eyebrows accentuated her almond shaped eyes--but they were amber. *Japanese have dark brown eyes, almost black.*

The floral essence of a woman he once passed on a dark street in Tokyo enveloped him. He recovered from the trance. "You speak English so well, I suspect you don't have trouble understanding the assignment."

She reached over and touched his hand that lay on the sofa between them. "Did you see much of Japan other than your trip to Osaka"

Harvey looked down at her fingers touching his hand and couldn't speak. *How did she know I'd been to Japan, and especially Osaka.* He moved his hand away and crossed his arms. "Pretty much. I taught in Tokyo for nine months as an exchange professor. I went to Osaka for one day to learn about the exceptional marketing curriculum they have there. If you're from Japan, why did you come to Lansing to study when you have such a fine program there?"

"I wanted to see more of the world, and your city came to mind as the place to go. As you know, Osaka is a sister-city to Lansing."

"I remember, now that you mention it. . . . What do you need help with, Miss Sakuma?"

"Would you like to see more of my country?"

15

"Yes, someday."

"Good. I'll be your guide and give you personal tour of Japan." She put her hand on his leg, sending an electric charge throughout his body. He moved his leg away from her. The hand remained. He placed his hand on top of hers to remove it, but her hand didn't cooperate. He wrapped his fingers around her hand and pulled, but it stayed put, holding like a vise.

He glanced up when he heard the clearing of a throat. Dean Pigeon was staring at the two hands playing tag on the upper part of his most staid professor's leg.

Harvey groaned. "Good morning, Dean Pigeon."

The dean gave Harvey a fake, two-second smile. "Good afternoon. I would appreciate a conference with you in my office when you finish whatever you're trying to accomplish with that young lady, whom I presume to be a student. . . . On second thought, I'd just as soon forget what I have seen that you feel is so important to do in view of the entire student body." He gazed at the two hands that now appeared to be content wrapped around each other, cleared his throat again, and stomped into his office.

A hefty tug removed Megumi's hand, but a cold spot remained where it had been. He peeked at his leg, expecting to see the outline of fingers in frost. Seeing none, he returned his gaze to her smiling face. "What's your question, young lady?"

"I have no question now. I resolved it while you were engaged in conversation with that nasty man."

Harvey stood. "That nasty man is my immediate supervisor, and the conversation would not have taken place if you had kept your hand to yourself."

"I don't like him, and I believe you are vastly his superior. Did you enjoy having my hand on your leg?"

"Yes." He frowned when he realized he hadn't meant to say that.

"How you say in American movies--preview of coming attractions."

"If you'll excuse me, I have to go," Harvey said. He headed toward the front door but shifted his eyes to take what he considered to be a secret peek at her. She waved the fingers of her hand that lay beside her. He shuddered and left.

When Harvey arrived at his house, he went directly to the bathroom and stood in front of the medicine cabinet. He scrutinized the image of his ruddy complexion and frowned. There was a time he thought the streaks of gray in his hair gave him what Sophie called a distinguished look, but now they reminded him he was getting old. At one time, he had been proud when told he resembled a rugged he-man. Now, he compared his skin to Megumi's smooth olive tone; her face, her arms, her legs. He felt like an old man.

Still wearing the tan sweater and khaki slacks he wore in class, Harvey carried his beat-up old cornet and a bottle of Merlot onto the deck. He tossed down a glass of wine and poured himself another. Glancing at the light blue sky over the pine trees on the far side of the pond, he was startled to see the moon wink at him. He pushed his glass away and looked again. It had changed back to an ordinary, everyday moon. He leaned back in the chair, sighed, and picked up his glass to take another sip of Merlot, but before he had a chance to lift it to his lips, he did a double-take and sat up straight. The reflection of the moon on the calm surface of the pond smiled at him, showing white teeth beneath a raised upper lip. He set the glass down.

Many evenings Harvey had sat on the deck and watched a faceless moon. Why was this one different? A falling leaf probably caused a ripple that just seemed to reflect a face and a smile, probably enhanced by the Merlot. He pushed the glass further away.

The cornet mouthpiece felt cool on his lips when he raised it to play the refrain of "Stardust." After the echo of the last note died, he laid the cornet next to his chair and gazed at the spot on his leg where Megumi's hand had rested, trying to remember the last time a woman had put her hand there. He touched it.

That evening, Rosie charged into the house. "Daddy, where are you?"

"Here in the kitchen having a sandwich and soup."

"I should have guessed--the house smells like chicken broth." She leaned against the door jam and looked at her father sitting at a table for two, with an empty package of dried chicken soup next to his plate. "Why are you alone?"

"Evidently your brother doesn't need money."

"I'm talking about Megumi. I thought you two would be shacked up by now."

"What language, Rosie." He put his lips to the cup of soup and spoke with them still there. "She never showed."

Rosie sat across from her father. "Bummer. You were ready for each other."

"No. I'm not ready for anybody, especially a student."

"You were absolutely intrigued by her. I could tell."

Harvey shook his head. "Can it, Rosie. Don't you understand that even if I was, as you say, intrigued by her, I still wouldn't get near her?"

She cupped a hand under her chin. "I saw a glimpse of life in you yesterday. Now it's gone. You didn't want me to know, but you were tied up in knots, struggling with feelings about her, even before Yoshi showed and even moreso when Yoshi talked about her. And you knew she was a witch then."

"I don't believe in witches."

Rosie poked him on the arm with her thumb. "I'll

rephrase it. You knew she had magical powers even before I got here." Harvey ignored her and sipped his chicken soup. She poked his arm again. "You knew it, didn't you?"

He set the cup on the table. "You're going to spill my soup."

"Well, answer my question."

"I only knew there was something unusual about her."

She cradled her chin on her hand. "Is that what attracted you to her?"

"Look, I've answered enough questions. Now, change the subject. Forget it."

She stood. "You really expect me to be able to forget what happened yesterday?"

"Probably not, but change the subject, please."

"I'm not going to forget it, and I'm not going to change the subject. I'm going to find out what happened to kill what would be a new awakening for you. You need someone like Megumi to bring life back into your life."

"What makes you think you know what I need?"

She glared at him. "It's obvious to everyone but you. . . . Was she in class today?"

"Yes."

'Well?"

"Well, what?"

"Did she say why she didn't show last night?"

"No."

"You're hopeless," Rosie said and stalked out.

He dumped his half-eaten soup and sandwich in the sink and watched her drive off, creating a dust-devil behind her. *Just like her mother.*

Late the next afternoon, Rosie rushed onto the deck. She pulled a chair over and faced Harvey. "She's beautiful, but now she's gone, and you didn't check. You didn't even know she dropped your class."

He crossed his arms and peered at his daughter. "What do you mean?"

"She dropped all of her classes."

"How do you know that?"

"The secretary told me when I went to the business office to locate her. It's your fault."

He stood and leaned on the rail, looking over the pond. "I didn't do anything."

"You did too. I located her, and we talked. She's in the same sad shape you're in, but she has a problem you don't have. She's on a student visa,"

Harvey glanced over his shoulder. "That means she goes back to Japan."

Rosie stood and moved over next to him. "She's already gone. She has a problem she can't deal with. She say's she's a witch and doesn't want to be."

"I don't understand what you expect to achieve by giving me all this information."

"Megumi told me she used her power to trick you a couple of times, and what she did was wrong. She's in love with you, and that's caused her to regret being a witch." Rosie's shoulders sagged as if she were tired. "She's gone."

Harvey gazed over the pond. Rosie wrapped an arm around her father, and her tears came. "Before she left, she told me something strange. She said if you knew the truth about her, you'd run and hide. I told her she could change your life for the better by staying around. She said, 'No,' and started to cry. I remember the crazy things you and Mom did that made life exciting for the whole family. I pictured those same things happening with you and Megumi. You both fit the mold, but now it's all screwed up. I feel so bad for you and for her too.

I'm supposed to go hiking tomorrow, but I can cancel and stay with you if you'd like."

He held her hand. "I'm fine. The hike will be good for you. I don't need or want any more excitement in my life. And I'm not the type to go nuts about someone I just met."

"That's exactly what you did with Mom."

"Yeah, I know. But it's not going to happen again."

Rosie put her hand on his chin, eased his head around, and kissed him on the forehead. "You sure you're okay?"

"Yes."

She backed toward the door. "I'll give you a call when I return." She ran back to him, hugged him, and kissed him on the cheek, leaving the side of his face wet.

The pond had drawn Harvey to the lot. As he stood on the bank with a real estate agent, he watched circles appear and bubbles rise in the water. The water was alive. Later he returned to show the lot to Ami and get her opinion. She gazed at the pond and the white pines that ringed it. After a long silence, she tapped her foot. "Right here from our deck, we can share this view forever." Before the house was finished, her forever was stripped away by cancer.

Sometimes he and Rosie reminisced against the backdrop of pines, and occasionally Jason joined them. Now, both of them were in college, so most of the time he shared the view with memories. That night he did so until the cool drove him inside, where the croak of frogs, splashes in the water, and other night sounds crept in through an open window and lulled him to sleep.

Harvey wasn't sure how long he had been asleep when the doorbell rang. He put on his robe and flipped on the porch light but didn't see anyone through the peephole. He opened the door. Yoshi stood on the porch wearing a light green brocade kimono. She raised her head to look at his face. "Hi, I'm lonely. May I sleep with you? Oh, forget I said that. Actually, what I meant to say was, may I stay with you. I would like to sleep with you except I wouldn't want to kill my daughter's future husband."

He squinted at her. "What was that you said about killing?"

Yoshi put her hand over her mouth. "Oh, nothing. It was a bad joke."

"Pardon me if I don't laugh. Most bad jokes have a touch of truth in them."

"You're pardoned. May I stay with you?"

He waved his hand. "Come in. You can sleep in my son's room. He lives in a dorm and doesn't use it anymore. How long do you think you'll be lonely?"

She stepped into the living room. "Until Megumi gets back here."

Harvey held the door open. "Are you saying she's coming back?"

"I don't believe I should say."

He closed the door and followed Yoshi into the room. "Why'd she leave?"

"Megumi wouldn't want me to tell you it was to get you out of her system, and I don't want to lie to you, so I won't say any more than that."

"Are you insinuating you always tell the truth?"

"Truth is difficult for me, but my last statement was true, not complete, but true, nevertheless. What is completely true, is that I've been with her almost every night for over a hundred and fifty years, and I've gotten used to being around her. Do you snore?"

"I don't know, but it won't make any difference. You won't hear anything from where you'll be. Come with me. I'll show you to your room." He started to walk away.

"First, would you do me a great favor and show me a glass of wine?"

Harvey stopped and held his hand up as if he were holding a glass. "You want me to show you one?"

She bowed her head and grinned. "Allow me to rephrase my last statement. I'd like one"

"I understand. The occasion deserves at least one." He opened a cabinet and pulled out two red wine glasses and a bottle of Merlot. He poured the glasses half-full and handed one to Yoshi, then he sat next to her on the sofa.

"Aren't you afraid I'll take advantage of you?" she said.

"You already have, Yoshi."

She raised her glass in a toast. "That's not the manner I was referring to."

They touched glasses. "I'm beginning to get an understanding of the Kitsune mission."

"That's only half of it." She took a drink. "You don't want to hear the rest."

"There you go again--another bad joke--what's the bad part that you're not telling me?"

Yoshi lifted her glass to her lips again. "Enough about us. Here's to my daughter spending a lifetime taking advantage of you."

Yoshi drank to the toast, but Harvey didn't join her. "I'm also beginning to realize how adept you are at changing the subject," he said. He glanced at his watch. "Before I go to bed, tell me: If you enjoy being around Megumi so much, why do you want to get her married off?"

"My daughter's been waiting years for the right man, and I have too. That's you. Another couple hundred years and she'd be an old maid." Her chest heaved as she sighed. "Then I'd never have grandchildren. No Kitsune has ever had grandchildren."

"That doesn't make sense. What do you call the offspring of Kitsune children?"

She drained her glass. "I'll explain that to you after I've become a grandmother."

"You're like every American mother--they all want to be grandmothers."

"Will you help me?"

"That's not an appropriate question to ask."

"Will you help me?"

Harvey perused the room when, in what sounded much like his voice, he heard, "Probably." He glanced at his glass that still had wine in it and then at Yoshi, who was smiling. "I think I'm in trouble."

He showed Yoshi to her room. The next morning when he knocked on her door to announce breakfast, he found she was gone.

CHAPTER 3

That afternoon in Marketing 110, Harvey was counting heads when he heard a clack, clack down the hall. He stopped talking and watched the door along with his students. His heartbeat sped up when Megumi walked in, wearing a very short red denim skirt. She went straight to Harvey and handed him an eight-by-eight, flowered package tied with a red ribbon, then continued on to her usual seat, opened up her doggie pencil case, and put a pad of paper in front of her. She smiled at Harvey. The students gazed at him, at her, and at him again.

At the break, two young women waited to talk to Harvey. When Megumi joined the line, one of the women nudged the other and waved Megumi forward. She bowed to them as they left the room, then she touched Harvey's arm. "Please open your gift."

He picked up the package. "Not here. It would be better if we go outside and sit at the picnic table near the fountain." He stuck the package beneath his sport coat and waved for her to follow him. She reached underneath his coat, pulled the package out, and placed it in his hand. Then they walked outside together.

He set the package on the tabletop, sat on one side of the table, and motioned for her to sit on the other. She didn't have to hike her skirt up to place one leg on each side of the bench as she sat next to him with her hands clasped on her lap.

"Open your gift. It's important."

Harvey glanced at her legs before picking up the package and sneaked another look at the knee pressed against his, that caused a pounding in his chest. He opened the box and removed a six-inch framework of four bamboo sticks with the embroidery of a smiling moon suspended in the middle. He held it up. "What is it?"

"It's similar to your Native American dream catcher. You can catch all your dreams as long as I'm part of them."

"Thank you. Very appropriate. But what if I have an occasional dream that does not include you? Will it still work?"

"Yes, but in a different fashion. The moon contains a hidden camera to record your every move, and if the camera sees the image of another woman in your eyes, you'll be sucked into the moon, and your body will remain a flat fixture on the wall. Flames will appear at your feet and rise higher each day until you are burned to a crisp." She smiled.

He surveyed the area and didn't see anyone else in sight. He placed one of his hands on hers. "You are an exciting young lady and so different from anybody I've ever known, but school regulations prohibit me from being with you other than in a teacher, student relationship."

She squeezed his hand. "That's what we shall have. I look forward to a warm, close relationship as your favorite student."

"Young lady, I don't believe you understand what I just told you."

"I understand completely. Now, you listen to what I say. We will have a close relationship, a torrid relationship, but I'll protect your professional reputation by being discreet about our lovemaking. I'll even let you announce our engagement." She took his other hand in hers, and he felt as if their hands had molded into one.

He regarded the hands. "Would you have a glass of wine with me at my place tonight? We can talk further on this subject."

"I would like that."

He wondered why he had invited her to his house since that was an improper thing to do. He heard his voice say, "Seven o'clock?"

She placed her hand on his leg. "So you don't forget me." She removed the hand, and a cold spot remained where the hand had been.

"My daughter said you regretted using magic on me."

"Excuse me." The cold spot returned to normal.

Harvey checked the time on his watch. "We'd better get back to class." They were ten minutes late in returning to the room where they were greeted by two dozen smiling faces.

At exactly seven that evening, Harvey's doorbell played "Happy Days Are Here Again," something it had not done before. He answered the door. Megumi stood on the porch, wearing a dark flowered skirt and white peasant blouse, looking more like a demure Spanish senorita than a Japanese half-witch.

He ushered her in. "I thought you agreed to quit using magic on me."

"I didn't use magic. When I pushed the button, I just wished, and the music began."

Harvey heaved a big sigh. "You're going to take some getting used to."

"You may as well start working on it. I'll be around for a long time." She handed him a ten-inch stuffed Minnie Mouse in Japanese dress. He took it and stepped back. She followed him. "I wish I had come last Wednesday when you invited me."

He stood in front of the sofa. "Who said I invited you last Wednesday?"

"Mama told me."

"Does she ever lie to you?"

"Quite often. Kitsune have no respect for veracity, but you can tell when Mama hides the truth. She places a hand over her mouth like this." Megumi touched her upper lip.

"What about you?"

Megumi kept the hand on her lip. "I seldom lie and then only about important things."

He backed up to the sofa. "Would you like to sit?"

She moved even closer to him. "No."

He held Minnie Mouse up in front of her. "What's the purpose of Minnie?"

"So Mickey has someone to love."

"I mean why did you give Minnie to me?"

She smiled. "To keep you company if I ever have to leave you again."

"Why would you have to leave me again?"

She looked up at him. "I won't unless it's absolutely necessary. I didn't follow you all the way from Osaka just to leave you."

"Why did you leave last week?"

"Because of our differences, I had to go away to determine if I'd be the perfect wife for you. But during the flight to Tokyo, I decided our being different would be an asset rather than a problem." She took Minnie from Harvey's hand and dropped her on the sofa. She moved even closer. "I must admit I missed you almost as much as you missed me. You see, I'm like normal. I inherited that from my father."

"Why do you refer to yourself as being like normal?"

"I'm one of a kind." She placed a fist under her chin. "I know who you are, but I'm not quite sure about myself."

"But you do have magical powers?"

She slid her hand across his cheek. "Only the few most

women have, like reading minds, changing doorbells, and other simple tricks a child can do."

"Or making your hand immovable."

She giggled. "You like my hand on your leg?"

"Tell me. You read minds."

She touched the end of his nose with a finger. "You like it, even if it leaves a cold spot when I remove it." She pushed on his nose with the finger.

He took her finger and brought it to his lips. "Yes."

As if by magic, one of his shirt-buttons came undone, and she slipped her hand inside. She caressed his chest. "And in your heart when I leave."

He rolled his eyes. "I'm in trouble, aren't I?"

"Only if I see you checking out another woman."

Megumi moved to him until their bodies touched. She slid her arms around his waist and raised her eyes to look into his. "Sometimes you can read minds. Read mine now."

He looked into amber eyes. His shirt tail came out, and two small hands slid up his back. He leaned down, and they kissed. He kissed her again, then stepped back and studied her smile. "You are so beautiful--what am I going to do with you?"

"What would you like to do with me?" He placed an arm around her waist, one behind her knees, picked her up, and carried her to his bedroom. "What took you so long?" she said.

The silence of the night was broken by gentle sounds and heavy breathing. Once more, early in the morning, she aroused him again. At dawn he opened his eyes and studied the woman sleeping next to him, whose face reflected a touch of Orient and the innocence of a child. *You're anything but innocent--you're a witch--but Rosie would be pleased.*

"I can beam her here," a sleepy voice said. "then you can fix breakfast for the four of us."

"No thank you. That was a thought, not a request. Who

would be the fourth?"

"Mama."

"You two aren't a package deal, are you?"

"No. Her goodbye gift will be knowing that you and I will always be together. You are totally mine. I don't share."

"Your mother slept here. Did you know that?"

"It's a good thing she slept in the other room."

He climbed out of bed and put on a robe. "Young lady, there are times I'll have to be with other people, as in working. In fact, one of those times is today. In a couple hours, I'll be attending the Business Department Annual Picnic in The Park."

"All right. We'll bid Mama goodbye another day, but just remember, there'll be times I'll keep you so busy you won't be able to maintain your schedule."

"Oh, no. I'm not going to be your personal plaything."

She giggled. "We'll see how it goes."

"You're not thinking of going to the picnic with me, are you?"

She hopped out of bed and stretched. "Of course."

Harvey stared at her. "No way. I can't show up with a student, especially one with a body like that. No. And you're too young for me to take to a college function."

"I'll be the oldest person there."

"Well, you won't look it. Too many teachers and professors get in trouble because they become involved with students. It wouldn't look right. No. Stay away."

"I guarantee I won't look young, and no one will recognize me as a student."

He shook his head. "There's no way to stop you from getting me in trouble, is there? At least get out of the clothes you wore here and wear something more sedate."

She winked at him. "I'm always ready to get out of my clothes for you."

"Is there anything I can do to get rid of you?" She rummaged through a dresser drawer. "Not that I know of."

"Do you know what a clinging vine is?" She picked a red and white striped garment out of the drawer. "Yes."

"Well, I don't want one." He eyed his guest as she slipped his pajama top on over her delicate body. She gave a coy smile as she held the top open for a moment. "Sometimes you won't notice I'm around, except when I find it necessary to protect my interests."

He was amazed as he watched her button up a pajama top that seemed so ordinary when he wore it. "I don't think I'll ever get to the point where I don't know you're around."

She threw the pajama bottoms at him. "To make sure you know I'm there, when I join you at the picnic, I'll have on a frilly skirt, wear spikes, and put on gobs of rouge. You can tell your friends I'm a piece you picked up in Yokohama."

"You do, and I'll ignore you except to swear I've never seen you before."

"All right, you win. I'll do my best to be a presentable companion for a professor. See, I can be quite reasonable when I'm treated like a lady."

He glanced at his alarm clock. "I have to clean up. I have a class to teach before I go to the picnic. With a look of pleading, he said, "I really would like to go there alone."

"You win again. That'll give me time to move my stuff from our front porch." She yanked off the pajama top, grabbed his hand, and led him to the bathroom. "Come on, let's take a shower." She spun around and poked a slender finger at him. "But, you remember--no funny stuff with any females at the picnic, or I'll change your name from Mr. Long to Mr. Short."

CHAPTER 4

Harvey strolled across the street to the park along the Grand River. He spied one of his favorite people, Professor Craig Akers, leaning against a walnut tree on the edge of the field. Harvey approached him. "What's goes with you, Red?" Craig reached out to shake Harvey's hand. "You old scoundrel. Why didn't you tell me about Susha?"

Harvey shook his head. "What are you talking about?"

Craig pointed at a blue and white striped tent which contained tables of snacks, soft drinks, and bottles of wine. "Who do you see there?"

"A bunch of people I know and some I don't know. What's your point?"

"Standing near the wine table--who do you see that's special to you?"

Harvey moved his head from side to side checking the people around the table. "Come on, Red--I have no idea what you're trying to say."

"Your engagement."

"I have no engagements today. I'm off--finished."

"Susha." Craig pointed at a short woman with her back toward him who was talking with three female professors near the open end of the tent. Flaming red hair hung from a babushka, and she wore a baggy burlap dress with WELCOME printed over her rear end. She wore Zouri sandals. Harvey closed his eyes. Craig cradled his chin in his hand. "I'll say one thing about her: She's sure different."

Harvey opened his eyes at the same time the woman called Susha turned to face him. He let out the breath he'd been holding. It wasn't Megumi. This woman had wrinkles that could only belong to someone who spent every day of her life in the sun, in the middle of a desert, without a hat. She had two warts, one on her chin and another on the end of her nose. Her eyebrows were so bushy they certainly obscured her vision. He laughed. "Kinda cute, but I think I'm set."

"You don't know her?" Craig said. Harvey shook his head. Craig wiped his brow. "I'm glad, but you'd better get over there right now. She's been here for fifteen minutes, telling everybody you two are going to get married. Drinks like a fish."

They headed toward the woman. When they neared Susha, she winked and waved at Harvey. He groaned and placed a hand on his forehead as if he had a headache. "Excuse me. I do know her. I met her at a conference in Saginaw. She was cleaning rooms, and I thought she did a nice job. She's not my fiancée. She's my cleaning lady. She has problems with the English language."

"She has more problems than just the language."

"Unfortunately, yes."

Harvey stepped up close to Susha and the three professors in time to hear her say, "We met at Hotel Lenin in Petrograd and did cha cha many times that night. At least that's name he called what we did. It felt so good. You ought to try cha cha."

A professor with her hair in a bun, nodded. "I think I already did. An Italian pulled the same trick on me on a riverbank in Verona."

Susha grinned. "Good, huh?"

Harvey approached the professors and grabbed Susha's

arm. "Excuse me, there's been a misunderstanding." He yanked her away from them.

The professor, with the bun, turned to the others. "I didn't misunderstand her."

Susha stopped and pulled her arm away. "What are you doing?"

Harvey grabbed it again. "What are you doing?"

She grinned. "I'm socializing with your friends." She pulled her arm loose from his, walked over, and grabbed a glass of wine from the hand of an older man, drank the wine, and handed the empty glass back to him.

"Quit that," Harvey said. "You're going to make me the laughing stock of the college. On top of that, I'll be fired. You go back there and tell those women a different story. We are not going to be married. If you keep up this act of yours, I'll give Minnie back to you and never even think of you again, much less spend time with you. I don't care what magic you use on me. Do you understand that?"

"I understand. It must have been the wine. You have excellent taste in Merlot. I had some earlier as I was moving your things out of one of the dressers in our bedroom. Now, you understand this--we are going to be happily married."

"You'll be headed back to Japan in a box if you don't follow my directions for the rest of the afternoon." Harvey took Susha by the arm and guided her back toward where the professors were watching his antics. Out of the corner of his eye, he saw Craig approaching. He held her by the arm and stopped. "Hold it. Be nice. The man coming this way is a good friend of mine."

She curtsied to Craig. "Much pleased to meet you."

"I met you fifteen minutes ago."

"That was Susha. I'm Megumi, but you can call me Meg now that I'm sleeping with Professor Long." Harvey closed his eyes and shook his head.

Craig turned his head toward Harvey with his eyes wide open. "I have a Megumi in my class, but not this one."

"This is the same one. You must excuse her. She's been drinking and has been invited to a costume party. She's trying out the costume to see if it works."

Craig waved at Harvey. "It works. I'll see you later, and you can explain the whole thing to me." He bowed to Megumi. "Much pleased to meet you, Meg." He left them and strolled over to a group of men who had been staring at her.

When Harvey figured his friend was out of hearing range, he whispered to Megumi. "Quit doing stuff like that. You're ruining my reputation."

She smiled. "I shall replace it with one, people will envy and yearn to duplicate."

"Where'd you get that outfit?"

"Mama made it for me with odds and ends she found in your foyer."

"That rug she used for a skirt has footprints on it."

"Oh, I thought those were decorative designs."

He noticed the professors, with whom Susha had been socializing, were staring at him. "You go back there right now and tell them you're my housekeeper, not my fiancée."

"I am not your housekeeper and never will be."

"I understand that. Megumi will not be my housekeeper, but Susha, who will disappear forever after this picnic, is my housekeeper until then. My friends may have a chance to meet Megumi later."

"You also may call me Meg. And as long as I'm your housekeeper, should I clean the wine off the professor's dress? While waiting for my fiancé, I mean my employer, I inadvertently spilled a glass of red wine on the dress of a skinny professor who said you were cute."

They joined the female faculty, and Harvey cringed when he saw red splashes on the front of Mitzi St. Marie's white dress. He spied a nearby table that had glasses of wine on it. He reached for a red wine and downed it.

"Pardon my English," Susha said to the women. "She is not too good. I made error. I am Mr. Long's housekeeper he purchased from employment agency in Detroit last week. I am much pleased to meet you." She gazed at Harvey when he returned to her side, smiled, and gave his hand a squeeze. "You are happy now?"

Harvey sighed.

Dean Pigeon and his wife, Pricilla, approached Harvey, stepping around Susha as if she were a leper. The dean pointed at his marketing professor. "Is this your idea of a joke, inviting this--this creature to the faculty picnic?"

Still holding Harvey's hand, Susha turned to him. "This is the same nasty man we saw in the hall, and I'll bet you the fat woman is his wife."

Pricilla rolled her eyes upward. "Oh!"

"How crude," the dean said.

Harvey closed his eyes and murmured, "No." He opened them when he heard an almost inaudible whirring sound. He saw the dean's fly hung open. "Your fly's unzipped, Dean Pigeon."

"I know."

Pricilla scowled at Pigeon. "You knew your fly was unzipped, and you left it that way?"

"Someone unzipped it. Did you have a hand in it?"

"I haven't had a hand in your fly for years."

Dean Pigeon glared at her. "I wasn't talking about that."

"Weren't talking about what? The last time I had my hand in your fly?"

"That's not what I said."

Susha faced Pricilla. "It surely is what he said. I'd never put my hand in his fly again."

"Why did you say again?" Pricilla said.

"I never did before or after, for that matter."

"Before or after what?"

"I have muchie problem with English. I never had my hand in that fly and do not intend to put it there in the future."

"If you did, you'd be disappointed," Pricilla said.

The dean glowered at her. "Quit discussing my fly."

Pricilla stepped back. "Then zip the stupid thing up."

Pigeon raised a finger upward. "Inanimate objects are not stupid, my dear."

"It must be more intelligent than you, or is it just more determined? Zip it up."

"I have done so a couple of times, but it seems to have a mind of its own."

Pricilla reached under his belly and zipped his fly up.

"Well," Susha said, "what do we talk about since that subject is closed?"

A whirring sound was heard, and those near the dean watched as his zipper headed to the open position without any apparent cause. He grabbed it and zipped it up, but as soon as he took his hands off, it flew down again.

Susha pointed at his fly. "This must be one of your new American parlor games."

"I wonder how a person scores in this game," a woman next to Mitzi said.

Mitzi nudged her. "I know how, but I wouldn't want to score with him."

"Probably the only man on campus you haven't scored with, dearie."

"Jealous?"

"The proper word is envious."

37

Dean Pigeon zipped up his fly again and struggled to hold it closed. He glared at Susha. "Woman, I suspect you're responsible for this." He shifted his attention to Harvey. "I regret what I said yesterday. Now that I've seen the type of person you're capable of taking to a college function, I'd be happy to have you do anything you want with that Asian student who was playing with your leg. Just promise I won't have to set eyes on this revolting person again."

Harvey didn't acknowledge the dean's remarks until a tiny elbow poked him in the ribs, causing him to jump. "Thank you sir," he said.

Virgil Pigeon placed one hand on his zipper and the other in his wife's hand. He worked his way through the crowd with both hands still in place as he and Pricilla made their grand exit from the Business Department Picnic in The Park.

An hour later, when Harvey and Megumi entered his house, the pretty woman who replaced Susha took her professor's hand. "Did you hear Dean Pigeon say he'd be happy to have you do anything you want with the young Asian student who played with your leg?"

"Yes."

She unbuckled his belt. "You should do what makes your dean happy."

Soon, with the sole purpose of making Dean Pigeon happy, Harvey was on the sofa doing what he wanted with the half-Kitsune student who had brought a cold spot to his leg and a warm one to his heart.

"Hello, Daddy," a female voice said. "Nice seeing you again, Megumi."

A male voice said, "Hello, Father."

CHAPTER 5

"Go on out to the deck," Harvey said. "We'll be with you in a minute."

Meg waved. "As you can see, we're almost done."

After they finished, she reached up and pushed a lock of hair back from Harvey's forehead. "The young man with Rosie--that was your son, wasn't it?"

"I don't know. I had my back to him."

"He is your son, isn't he?"

"Some witch. I thought you could read minds."

"I'm trying to give that up."

"Is that possible?"

"I hope so."

"Yes, that's Jason."

Ten minutes later, they stepped onto the deck. Meg wore shorts and a sleeveless top while Harvey had on a skaggy looking white shirt tucked into a ragged pair of pants. He pointed to a young man dressed in baggy jeans with the crotch at his knees and his t-shirt hanging out from under his jacket. "This is Jason. He's a sophomore at State. At least he will be if he treats you nice enough that I'll pay his tuition this fall."

"I didn't realize you had a son," Meg said, "until this handsome young man called you father." Rosie smiled. Jason scowled at her as if she'd just dropped a bug in his drink.

"Jason," Harvey said, "I want you to meet Meg. She's,

ahh--as you may have noticed, we have a thing for each other."

"What is she, Chinese?"

Meg stepped up to Jason to shake his hand, but he kept his right arm at his side. Suddenly his eyes opened wide, and he strained but couldn't keep the hand from reaching up, where it shook hers. She smiled. "My name's Meg. I'm part Japanese. My father was American."

Jason managed to gain control over his hand. He glowered at his dad. "I got to get back to the dorm--like I got stuff to do." He hurried into the house.

Rosie touched Meg's arm. "Don't pay attention to him. He was a miscarriage."

"Excuse me," Harvey said. "I'll be back in a minute. Rosie, get a glass of wine for Meg. She drinks the same stuff we do. And pour me one."

Rosie's gaze followed her father. "You're sure doing a lot of wine drinking lately."

"It's not my fault--it's the magic." He hurried into the house. "Wait up, Jason."

Jason stood at the front door, scowling. "Where'd you pick her up?"

"I didn't pick her up--she's a student of mine."

"So, what were you teaching her on the sofa?"

"Jason, I don't interfere with your life, so please don't interfere with mine. It's been a long time since your mother died, and this is the first time I've been enamored with anyone since then."

Jason turned to leave. "Like I don't want a half-breed Jap for a stepmother."

Harvey grabbed his son's arm. "Watch your mouth. The word is Japanese. You change your language, and you be nice to her, or you're out of school and looking for a job." Jason glared at Harvey and stalked out.

When Harvey returned to the deck, Rosie handed him a glass of wine. "This remarkable woman is all I could have hoped for," she said. "We've decided it's permissible for me to steal her away from you any time I get a chance."

"Good. I already see there are times I'll need a break."

Rosie tilted her head back and laughed. "That is the real you, Daddy." She reached up and hugged him, almost knocking the wine out of his hand. She backed away. "Did you show Megumi off at the college picnic?"

When Harvey stopped laughing, he said, "You should have seen her. I told her to look old, so she disguised herself as a Russian scrubwoman with a big wart on the end of her nose. By the time I arrived, she'd told everybody we were engaged."

"Are you?"

Megumi answered. "Yes, and as long as we are, you can call me Meg."

Harvey stepped between Rosie and Meg and put his arms around them. He squeezed Rosie. "She told Craig Akers he could call her Meg as long as she and I were sleeping together. Then she got Dean Pigeon and his wife to hold hands, probably for the first time in years." Both women leaned against him. He kissed the top of one pretty head and then the other. "You two are my new life." They stood on their toes, pulled his head down, and kissed his cheeks.

Rosie slipped from her dad's grasp and bowed to Meg. "In honor of your engagement to this hobo, I'll fix a light snack. I bought plenty of eggs, Daddy. How many would you like?"

"None, thank you. I had a dozen for breakfast."

Conversation came to a violent halt when a platinum blonde in a white bikini strutted across the lawn to the deck.

Harvey had met Lillian a month earlier when she and her husband were moving in next door. He was sitting on the deck, contemplating a flock of Canadian geese flying over, honking their horns, when she pranced over, wearing a flimsy white blouse and red short shorts that had gone out of style years earlier but still accentuated her current attributes. She posed against the deck rail in front of him. "Hi, I'm Lillian."

Harvey waited for her to say something else but finally realized she was content to enhance his view with her body and watch for his reaction. "I'm Harvey Long. Glad to have the two of you move in next door."

Around the side of her curves, Harvey saw a pudgy man plod across the lawn. The man climbed the stairs to the deck, grunting with each step. "Lill, we got enough to do without you sashaying around the neighborhood."

Lillian pointed a thumb at the man. "Harvey, this is my husband, Arnold." She waved a hand toward Harvey. "Honey, this is Mr. Long. I thought it would be nice to meet him."

Arnold ignored Harvey. "I'll bet you did. Get your buns off this deck, and let's get moved in before you do your galavanting." He did an about face and stomped down the stairs. Lillian wiggled her fingers at Harvey as she and her buns followed Arnold off the deck and across the lawn. Harvey returned to contemplating the geese that had landed on the pond and hoped his quiet life wouldn't be adversely affected by his new neighbors.

This particular morning, Harvey waved at Lillian as she swung her buns across the top step. "This is Lillian Doerner," he said to the two women. "She and her husband, Arnold, live next door." He motioned toward the women. "My daughter, Rosie and Meg." Rosie smiled. Meg frowned.

"I guessed that was your daughter," Lillian said. "I've seen her here before."

Rosie extended a hand toward Lillian. "I was just going

42

to fix a snack. Would you care to join us?"

"No, thank you. We're putting on a pool party this afternoon, and I came over to invite you to join us." She waltzed over to where Harvey sat. "I didn't mean to bother you while you had company, but I saw you on the deck and thought it would be nice to invite you to the party. It begins one hour from now with a light lunch and refreshments. Your daughter and her Korean friend are invited to join us, too."

Lillian turned her attention to Meg. "I don't know how well you know Harvey, but he's a wonderful, charming man to have as a neighbor--and would be so in other roles, I suspect." She reached over, pinched Harvey's cheek, gave a little squeal, and pranced down the steps.

After a moment of silence on the deck, Meg strolled over to Harvey and sat on his lap. She pinched his cheek, harder than Lillian had. She imitated Lillian's squeal, put her hand under his chin, and pulled his head around to face hers. "You wonderful, charming old man; are you going to take your Korean friend to the party with you?"

"Yes, older than I."

"And what were those other roles she mentioned?"

"I have no idea."

"It's a good thing for you she only suspects." Meg jumped as he pinched her on the rear. She slipped an arm around his neck and nipped the top of his ear.

"Ow."

Rosie smiled. "Love in action." She went into the house and returned minutes later with a bottle of wine and three glasses. "To repair your bodies from the rigorous antics of earlier." She set the glasses on the round table.

Harvey tried to move to the table, but Meg still sat on his lap. He pushed and shoved but couldn't budge her. He spoke to the ear in front of his face. "Would you grant me the

43

honor of having a drink of wine with me?" She didn't respond. "Meg, I would like to--"

"Don't talk to me you, you--you charming man." She hopped off his lap and sat at the table. He sat next to her.

Rosie poured their Merlot. "To help us enhance the day with new antics."

After they emptied the bottle, Harvey rose from his chair. "It's time to go next door, hopefully for more wine." He gazed at the sky. "It's going to be a hot one."

Meg still had not spoken to Harvey, but she held his hand as they crossed the lawn to the two-story yellow brick house. Lillian greeted them near the back door, wearing a grin that telegraphed her excitement. "Hello, Harvey," she said in a voice that sounded like she was singing a love song. She noticed his hand entwined with Meg's. "You certainly have a nice relationship with your daughter's friend."

"She's not my daughter's friend--she's a student of mine at the college."

"Oh, she must be an exceptional student to deserve such a close relationship with her teacher."

Meg glared at Lillian. "Yes, and I've taught him a few things. I'm not just a student--I'm also a bimbo."

"Oh. Well, miss, please forgive me for my past errs."

Meg bowed her head. "I didn't realize you had passed air. Is that something you did on the deck this morning or did you do so just now?"

"I was speaking of when I erred this morning by assuming you were with someone your own age."

"That's quite all right, Mrs. Doorknob. The wind probably blew it away."

"The name is Doerner."

"Excuse my mistake. I have muchie problems with

English. Now I understand. Doughnut, a little round tart with a hole in it."

Lillian gave Rosie a look of pleading, but Rosie seemed not to notice. Harvey faced Lillian. "Thank you for the invitation, Mrs. Doerner." He grabbed Meg's arm and led her into a glassed-in porch containing a table loaded with food and bottles of wine.

Meg grabbed Harvey's ear, pulled on it, and whispered to him, "If I ever catch you hanging around that vamp, I'll turn you into a toad."

"Why do witches always turn men into toads? Why not white rats or mice?"

"Tradition. Probably because we like to see men jump." She stuck her hand in his rear pants pocket and did something that caused him to jump. "See?"

The threesome ignored the other guests on their way to the refreshment table, then did their best to keep the wine from turning to vinegar out of neglect. After a half-hour making sure that wouldn't happen, Rosie raised a finger. "Let's go swimming." Harvey agreed it was a great idea, but Meg indicated she didn't have a swimsuit. "I have extras at the house," Rosie said.

As Rosie and Meg headed toward the back door, Harvey waved a pair of bathing trunks above his head and shouted over the other guests' conversations, "Last one in's a wart hog." He staggered between couples who shied away from him as he searched for one of the Doerners to ask about a place to change. He didn't see Lillian or Arnold, so he wandered up a staircase and knocked on the first door he came to. Hearing no answer, he entered a room furnished with a king size bed and living room furniture.

He had just flung his shirt and trousers on a chair next to the bed and thrown his shorts in the same general direction when he heard a doorknob being turned and a woman's voice from outside the door say, "I'll be back to join you in a few minutes, Dorene."

Harvey forgot where he threw his trunks and opted to run rather than try to locate them. He bolted through what he thought was a closet door but led to a bathroom that reeked of violets. Standing in the dark, he heard the bedroom door open and someone humming. The door slammed, and the humming stopped. He heard no sound for a couple of minutes. He eased the bathroom door open. Lillian Doerner posed there wearing a bra, undies, and a smile. "Hello, Harvey. I thought those were your clothes on the chair." She surveyed his naked body. "Nice to see you."

"May I get past you to my trunks?"

She reached back and unhooked her bra. "I saw them on the floor next to the bed."

"May I get my trunks?" He tried to squeeze around one side of her and then the other, but she slid over in front of him each time.

She stretched a hand out to each door jam, spread-eagled to block his way while she scanned his body again. "You have a wonderful physique. Not particularly attractive, but it appears to be quite functional."

"I'm not interested in functioning. I want to swim."

"Wait while I finish putting on my bikini." She pulled off her bra and held it in her fingertips before letting it drop to the floor. "You can help me hook the top. I'm sure you're good at hooking as well as unhooking."

"I may be, but I don't believe it would be in my best interest."

"How will you know what benefits you may derive if you don't try?"

"I'd better go swimming. Please let me get--"

A male voice rang out in the hall. "Lill, who are you talking to?"

Lillian put a finger to her lips. "Shh. It's Arnold." She pushed Harvey backwards into the dark bathroom, followed him in, and eased the door shut. She leaned against him. "Shh. Don't move an inch." She giggled.

The door from the hall to the bedroom opened and banged into the wall. "Lillian, I know you're in here. I see your clothes on the bed."

Lillian switched on a light, turned the shower water on, and whispered, "Get in."

Harvey hesitated. She pushed him under the cold stream of water and closed the curtain. He shivered but remained silent. "I'm in here, darling," Lillian shouted. "Wait downstairs. I'll be there in a minute."

"Why are you taking a shower now?" Arnold yelled.

"One should always shower before entering the pool, darling."

"Why are you calling me darling? Something's fishy here. And whose clothes are these? There's only one person I know who wears pants that long. Harvey Long's in there with you, isn't he?"

"Sorry, darling, I can't hear you with the water running."

"You'll hear me when I get my thirty-eight and shoot him full of holes."

Lillian stuck her head around the edge of the shower curtain and giggled. "Just like in the movies. He's going to defend my honor."

Harvey didn't think it wise to make a comment about that or stay and become an easy target. He bolted out of the shower, through the door, and past Arnold who was shoving rounds into the cylinder of a revolver. "I can explain," Harvey hollered as he dashed through the open bedroom door.

He opened the next door down the hall and found himself facing a startled redhead, who wore a watch on her wrist and a white towel around her waist. Harvey gave her an admiring glance, hurried into the room, and slammed the door shut. "He's trying to kill me."

The redhead watched with wide eyes as Harvey raced across the room, hid behind a drape, and peeked out through a slit. The door burst open, and Arnold entered with his pistol aimed at the redhead. She screamed and covered her face with her hands. He pointed the gun at the floor as he inspected her. "Excuse me lady. I'm looking for a naked man."

She peered between her fingers. "From the way you're checking me out, I expect you can tell I'm not one."

He scanned her again. "True."

She took her hands from her face and placed them over her breasts. "Then get out of here and look for your naked man somewhere else."

"But I know he's in here."

"Does your wife know you spend your spare time looking for naked men?"

Arnold glanced around the room, then back at the redhead. "Just tell me where he is."

The redhead pulled one end of the towel up to cover her breasts and poked a finger at Arnold while holding the bottom end in place with her elbow. "Do you really believe I'd be standing here, making small talk with you if I had a naked man in my room?"

"Just tell me where he is, lady?"

She tilted her head back. "Describe him."

While still studying exposed areas of the redhead, Arnold wrapped his hand around his chin and grinned. "Don't you know what a naked man looks like?"

"Of course I do. I just want to know what your naked man looks like."

"He's not mine. I just want to shoot him."

"Why?"

"For running around stark naked in my bedroom with my wife."

"Was she naked too?"

"Not completely. I got there just in time."

"Just in time for what?"

"To make sure it didn't happen."

"What didn't happen?"

He raised his eyebrows. "You know what."

"Oh, that. What are you going to do if you find him?"

"I'm going to shoot him full of holes."

"Oh." She checked her watch. "Tell you what. We have plenty of time. You go back and take advantage of your wife while she's still naked, and I'll take care of your naked man's hormones, so they'll no longer be a threat."

From outside the door came a female voice. "Miss, you get anywhere near his hormones, and I'll calm yours down to the point they'll never flare up again." When Harvey heard Meg's voice, he shuddered, causing the drape to move. Arnold fired his revolver at the movement, shattering a window behind the drape. Meg burst into the room. "Run, Harvey," she yelled.

"He'll shoot me."

"No he won't. Get out of here."

"If you say so." Harvey flung the drape aside and flew full speed across the room. The sight made three people gasp as he raced past them. From the corner of his eyes he saw Meg in a bikini, a redhead with a towel wrapped around her middle, and Arnold Doerner holding what may have once been a revolver but was now the nozzle of a water hose, all frozen in place as the mass of naked arms and legs flailed past them.

One of the arms reached out and snatched the towel from the redhead, and Harvey took a quick look back to see if she was all right. She appeared to be in excellent shape. She didn't seem to miss the towel but frowned when the naked man left her room. Arnold Doerner didn't seem to mind losing the towel or the naked man and paid only minor attention to the mass of skin and bones that whizzed by. He was busy surveying newly exposed areas of the redhead's body.

Harvey wrapped the towel around his waist and sprinted down the stairs. Meg stood at the top and watched him bound down, only to see him trip on the last step and sprawl on the floor among the guests. He lay there stunned, and the towel came off. A woman, next to where Harvey lay spread out on the floor, turned to a man standing beside her. "Perhaps this signals the beginning of the entertainment."

"I think the entertainment's already taken place," the man said.

She smiled at him. "Do you suppose they have a sign-up sheet?"

"I don't know. I could start one if I had pen and paper."

She opened her purse to pull out a pen and a pad. "The name's Ethel, E-t-h-e-l."

Meg pointed at Harvey, and an unseen force wrapped the towel around him. He came to life, regained his feet, and ran through the room. Conversation between guests ceased as he hurtled past them and out the door. He sprinted across the lawn with one end of the towel trailing behind him like the white tail of a Great Albino Pheasant.

Meg returned to Harvey's home, still wearing her bikini, and spied him sitting on the living room sofa, staring at his bony feet. She sat next to him and put a hand on one of his. "Do you want to talk about it?"

"I don't know if I'm able. It all took place so fast, I was never in control."

"I understand."

"You saw me with two naked women and a madman with a gun, and you understand?"

"I didn't know there was another naked woman. I don't understand quite as well now."

"Lillian Doerner."

"My understanding has evaporated completely. How could you possibly dilly-dally around with that tart less than ten minutes after I promised to turn you into a toad? Is what she has that good? I'll dilly your dally for you. I'd turn you into a snake, except that's what you already are, a low down, dirty snake."

"I'm innocent. She tried to trap me in her room before she was naked. She got that way in a hurry, so I ran out. Then her husband chased me down the hall with his gun. I took the first door I came to. That's where I ran into the redhead."

"Into her?"

He raised his hands above his head as if surrendering. "Into her room."

"That's better. Life around you is as exciting as I hoped it would be but extremely complicated. Why can't you be more sedate?"

"Are you sure that's what you want me to be?"

"No. Forget I said that, but you must admit you do lead a wild life."

"Only since I met you. Which has made my daughter happy. . . . And me too."

"But you know we'll have a problem because we're so different." Meg said.

"You mean because you're a witch and I'm not?"

"No. Because you're naked and I'm not." She unhooked her bra, slipped out of the bottom of her suit, yanked his towel off, and tossed it across the room.

He sprawled out on the sofa. "You know, Jason and Rosie might walk in on us again,"

"Slide over, snake."

CHAPTER 6

During class, Harvey did his best not to show interest in Meg, fearing she might blow him a kiss or do something worse to embarrass him. She surprised him by being pretty much a model student. She remained silent, took notes, and the only time she left her model student mode was when the petite blonde, with the skirt pulled above her knees, raised one hand and hiked her skirt up even further with the other. Meg scowled when Harvey's gaze locked onto the display like a cat that spied a songbird, but she regained her composure when Harvey answered the blonde's question without stuttering.

At the break, Meg walked within two feet of him on the way out of the room without acknowledging he existed. He approached her in the hall, but she ignored him to talk to a fellow student. After class, Harvey saw her standing alone on the lawn outside the front door of the building. He stopped. "Hello, beautiful. Would you do me the honor of having--"

She glared at him. "Don't you cozy up to me, you Romeo, you."

"Now, what did I do wrong?"

"Don't pretend you don't know what you did, you carnivore."

"Carnivore? What are you talking about?"

"You practically drooled when your eyes gobbled up that skinny blonde's legs."

Harvey placed his fingers on his forehead in thought. "Oh, the young lady next to you who asked about greeting customers. I just answered her question."

"And devoured her lilly-white legs with hungry eyes."

Harvey grinned at her. "I never devour legs, in that class, except yours. Your legs get me so excited I can't think, I can't talk, and I can't eat. But right now I'm going to have cappuccino and a roll by myself unless you care to join me to hear more about how you turn me on."

A smile spread to replace Meg's frown. "My legs really get you excited?"

He crossed his arms. "Didn't you know?"

Her head bobbed up and down like the toy dog in the back window of a car. "Join me in a nap instead of having cappuccino, and I'll show you how much more excitement they generate when they're wrapped around you."

Harvey checked around and didn't see any faculty, only a few students. He grabbed her hand. "I'm more sleepy than hungry. Let's go take a nap."

After their lunch break, Meg smiled on her way to her next class, and Harvey strutted through the hall with a renewed spring in his step.

Late that afternoon, Rosie carried a day pack as she stepped onto the deck where Meg and Harvey sat on the glider, holding hands. "You have no wine," she said.

Harvey smiled. "It's too early in the day to drink."

"What do you mean? I drove all the way down here to have a glass of wine and dinner with you." She opened the pack and pulled out a bottle of Merlot, a corkscrew, and three glasses. "Guess where I learned this."

Harvey grinned. "From Yoshi."

Meg elbowed him. "My mother? No way."

They drank to Yoshi, then drank to her again. By the time they climbed into his ancient Oldsmobile station wagon, they weren't as tight as good old boys at a reunion, but they weren't sober either. Harvey and Rosie laughed and sang "If You Knew Meggie Like I Know Meggie" as they cruised down Michigan Avenue and into town. Harvey drove carefully, so he wouldn't attract attention, but so slow he was liable to. He pulled up to valet parking at the Radisson, where a young valet bumped his head on the door while ogling the two women.

Harvey and the women stumbled into the hotel. As they passed the front desk, he heard someone say, "Welcome to the Radisson, Mr. Long." He glanced to where the voice came from and recognized the clerk as a student of his. The clerk stepped from behind the counter. "I'm Ted Nelson from your Marketing 110 class. I recognize Miss Sakuma but not the other pretty lady." The three of them stopped while Harvey introduced Ted to Rosie. She gazed at Ted through glazed eyes. "I'm happy to meet you, Miss Long," Ted said.

Rosie stared at him with her mouth open. Harvey nudged her. "Say something."

"He's beautiful," she murmured.

"You'll have to excuse her," Harvey said. "She contracted mono and has lost her speech. That's why we stopped here, to get her a sip of alcohol. . . . It seems to help."

"I'm off duty in ten minutes. If you don't mind, I'll come to your table to see if she's recovered."

"That would be nice. Join us and have a sip yourself in case you contract it."

The three strolled into the dining room and sat at a table. Harvey ordered a bottle of Merlot. He noticed Dean Pigeon sitting alone two tables away and yelled over the heads of an older couple, "Hey, Pigeon, where's Pricilla?"

The dean cupped his hands in front of his mouth, and

spoke in a loud whisper. "She left town to visit her mother."

"How's your fly?" Harvey yelled.

"Shut up."

"See if you can keep it that way. At your age, forgetting to zip up is a problem you'd better get used to. That's what I've heard."

The older couple in the line of fire between the tables left, leaving their food uneaten. Dean Pigeon stood and pointed at Harvey. "I regret the reprieve I gave you at the picnic. I don't ever want you to teach another class in my college. Your contract is terminated as of now."

With Meg hanging on his arm to keep him from standing, Harvey grinned and pointed at Pigeon. "I didn't realize it was your college."

Pigeon stomped out. A minute later, an official looking man wearing a tuxedo came into the dining room with the couple who had left. The woman pointed at Harvey as the culprit, and he was asked to leave. When he and his two lady friends walked through the lobby, Ted left the desk and followed them out. "I'll get your car for you, Mr. Long."

"That would be nice. . . . Ted, wasn't it?"

"Yes, sir." Ted called for the station wagon, and when it arrived, he seated Rosie in front, then opened the rear door and waved Meg and Harvey in. "I'll be your chauffeur to make sure you all get home safely."

"That's excellent service," Harvey said. "I'll take that extracurricular duty into consideration when I compute grades."

By the time they pulled out of the driveway, Rosie's head was on Ted's shoulder, and she was asleep. Harvey tapped Ted on his other shoulder. "On the way, I'd like to stop at the Winkin' Pup Saloon in Old Town. I'm doing research for my marketing class. Please take us there?"

"Yes, sir, but first I'll drive to Lake Lansing if you

don't mind. You can walk along the shore to get freshened up. I'll stay in the car with your beautiful daughter. I don't want to wake her while she's getting needed rest for her mono."

"Well put, Mr. Nelson."

Harvey and Meg strolled barefoot in the shallow water along the beach. With a sad face, she gazed at him. "I've caused you to lose your job."

He leaned down and kissed the top of her head. "I caused me to lose it. I really shouldn't have done that. I'm sorry I embarrassed you by having too much to drink. I've meant to ask you why Rosie and I are practically disabled by wine, while you seem to remain unaffected."

"I guess I'm enough of a witch it doesn't affect me as much as it does humans."

"Why do you talk that way? You're as human as I am."

They walked in silence until they came to a bench on the edge of the sand. "You'll be better off sitting when I tell you this," she said. Harvey sat, leaned back, and stretched his legs out, while she sat up straight and made a little house with her hands. "You see me as human, but I'm not. You have no idea what I am. If you knew, you'd run away."

He put his arm around her. "I'll never leave you."

"I should have stayed in Japan instead of coming back to Lansing."

"Why do you say that?"

"I might be killing you. When Kitsune make love--"

Harvey sat up straight. "You sound like your mother. What's this nonsense you two have in your minds about the possibility of killing me?"

"It's the curse. Kitsune aren't human. They're wild foxes that shapeshift to women with the sole purpose of seducing men, causing them to waste away and die."

57

"What are you talking about?"

"It's true. That's why I left you and went to Japan. My mother is Kitsune."

"But you came back to me."

"Yes, because I realize I'm only part Kitsune. Since I met you, I've begun to act human--I have human feelings. I reasoned that Kitsune seduce and kill, but they don't fall in love. I did. I'm in love with you."

He put a hand under her chin and kissed her, tasting the salt of her tears. "Since we met, I've been more alive than I have for years--you can't be carrying that curse."

"I hope not. I feel human when I'm with you. Perhaps that's a good sign. I want to love you a long time."

"And lots of times too, I'm finding out."

Meg laughed. "You like?"

"Yeaahh."

They strolled the beach until Harvey was able to walk a straight line back to the Olds. Rosie was snuggled up to Ted in the front seat. Ted took care not to disturb her when he slid over to drive. Fifteen minutes later, the Olds pulled into a parking lot across the street from the Winkin' Pup. He glanced back at Harvey. "I don't want to disturb Rosie. We'll stay in the car while you conduct your research."

"Great idea. We'll be back soon."

The saloon resembled a dark cave which reeked of stale beer and smoke. A rock band blared away, pounding patrons sitting at two-foot-square tables crowded around a dance floor. A good-looking woman in her late-twenties, wearing shorts and a well-stocked halter, waltzed to where Harvey and Meg sat. "Welcome to the Winkin' Pup. I'm your server, Jamie."

Harvey waved at her. "Hi, Jamie. We'd like two glasses of Merlot."

"What's that?"

"It's a red wine, almost as red as your hair."

Jamie bent over toward him, her breasts straining to climb out of their halter. "We don't serve wine here--just beer and booze." When Harvey inspected Jamie's cleavage, they both jumped, he from a kick in the shin, and she when her halter was yanked up to where the cleavage was not so prominent. Jamie looked around to see who had caused her prized possessions to be hidden from view. She saw no one. "What'll you have?" she said to Meg.

"I see a bottle of Merlot next to the Canadian Club. I'll take a glass of that."

Jamie surveyed the back bar. "Oh, we must have just got that in. I'll give you the same," she said to Harvey.

As Jamie left she jiggled her halter, trying to loosen it to where it had been. Harvey leaned over next to Meg and whispered, "Now I see what you mean about tricks even children can do."

"Keep your eyes in your head, or you're liable to see stars next time."

"Do you have any tricks that don't hurt?"

She perused the room, then pointed at a platform above the bar where a plastic bulldog sat on his haunches with one eye closed and the other flashing on and off like a pink caution light gone mad. As Harvey watched, the dog jumped down, ran along the bar, and knocked glasses over, spilling beers and mixed drinks. Patrons pushed their stools back from the bar and ram for the door. Others just laughed and wiped their wet clothes as if the dog's actions were a normal part of a night on the town.

Harvey watched wide-eyed as the dog jumped off the end of the bar and ran around the room, yapping at customers. Upon arriving where Meg sat, the pup sat and wagged its stubby tail as she scratched behind its ears. She took her hand away, and the pup raced to the bar, hopped up, and ran in front of the few remaining customers. Glasses, it had missed on the first pass, clattered to the floor. The pup jumped up onto the platform and returned to its original plastic state except for the addition of a wide grin.

Harvey shuddered. "Wow."

One of two men sitting at a nearby table said to the other, "I'll bet you ten dollars that didn't happen."

"What didn't happen?"

The first man thrust a hand in the direction of the platform behind the bar. "That dog didn't come to life and run around the room."

The other man stood. "What are you talking about? I didn't see anything." He dropped two bills next to his glass and pushed his chair to the table. "I'm leaving. My mother told me not to drink on an empty stomach."

"What's going on here is enough to empty a stomach," his companion said. Then the two of them pushed and shoved their way to join the crowd headed for the door. Jamie didn't pay attention to the pup or to the patrons leaving. She was too busy shaking her halter, trying to loosen it. She gave up and served Harvey and Meg.

A couple entered the bar and sat at the table the two men had vacated. The woman was Dean Pigeon's secretary, Sophie, decked out in tight jeans and a see-through blouse. The pudgy man, who pulled a chair out for her, could have been Pigeon except for his bushy hair and matching mustache. Harvey touched Meg on the shoulder. He poked a thumb at Sophie and her escort. "That's Dean Pigeon and his secretary."

Meg first peered at them, then frowned and made a sliding motion with two fingers. The dean's hair slipped to cover his left ear, and the mustache slid around to rest on his cheek. Pigeon tugged on his mustache and hair to return them to their proper locations, but neither hairpiece budged. Harvey nudged Meg as he watched Pigeon fiddle with his fake hair that had become displaced. "Don't you think that's a little much?"

One of two women, sitting at a nearby table, turned to the other. "Look at that showoff. Men--they'll do anything to attract a woman."

"He doesn't attract me. I think he should put both of those things back in his pants where they belong."

"I don't think they belong there either. I've never seen anything like that in a man's pants. . . . Of course, I'm not really an expert on the subject."

"I find that hard to believe, Myrtle." Myrtle shrugged and took a drink.

After listening to the conversation between the two women, Harvey stepped over to Pigeon's table. "Good to see you, Dean. And how are you, Sophie?"

Pigeon reared his head back and closed his eyes. "Lord, not again."

Sophie either didn't see Meg or ignored her. She stood and staggered up close to Harvey. She fluttered her eyelashes. "Hello there. Since I met you, I've wondered if Mr. Long was your real name or if it was a nickname." Before he answered her, one of her eyelids closed, and the other fluttered, causing her to resemble the winking pup. She backed up, took her seat, and fidgeted with her eyes, trying to get one to open and the other to stop blinking.

Harvey approached the dean. "Dean Pigeon, I apologize for my words and actions at the Radisson. Next time I see Pricilla, I'll apologize to her too."

Pigeon stood. "That's quite all right. She was unable to make it tonight. Don't bother apologizing to her--I'll relay your kind words. I'm sorry I spoke to you in the manner I did at dinner. I'm sure we can both forget this evening and continue preparing our students to lead fruitful and prosperous lives as we ourselves do." He turned toward Meg. "Miss Sakuma, it is indeed a pleasure to see you again." He bowed with a look of pleading. She smiled.

Jamie came to the table. "The manager, who wishes not to be identified, is not blaming you, but he says everything bad that's happened tonight has been centered around this table. He says it's time for you to leave. Your drinks were on the house."

Harvey and Meg chugged their wine down and headed for the door. Harvey nudged Meg while looking at the dean and his secretary. "Don't leave them that way." Meg flipped two fingers. Sophie's eyes behaved, and the dean's hairpieces resumed to their proper locations.

Next, Harvey pointed at Jamie, then watched with his mouth agape as Jamie's breasts shrunk to half of their original size. "She'll be more comfortable now," Meg said.

Jamie stared at her breasts, at Meg, and at her reduced breasts again. She picked up a shot of whiskey from in front of a customer, chugged it down, and said to the bartender, "Give him another and put it on my tab."

Harvey and Meg left the bar and crossed the street to the Olds. The front seat was vacant. Harvey knocked on a rear window and motioned for Ted and Rosie to get in front. After they did, Harvey and Meg climbed into the back seat. When they arrived at the house, Harvey said to Ted, "I've taken you out of your regular groove. You can stay here tonight." He showed Ted to the guest room. "Sleep here, please." He made sure Rosie found hers. "Stay here," he said.

Harvey yawned as he ambled to his room where Meg sat on the edge of the bed. He sat and put an arm around her. "I'm so looking forward to tomorrow. We're going to have a normal, sane, quiet, relaxing day--just the two of us."

CHAPTER 7

After Harvey and Meg took their morning shower, she frowned when she saw the ragged jeans and polo shirt he donned while she decked herself in pressed white shorts and a white blouse with an embroidered rose on it. She still wore the frown as she followed him to Rosie's room. Nobody was in the bed, and it didn't appear to have been slept in. He checked the guest room. Nobody there either, but it looked like a wrestling match had been held on the bed.

"I smell bacon," Meg said. They walked toward the kitchen. Nobody was there, but conversation came from outside. They turned and walked out to the deck where Ted and Rosie had left breakfast dishes on the table in favor of sitting on the glider, holding hands, and soaking up sunshine.

Meg bowed while Harvey said, "Good morning. Did you sleep well?"

"Wonderful," Rosie said. . . . Ted didn't answer. Rosie poked him in the ribs.

"Oh, yes," he said. "Me too. Wonderful."

Rosie stood and bowed to Meg. "You are so beautiful. What in the world are you doing in the company of that hobo?"

"You're right--he is sort of a mess, isn't he? We should start reforming him."

Rosie picked up the dirty dishes. "I don't think it'll work, but as a reward for your concern, I'll cook breakfast for you. How do you like your eggs?"

"Scrambled, thank you."

Rosie raised four fingers in front of her father. "And for you, sir? Four?" She added her thumb. "Five?"

"Two will be fine."

Ted rose to leave, but Rosie put her hand out and blocked his way. "Stay and introduce yourself to these two-- you may be related to them someday." He stared at Rosie as she headed to the kitchen.

Harvey shrugged. "Women." Ted nodded.

Soon, the aroma of bacon cooking drifted to the deck. Harvey sat up straight and placed a hand on Meg's arm. "I just thought of a nice way to bid your mother goodbye. We can take her to dinner at the University Club."

"Excellent idea. Rosie and Ted can go with us."

Rosie caught the end of the conversation as she brought out a tray containing two plates, one with two scrambled eggs and the other with four eggs sunny-side up. "Thank you, Meg." She set the plates on a table in front of Meg and Harvey.

"That settles it," Meg said. "See you tonight at seven."

After Meg and Harvey ate, Rosie brought a cup of green tea for Meg and coffee for her dad. Meg picked up Harvey's cup and inhaled the aroma. "I wish tea smelled like this." Minutes later, after she drank her tea, she stood, "I have to go now to invite Mama."

Harvey set his cup down. "I'll give you a ride."

"No, thanks. I'll walk."

"Let me drive you."

"No, I need the exercise."

"I'll walk with you. I could use the exercise too."

Meg waved a hand back and forth. "I'd rather go alone."

"Why don't you want me to go with you?"

"You'll slow me down."

"I'll drive to the club tonight if that's all right."

She picked up his coffee and inhaled the aroma once more. "Fine with me." Harvey took the cup from Meg, placed his hands on her cheeks, and gave her a kiss. "I'll miss you."

"I am in love with you," she said. She walked to the door, turned to blow him a kiss, and left.

Rosie faced Ted. "And I'm in love with you." Then she blew him a kiss. "See how it's done?" She waited.

"Oh, yes." Ted put his hands on her cheeks and gave her a kiss. She kicked his ankle. "And I'm in love with you, too," he said.

Harvey picked up his cup of coffee, still untouched. "I'll be inside if you two lovebirds need me."

Ten minutes later Meg returned. Breathing hard, she walked into the kitchen where Harvey was cleaning the stove. "Mama will be here at seven."

Harvey put down the dish towel which now had brown streaks of grease on it. "Good. Rosie and Ted should arrive at about the same time."

Minutes before seven, Harvey and Meg were sitting on the sofa when Yoshi materialized four feet in front of them. Harvey jumped. Meg glared at her mother. "Mamasan! Don't do that. Harvey isn't used to it."

Yoshi frowned, but when Rosie and Ted walked in, her frown disappeared and a smile took its place. She bowed to them. "What a beautiful couple you make."

"Thank you," Rosie said. "You're beautiful too." She nudged Ted.

"Oh. Thank you, Yoshi. You're beautiful too."

"Nice of you to notice."

Harvey parked the wagon in the University Club lot. He touched Meg's arm with the back of his hand. "Definitely no magic tonight--and please remind your mother."

"I promise." Meg glanced at her mother in the back seat. "Hear that, Mama?"

"Oh, all right."

They strolled through a lobby rimmed by freestanding vases filled with flowers casting their perfume toward the entryway, then paraded across a dance floor circled by tables of diners. The diners quit eating to talk in hushed tones as the entourage followed the Maitre d' across the center of the room. Members and guests cast admiring glances at the tanned young lady wearing a white silk dress that covered her form from eight inches above her knees to her bosom where the cleavage tickled the imagination. Another who attracted attention could have been an exotic model. She wore a long, tight, chartreuse brocade dress with a split up the side that showed off shapely legs. A white rose decorated the left side of her oriental bun coiffeur.

The one who received a majority of the glances of admiration and murmurs of approval, from both staff and members, strutted in front of the others as if she were the Empress of Honshu--a mature woman, dressed in traditional Japanese garb. She was a full four feet tall and had a hairdo that added another four inches. She waved her hand for her entourage to stop while she bowed to her admirers, then held her head high and led her subjects to their table. Last in line came two ordinary men.

The tall man was sure Meg would honor her promise not to indulge in magic, and he was sure Yoshi would keep hers in order to maintain continued admiration. As he followed Yoshi across the dance floor, he was comforted by the awe he sensed from the diners and was certain she would keep her image of royalty intact.

66

Conversation returned to a normal level after the Maitre d' escorted the group to a round table overlooking the dance floor. Another man in a tuxedo hurried over to pull a chair out for Yoshi. She bowed and winked at him. He hurried away with a flustered look, leaving the others to seat themselves.

Harvey called the Maitre d' back. "What time does the music start?"

The man checked his watch. "In a half hour. The Jazztones are playing tonight."

"Sounds like old folks' music," Rosie said.

"Not entirely. They play big band sound but do rock also. I believe you'll find their music will appeal to all of you."

Harvey looked at Meg. "Do you dance?"

"I love to dance. Do you rock?"

"Sure, but first I want to dance a slow, romantic ballad with my fiancée."

Tears made Meg's eyes glisten.

"I'm out of practice," he said. "It's been four years."

"Me too. It's been eighty years."

Yoshi frowned. "It's been two hundred years since I've had a drink."

A young woman wearing a short black dress and white apron came to the table and bowed to Yoshi, who nodded. She moved over next to Harvey. "My name is Sheri. Would you like an aperitif?" She glanced around the table as everyone signaled approval. Harvey raised five fingers. "How appropriate--we'd like five dry sherries from Sheri."

Sheri fixed her gaze on Meg. "Are you twenty-one?"

"Just barely."

"How old is barely?"

"One hundred and fifty-five."

"That should be enough."

Harvey was glad to see the glasses of sherry delivered to the table were tiny, so the party would stay sober and retain the air of dignity that surrounded them. At a time when conversation was minimal, the mature little woman, who was still receiving admiring looks from diners, picked up her glass between her thumb and first finger and held it high. "What the fuck is this?"

All movement and sound in the dining room was suspended except for the echo of Yoshi's words and Meg's admonition, "Mamasan."

Yoshi held the glass out in front of Meg. "What do you expect? Look at this tiny little thing I have in my hand. Am I supposed to get a buzz on from that?"

"Shh, Mom. You're not here to get a buzz on. This is a going-away party."

"Well, if I don't get a decent drink pretty soon, I will be going away."

"That's only to whet your appetite," Harvey said.

Yoshi scowled. "I don't want to whet my appetite--I want to wet my whistle." She downed the sherry in one gulp, sat the glass down, and pulled a bottle out of her purse. While many of her admirers watched, she dumped her glass of water on the carpet, filled the glass with sake, and plopped the bottle in the middle of the table.

Harvey grabbed the bottle and handed it to Meg. "Yoshi, you can't do that."

"I'll make it invisible, and they'll never know."

Meg handed the bottle to Yoshi. "Put it back in your purse--remember your promise."

Yoshi put two fingers over her mouth "Oh, all right." She used her other hand to shove the bottle into her purse. Harvey heard a distinct plop when she brought the hand back to the table top but didn't see anything that could have made the sound.

As the others read their menus, Yoshi picked up a fork and admired it. Harvey saw her studying the fork. "It's real silver," he said. Meg reached over to remove a knife, a fork, and a spoon from her mother's purse and placed them on the table in their original positions. Quiet reigned until Harvey noticed that Yoshi wasn't smiling. He picked up his glass and held it up to her. "A toast to you, Yoshi. Where will you be going?"

"Going?"

Yes. When you leave here."

"Back home, I guess. It's too crowded at your place."

"To Japan?"

"No. To the south side of Lansing. I'm not leaving this country. Not until I know for sure I'm going to be a grandmother."

"You can't stay here without a permanent visa."

"I can do anything I want except get a decent drink in this place."

Meg nudged Harvey. "She's been trying to get rid of me for fifty years. She wouldn't consider living with us."

The lights dimmed when the music started, so Harvey's guests were able to hide the fact that their aperitif glasses never got empty. Harvey checked his watch. "We should probably eat someday." He signaled to a waiter, who came to the table. "When you get back here with a bottle of Merlot, we'll be ready to order." The combo played the opening notes of "Blue Moon," and diners headed to the dance floor. Harvey placed his hand on Meg's. "May I have this dance?"

"Yes."

Yoshi picked up her purse. "While you two are rubbing bellies, I'm going to the *benjo*." Hand in hand, Rosie and Ted swayed to the music as they followed Meg and Harvey to the dance floor. The four of them demonstrated how a love song should be danced and stayed on the floor for another ballad. When they returned to the table, Yoshi was back from the ladies room.

They ordered and ate dinner, danced again, finished the wine, and smiled a lot. Harvey looked around to signal for his check and noticed an officious looking man in a business suit huddled with three waiters. One of the waiters pointed at Harvey's party. The one in the business suit evidently concurred with the waiter, but instead of heading to the table, he and the waiters walked in the other direction. A different waiter came with the check. He dropped it in front of Harvey, and without a word, turned and left.

Harvey's party made their way across the dance floor and again received admiring glances from the other patrons. Harvey noticed Yoshi was lagging behind. He stopped and saw she was having trouble with her purse. He was about to ask what the problem was when one of the handles snapped. The clatter of metal, colliding with wood, echoed through the dining room and caused diners to focus attention on the petite woman they had earlier admired. Now, she stood in the middle of the dance floor staring down at an expanding sunburst of knives, forks, and spoons.

Yoshi waved at the rest of her party as she was carted from the University Club in a sheriff's black and white. Harvey followed the patrol car in his Olds, carrying Meg, Ted, and Rosie. When they entered the county booking room at the court house, one of two young men sitting on a bench next to a deputy, waved at Harvey. "Hello, Professor Long."

Harvey recognized the two as students of his. He kept walking, hoping they'd forget they'd seen him. He, Ted, Rosie, and Meg sat on the front bench while the arresting deputy and

Yoshi stood in front of a desk perched on a raised platform. A short sergeant with a pot belly, stepped up and sat behind the desk. He surveyed the room. "Okay, Gordon, what you got?"

"A woman charged with grand theft."

"Which one of these broads is the culprit?"

"The little one."

The sergeant glared at Rosie and Meg. "Which one, the girl in white or the Viet Namese?"

A voice came from down in front of the desk. "Japanese-American."

The desk sergeant's eyes searched the entire room. "Who said that?"

Gordon pointed down at Yoshi. "The culprit did."

The sergeant leaned forward. "I can't see her. Is she a juvenile? If she is, you brought her to the wrong court."

"No, she's old, but she's a runt. . . . Ow!"

"What happened?" the sergeant said.

"She kicked me."

"Where?"

"In the shin."

"Hold her up here so I can see her."

Gordon bent down but jumped back up. "Ow! Ow!"

"What did she do now?"

"I don't want to say in front of the ladies. I'll tell you later in the men's room."

"Why in the men's room?"

"It just seems like an appropriate place to discuss what she did to me."

"Do you really believe it's necessary to discuss what she did?"

"No. I'd just as soon forget what she did if they ever quit hurting."

The sergeant leaned over the desk and glimpsed Yoshi

for the first time. "Miss, I don't know what you did to Officer Gordon, but if you did what I think you did, it's not the proper thing for a lady to do."

"Next time he calls me a runt, I'll turn him into a toad."

"I'd suggest you not turn him into a toad--that would bring another charge against you."

"What do you suggest I turn him into?"

"Nothing."

"You want me to make him disappear? I can do that."

"That's not what I meant."

"Then why didn't you say what you meant?"

"Young lady, I'm supposed to ask the questions here."

"It's a good thing you called me young, or there'd be two toads hopping around. I could make you both invisible, and somebody would step on you."

"Can you come up here where I can see you without lying on my belly all night?"

"If you're insinuating we should spend the night together, I'd suggest we get to know each other better first. We can start with a quiet evening at the University Club."

"From what I heard over our radio, the last time you were there didn't turn out to be a quiet evening."

"My daughter and her teacher were a bit rowdy, but they can't go with us because they sleep together and have to get up early in the morning."

"That so?" As soon as the sergeant said those words, Yoshi appeared, sitting in the middle of his desk. He jerked back in his chair. "How'd you do that?"

She pointed her thumb behind her. "He lifted me."

"I didn't see him do it."

Yoshi touched the sergeant's chin. "There's a lot you ain't seen yet, sweetie."

"I'm seeing more tonight than I want to see. Let's get

72

down to business."

"In front of all these people?"

"Officer Gordon, what's this woman's--ah--this young lady's name?"

"She has no ID, but she says her name is Yoshiko."

The sergeant glared at Yoshi. "What's your full name?"

"Yoshiko." She smiled and touched him on the chin with her finger. "But my friends call me Yoshi. You can call me Yoshi if you'd like."

"Why don't you have a last name?" he said.

"I don't know who my father was."

"What about your mother?"

"I don't know if she knew his name either."

"I was asking if you know your mother's last name."

"I never asked her."

"Is your residence here or in Japan?"

"Are you insinuating we should go to my place instead of the University Club?" Yoshi put her hand under her chin and fluttered her eyes. "I really should know more about you first. What's your name, sweetie?"

"Homer."

"Okay, that's enough. You're cute, a little pudgy but cute. Let's go to my place."

Homer sucked his belly in. "Thank you. It's been years since anyone called me cute. I think you're cute too, and I'd like to go home with you. I'd even like to go to the University Club with you, but I'd have to explain those actions to the sheriff and to my wife, so I'm going to put you in jail overnight to answer these charges in the morning."

Yoshi blew Homer a kiss, then pointed two fingers at him and Officer Gordon. They disappeared. She jumped down from the desk and joined Harvey, who sat with his eyes open wide. "Let's go have a drink," she said.

Harvey didn't move. "What happened to them?"

Yoshi pointed to the floor at the side of the desk where two toads hopped around, one with a little pot belly.

Meg shook her head. "You can't leave them like that."

"They're on a timer. They'll become themselves again in an hour if nobody steps on them in the meantime." Yoshi stopped in front of the two young men waiting for their turn in front of the sergeant. "You can leave now. I don't know what you're in here for, but they'll find you innocent of all charges. If they don't, you let me know, and I'll come back to reason with them." The two students hustled out the door.

Yoshi stomped her foot in front of the toads. "Did you hear me? . . . Answer me. Did you hear me?"

"Beedip."

"Beedip."

Harvey hurried toward the exit. "Let's get out of here."

CHAPTER 8

It was dark by the time they returned to the house. Harvey and Meg sat on the living room sofa while Yoshi curled up on a recliner. Through the open door to the deck, Harvey heard Rosie's voice. "Ted, is this something you want to get involved in?"

"I think Yoshi's a hoot. And you're part of it, so it's where I want to be."

"What about my dad and Meg?"

"They're cool." Soon, Ted's and Rosie's footsteps faded as they went down the stairs from the deck to the lawn.

Harvey opened a bottle of Merlot and filled three glasses. Yoshi raised her glass. "Weren't you guys proud of me at the club?"

"For what? For getting so much silverware in one purse?" Meg said.

Yoshi glared at her. "No. For holding up my end of the bargain. I could have had that silver float out the window to the car or to the den, but I kept my pledge and stole it honestly. Remember? No magic?" She chugged down the Merlot.

Harvey touched the Merlot bottle. "What about the disappearing sake?"

Yoshi held her glass out, and the bottle floated over to fill it with wine. "I knew you'd hold that against me. Watch your step, or I'll give those two cops a companion."

75

Harvey closed his eyes and shook his head. "Down what road am I headed?"

"You ain't seen nothing yet, sweetie."

He opened his eyes. "Last person you said that to is now a toad."

Yoshi held her glass high as in a toast. Meg shook a finger at her mother. "Stop that, Mamasan. Go entertain that young man who thinks you're a hoot. Forget I said that. Go home and let me spend time with my professor." Yoshi tossed down the rest of her wine and vanished.

"I wish she wouldn't do stuff like that," Meg said.

Harvey smiled. "Why not? It doesn't hurt anybody."

"No, but it reminds me too much of what I am." She reached over, turned the lamp off, and curled up to him.

In the dim light that seeped in from the other room, he put his hands on the sides of Meg's head, eased it around until she faced him, then kissed her. "I love you like you are."

"A half-witch?"

"I love Megumi and don't mind the magic part."

"It's not just the magic. In fact, I seem to be losing some of my power, and I don't care--I don't want to be Kitsune--I want to be your lover, your woman."

He held her close. "You are."

She looked away. "You don't know the whole story about me."

"Look, I'm not concerned about the past. I love you as you are."

She wept. "But it's true--I'm part Kitsune."

"I know."

"But we don't know what I may have done to you or may do to you. Kitsune are not people, they're foxes that only take the shape of women. Kitsune blood runs in my veins. I'm scared." Tears rolled down her cheeks. She covered her face with her hands.

Harvey ran his fingers across the top of her head as if he were combing her hair. "I saw what was happening, my sudden attraction to you, the statements I made that were unintended. The cold spot on my leg, and a smiling moon were pretty good clues that you weren't an ordinary woman. I fell in love with you in spite of that. I fell in love with you when I discovered you were the person I'd been waiting for. You're so much fun to be with. Rosie says she likes me now that I'm alive again. I'm that way because of you."

She wrapped her arms around him. "Love me." He kissed her tears away and carried her to the bedroom. After they made love, she said, "This may be our last night together."

Harvey sat up in bed. "What did you say?"

"I'm going to Japan."

"You can't mean that."

"Yes. I'm scared."

"Scared of what?"

She put her hands over her face. "You may be dead in three months. That's how much time it takes to die from the curse. I don't want to do that to you if I haven't already."

"Your fears are exaggerated."

"You're still under the impression I'm a woman."

"You are a woman, and I'm not wasting away."

"It's only been a few days. Don't you remember what happened to my father."

"Well, you're different. You mother's Kitsune, but you take after your father. Have you ever been a fox?"

"Not that I know of."

"Have you ever caused a man to waste away or die?"

"I've never been with a man other than you. I never met one I wanted to be with. I knew I wanted you the moment I first saw you--I fell in love with you. I know I have human traits, but I have to find out how much Kitsune may lurk in my genes. I can only discover that in Japan."

"How do you expect to discover anything by going back there again?"

"I don't know. I'll find a lair of Kitsune and see if I'm like them. I'll emulate them and see if they accept me. I've already made the decision. I'm going, and I'll only come back if I determine I won't cause you harm."

"Will you marry me before you go?"

"No. I'm leaving tomorrow morning."

"Do you need money?"

"My mother has plenty."

"I believe that. You picked a good time to go, though. Thursday I'm to speak to a conference at the Grand Hotel on Mackinac Island. I'll drive up tomorrow."

"Any hotel would be grand if I could be with you."

"A student, as young and pretty as you, would be as welcome at this college conference as Susha was at the picnic."

"Where's Mackinac Island?"

"In the middle of the straits that connect Lake Huron and Lake Superior--an amazing place--no automobiles allowed on the island--only horse-drawn carriages and bicycles."

"Sounds like a nice place for a honeymoon."

Meg's plane flew away early in the morning. Harvey stood next to Yoshi and watched it disappear into low hanging clouds, through a window that appeared streaked because of his tears. He had known she was leaving, but now the realization hit him hard. Yoshi climbed onto a chair and wiped his face as he stared at the hole in the cloud layer where the jet had disappeared. He drove Yoshi to her place across from the cemetery and then continued on to the college.

As soon as he checked into the business office, Sophie hurried from behind her desk. "Dean Pigeon wants to see you in his office, but first I want to tell you what it's about." She led him into a storeroom and closed the door, leaving them in the dark. "One of the instructors told Mr. Pigeon you were involved in a major incident at the University Club last night. An Asian woman was caught stealing silver, and you were arrested along with her." Sophie pulled his hand up and placed it on her left breast. "My heart pounded when I heard that."

Harvey removed his hand from where she had put it. "Thanks for the information."

"There's more. The dean asked me to check it out with the Ingham County Sheriff. I did but haven't told him the results yet. The department has no record of you or anybody else being charged with a theft at the club. I thought you'd like to know that before you had to face him." She pulled his hand up to her left breast again and held it there. "I'm glad I talked to you first."

Having more trouble prying his hand loose this time, he put his hands in his pants pockets. "Thank you, Sophie. Is there anything else I should know?"

She reached back and opened the door, letting light shine on her smile. "Your student, Megumi Sakuma, took a temporary drop and left no forwarding address."

"Thank you again, Sophie. I'd better see the dean now." He stepped past her and escaped.

Minutes later, Dean Pigeon glared at Harvey from behind his desk. "One of our professors informed me he was present at the University Club last night when you were involved in a fracas there. He said you were arrested."

Harvey frowned and shook his head. "I am deeply hurt that any of our staff would suggest such a thing. I had dinner at the club with my daughter and friends, then spent a quiet evening at home, preparing my lessons for today. I'd appreciate it if you'd check with the authorities. It must be a case of mistaken identity."

"I sure hope you're right. Otherwise, it would reflect badly on the college and on our staff. If you're found guilty, I'll have to terminate your contract."

"Please check. I'm sure you'll find no record of my being arrested."

"That would certainly go a long way to relieving my mind. By the way, did you know that Megumi Sakuma has taken a temporary drop?"

"Yes. I understand she had to go to Japan on business."

"An interesting woman, don't you think?"

"Yes, sir. Now, if that's all, I must get ready for my class." Harvey hurried out of Pigeon's office and touched his brow in a little salute as he passed Sophie. In the lounge where he had spent time with Meg, Yoshi sat with her hands folded. He hurried to her. "What are you doing here?"

"I want to see if you're holding up better than I am."

Harvey reached out and covered Yoshi's hands with his. "Yoshi, I was so involved with my own problems I forgot about you. Let's have lunch together and talk." Dean Pigeon chose that exact time to walk out of his office. He stopped in his tracks, as if stunned to see Professor Long had taken up with another Asian woman. He turned, jerked his head up, and marched away.

Harvey and Yoshi crossed the street to the Downtown Deli, where they walked past a hissing cappuccino machine, and sat at a corner table away from the other patrons. He pointed at a menu board on the wall. "What would you like?"

She didn't look at the board. "I'd like a glass of wine, but I've caused you enough trouble to last a while. Get me a bowl of soup. I'll sit here and try to be good."

Harvey laughed. "It depends on whose interpretation of good you use. Personally I believe most of the things you do are good. I'll be right back with some food that will make you forget everything else."

"Will it taste like wine?"

"I don't think so."

"Will it make me taller?"

"No."

"Then it won't make me forget anything."

Harvey returned from the counter, carrying a tray loaded with bowls of soup, rolls, and cups of tea. He set them on the table.

Yoshi took a spoonful of vegetable soup, tasted it and nodded approval. "One thing I'll never forget," she said. "I like you so much, I've tried to push you and Megumi together. But I really didn't have to. Now, I realize you two have sought each other for a long time."

"I believe you're right about that."

"I know what my daughter's going through. She's afraid she'll do to you what I did to her father. Did she tell you about him?"

Harvey hesitated while buttering his roll. "Only that he died. She didn't say it was a result of your relationship, but that in your mind, it was."

"Yes. It was in reality as well as in my mind. I was young and had never felt that way about any man I was with until I met Elmer."

"So you did know his name."

Yoshi spoke while Harvey ate. "Yes, but this is the first time I've spoken it since he died. It was the last word he heard. I decided I would never repeat the name, and now that I have, I may never say it again. Hopefully, my daughter will have the opportunity to enjoy the lasting relationship I never had. I tell you this because it depends on you, or should I say on you being able to survive the curse of the Kitsune." She picked up her tea and sipped it.

"I believe in what Meg and I can do together."

She set her teacup down and opened her eyes wide. "Oh! You want children?"

"I was talking about surviving the curse."

"I don't believe you have to worry. Kitsune are foxes, but not Megumi. Because of my transgression with a mortal, I gave birth to a baby girl, a poor excuse for a witch, who seldom used what powers she had as she grew. Even today, part of her concern is that she used magic to make you fall for her."

Harvey shook his head. "No, no. I was excited about her the first time I saw her walk into my class, even before she knew I existed."

"Ha!" Yoshi pushed away the rest of her soup and roll, and lifted to her mouth a glass Harvey hadn't noticed before. She sipped a red liquid from it, then spoke. "She fell for you when she saw you in Osaka. You may not remember her, but she remembered you. She thought the unexpected attraction would disappear, but after a year of trying to rid herself of the feeling, she gave up and came to Lansing. From then on you were doomed. Everything you experienced with her those first few days here was contrived. Even the sound of her walking down the hall. "

"Question, Yoshi--why would someone who loves life, as much as she, be attracted to a man like me who had given up on life?"

She took another drink of the red liquid that resembled grape juice, then gave a satisfied sigh. "She saw the real you beneath the gloom."

"Another question--if as you say, I was doomed, then

why is Meg so jealous of me being around other women when I only have eyes for her?"

Yoshi set the glass down but kept a hand wrapped around it as if to protect the contents. "Simple. Kitsune cannot grasp the concept of being faithful. Their lives are devoted to servicing men who cheat. Even though Meg is faithful and knows you are too, that bit of Kitsune in her blood is always in the back of her mind. Logically, she trusts you, but the emotion of her heritage peeks through when other women are around. I passed that flaw on to her along with the ability to fall in love. You're lucky she just rags on you--it killed my man."

"So you don't think I'm a dead man."

She waved her hand. "Who knows? She's not Kitsune. She only has Kitsune blood in her veins. Now, she might kill you, but first you'd waste away. The problem is you look wasted away already." She put her hand on the back of his. "Excuse me for saying that again, but it's true. Evidently, mortal women have a motherly urge to feed and take care of their men."

"What do you think Meg will discover in Japan?"

"I don't know if she'll be able to accomplish anything, especially since I've been on the Kitsune shit list for hundreds of years." She sighed. "I believe I made two right decisions in my short life. One was to seduce that redheaded sailor, and the other was to raise the result of that interlude. So that's the good and the good of it."

"Do you want to stay with me until she comes back?"

"I want to, but I didn't want to ask. If I do stay, it won't be for long, because I have two relatives coming from Japan to keep me company until Megumi returns."

Harvey leaned toward Yoshi, wishing she hadn't said the word, relatives. "Kitsune?"

"Yes. Cousins of mine, but I'll make sure they behave

while they're here."

He relaxed. "Make sure--I don't want all of my friends to waste away and die."

"I understand, but I need their companionship until my daughter returns unless you let me sleep with you."

He put his dishes on their tray. "Bring them on." He checked his watch. "I have to teach a class."

Yoshi chugged down the contents of her glass and put it on the tray with her other dishes. "I've known her for a hundred-and-fifty-five years. That's a problem neither of you will be able to solve. She'll outlive you by hundreds of years."

"I hadn't given that much thought. It won't be a problem for me, but it will for her. It seems unfair." He tapped his watch. "I have to go."

She picked up the tray. "I do too. I have an appointment with a businessman."

Harvey laughed. "How much is silver bringing these days, Yoshi?"

Yoshi dumped the tray in the dirty dishes container and kept walking. "Sayonara."

Even though full of students, Harvey's classroom seemed empty. He taught a pretty good session, not counting the times he turned his attention to the door or listened for the sound of Zouris.

When class was over, one of the young men who had been present in the court house, joined Harvey at the front of the room. "That was a pretty interesting show the Japanese woman gave at County Booking," he said.

"You saw her turn those cops into toads?"

"Yeah. That was cool, man."

"I had lunch with that little woman today, and she said to let her know if I heard anyone repeat the story of what happened there. She said she'd like to meet whoever's telling the tales. She's unhappy with the type of toads she transformed those men into and says she could use a couple of young guys to practice on. She wants to develop a better looking toad. . . . You going to tell anybody what happened at the booking room?"

"I don't remember no booking room--I was out of town all last weekend."

"What about your friend?"

"Yeah--him too--guaranteed."

Harvey walked toward the classroom door. "Have a nice day."

On the way out, he thought about the coming visit of Yoshi's cousins and wondered if two full-blown Kitsune could cause four times as much trouble as one half-Kitsune.

CHAPTER 9

Harvey leaned against the rail on the bow of the ferry, inhaled mist from the turbulent water, and stared at Mackinac Island, a quiet sentry in the middle of the Straits of Mackinac. The hundreds of lights on the quarter-mile porch of the Grand Hotel reminded him of the marquee on the old Michigan Theater where he and Ami had gone occasionally on Saturday nights when they had money for two tickets.

The wind pushed him in the back as he walked the gangway to the dock. He hailed a horse-drawn carriage and climbed on. With closed eyes, he listened as the horse trotted through the darkness and into the village, the clop, clop of hooves on pavement cartwheeling him back in time and reminding him of what first drew him to Mackinac Island, the sounds and aroma of horses which replaced the noise and odor of automobiles. As the carriage carried him along the waterfront past small shops lit up by flickering gas lanterns, he reminisced about how life must have been a hundred years ago.

The spell disappeared, and he became alert when he realized the woman he was attracted to, not only had been alive back then, but was fifty years old at the time. His head moved from side to side.

Thoughts of Meg retreated when he arrived at the Grand. He dropped his bags in his second-floor room and walked downstairs to a registration table at the entrance to the banquet room. He recognized the woman behind the table, Mitzi St. Marie, the travel professor who had red wine splotches on her white dress at the picnic. His mind wandered. *She's cute and sexy, the kind of woman who may have pulled me out of the rut I'd been wallowing in, without my getting into the trouble I'm probably headed for.*

Mitzi rose from her chair. "I'm glad you're here."

"Why's that?"

"I'm lonely."

Harvey's thought pattern switched 180 degrees from the advantages of spending time with Mitzi. He swung a hand around at the dozens of people milling about. "How can you be lonely with all these hospitable people here?"

Her voice was tiny as a little girl's. "But I don't know them, and they don't know me."

"You're a good-looking woman, and I'm sure you'd attract a bunch of them if you'd get out from behind that table."

Mitzi bowed her head and looked at Harvey out of the top of her eyes. "I know, but I thought it would be nice to take a break and have a drink with you."

"I'd enjoy that, Mitzi, but I have to get ready for my talk tomorrow." Her shoulders sagged, and she gave him a glum look as she handed him a conference packet. She gave a little wave, and as he walked away, he wondered if he should have spent time with her. The more he thought about it, the more he realized he had made the right decision not to become involved with her. Meg and Ami, were the only women who had ever generated electricity in his relationship with them. Strange as it seemed, he missed both of them.

He worked on his presentation but soon gave up. He opened a window and stared at the lights on the five miles of suspension bridge that connected the two peninsulas of Michigan. After a while he went to bed, knowing that the relaxing sound of waves breaking on the shore below would lull him to sleep. It didn't happen.

His thoughts reverted to the two women who had been, and were now so much a part of his life. It didn't make sense to have an honest-to-God witch turn his life into an upside-down world dominated by sex, wine, and outlandish situations, but until Meg came along, he couldn't have envisioned another woman in his life other than Ami, much less being drawn to one. Being drawn was a gross understatement--drowning in visions of her came closer to reality, similar in respects to what had happened when he gave up the serious life to follow Ami Long to the edge of sanity.

Harvey had been studious when he started at State and was well into the spring term before he tried to date a freckles-on-her-nose, dishwater blonde he'd been eyeing since day one. On a Friday after science class, he asked her for a date. He didn't think she'd accept, but she surprised him by saying, "Come to my house at seven."

He smiled all the way to the dorm because she lived only four blocks from college. He didn't own a car. After dinner at the dorm, he put on a white shirt, summer slacks, a sweater, and his new tennis shoes. She met him at the door of her parents' white colonial home, wearing khaki shorts, a white halter, and running shoes. Her pony tail swung as she stepped onto the porch. "I apologize. My folks just left to see a play in Detroit, so I didn't have a chance to run."

"Run?"

"Yes, I run every day. Can you run two miles?"

He thought for a moment. . . . "Sure."

She motioned for him to come in and grabbed the waist of his sweater. "Take that off, and let's go." She helped pull the sweater over his head and tossed it onto a sofa.

She led Harvey to a park and onto a path of wood chips that led through a pine forest. "This is one of my favorite places. I love the pine bouquet."

Ami took off running, and he followed, catching up and staying with her, even when his breathing became labored, and even though his legs objected to the exercise they weren't told about ahead of time. After two miles, they slowed to a walk. She grabbed his hand and held it. "That was tough, wasn't it?"

He saw she was hardly sweating while he was dripping wet. "Not too bad."

"Most guys come up with an excuse for not running, or if they do start, they give up. Then I give up on them. I've watched you for weeks and guessed you were not the quitting type. I'm glad you're here." Ami swung his hand with hers as they walked to her home, both keeping their thoughts to themselves. He was glad he had kept going.

She led him into her house and upstairs, where she pointed to a bathroom. "You'll find a clean towel ready for you." He hesitated. She nudged his hip with her elbow and walked away. "Go ahead." He felt uneasy taking off his clothes in a strange house but did so and stepped into the shower. A minute later, the door opened, and through the knurled glass shower door, he watched Ami pick up his clothes. "Don't worry, I won't look at you," she said. "I'll wash them and leave one of my dad's robes for you to wear until they're dry. . . . You sure are lean." She hung the robe on a hook, walked out, and closed the door.

He dried himself, put on the white terry cloth robe that would be short even for a short man, and stepped out of the bathroom. Ami waited in the hall. She wrapped an arm around one of his and led him into what appeared to be a bedroom converted to a reading room. "You can sit on the sofa while I shower, then we can tell each other lies until your things are dry." She left, and within minutes, he heard the shower running. He stared at the bathroom door until the sound stopped, and the door opened. Ami entered the reading room wearing a robe, the twin of the one he had on, except shorter. Anxiety raged through his body.

"I dressed the same as you," she said, "as long as we're on a date together." She sat on the sofa, bringing a moist warmth with her. She moved her knee over until it touched his, and her robe fell open, giving him a grand view of her legs. He was sure his heart beat out loud, and he blushed when he thought maybe she could hear it.

Harvey settled down when they talked about why they chose State and what their majors were. When twilight came, she left him but returned moments later. "Your clothes will be dry in a few minutes. No sense turning on the lights. This way we don't have to close the drapes."

"It's okay like it is. I can still see you. You're very pretty. How old are you?"

"Nineteen. How old are you?"

"Nineteen."

She cocked her head and gazed at him. "You look older. Are you a virgin?"

"What?"

"Are you a virgin?"

He surprised himself when he found how easy it was to lie. "No, I'm not."

"Me either." She looked down, then up at him. "Actually, that's not true. Most of my friends who were virgins when they came here say they aren't now. I didn't want to admit I was." She cocked her head again, and her eyes met his. "I'm still a virgin. You are too, aren't you?"

He bit his lower lip and lowered his eyes. "Yes," he

murmured.

"That's okay. We can relate." She put her hand on his knee. "Coke?"

The warmth of her hand excited him. He glanced at her, then away. "No, thanks. I drank water in the shower."

She laughed. "Me too."

It was quiet for a while as she gazed at him. He returned the look for just a moment and then averted his eyes.

She stood in front of him. "Harvey?"

"Yes?"

"Please stand."

He stood facing her. She untied her belt, then his, and their robes fell open. She moved against him and pulled both robes back. She lay her head on his chest, which was heaving as rapidly as when he ran. She put her arms around him inside the robe. "I want to feel you." Harvey'd had daydreams of being in a situation such as this, but now he was so nervous he thought he might actually faint rather than follow through as he'd always done in his imagination. He didn't faint. He placed his hands inside her robe and enjoyed the heat from her body, giving him feelings stronger than those he had imagined.

She looked up. "I can tell it feels good to you too." She pulled him against her. They drifted down onto the sofa and lay side by side, kissing and caressing each other. Her mouth was still touching his, and he inhaled her warm breath when she whispered, "Get on top of me."

Two months later, Ami and Harvey were married. A month after the wedding, the preacher who performed the ceremony, caught them engaged in their favorite form of exercise, in the woods behind the church, in the middle of the afternoon. Once, while doing it below a ledge on the bank of the river that ran through the campus, students in a canoe paddled against the current to watch the action. Harvey and Ami continued their lovemaking. When they received a round of applause for a job well done, they bowed from their prone positions. Their newfound freedom from concern, of what others thought about them, stayed with Ami and Harvey through the next thirteen years of exercise, sex, and devotion.

Years later, lying alone in bed, Harvey thought how strange to feel unfaithful to Meg for reliving his love life with Ami. He recalled, only days earlier, he had felt unfaithful to Ami because of his attraction to Meg. He had always thought maybe his being different had attracted those two strange women to him. Now, he realized they both had seen in him, a soul-mate who lurked beneath his serious exterior, and they both brought to his life the kind of excitement Rosie liked. They provided the electric spark that turned him on.

He didn't rest well that night and dozed three times in marketing meetings the next day. He received hearty applause for his breakout group presentation, and after trips in a carriage, on a boat, and in his car, he was in Lansing and asleep by ten.

The doorbell rang, and Harvey checked his clock-radio-- it was midnight. After he put on a robe and flipped on a living room light, he was surprised to see Yoshi standing in the middle of the room. She snapped her fingers. "Meet my cousins, Emiko and Kyoko." He didn't see anyone, but when Yoshi snapped her fingers again, two women, one Yoshi's size and the other only inches taller, materialized in front of the sofa. Yoshi gestured for them to move to the middle of the room.

He gazed at the taller of the two, a curvaceous woman in micro-miniskirt who appeared to be Rosie's age and could pass for a Japanese movie star. "That's Emiko," Yoshi said.

She pointed at the other, who wore a low cut t-shirt and low-rider jeans. "This is Kyoko." The sisters bowed. Harvey bowed in return. "Don't mind it if they flash off and on occasionally," Yoshi said. "They were invisible on their plane trip, and sometimes it takes a while to get back in shape." He surveyed them. *They're already in great shape.* They giggled. Kyoko reminded him of the shy young girl in a Norman Rockwell painting except for the expanse of skin showing between her jeans and her top. "Do you speak English?" he said.

Kyoko lowered her head and peered at him from the top of her eyes as she twirled a pigtail between her fingers. Emiko answered Harvey's question, "Yes. We speak many languages quite well and can do almost anything."

"I believe I'll find that's true."

"I know," she said.

"That's right, you read minds too. That's why you laughed a moment ago." They giggled again. Harvey bent down to Kyoko's level. "Do you speak?" She gave a tiny nod.

"She's shy," Emiko said.

"Quite different from the Kitsune I know." The sisters smiled. Yoshi glared.

Harvey waved a finger at the sisters. "Do you need a place to stay?"

Yoshi stepped forward. "I've already found suitable lodging for them. And you'll find they are self-sufficient."

"Good. There's something I'd like to do as a welcome treat for you. I'd like to take the three of you to participate in an American tradition."

"That would be nice," Yoshi said. "We've never been to a county fair."

Harvey laughed. "I still have trouble getting used to my thoughts being public domain. I'll have to be careful."

"Only when we're alone," Emiko said. "In a crowd, noise hides a person's thoughts."

"That's nice to know. We'll be in a crowd at the fair." He turned to Yoshi. "I do have one request though. Don't get me in trouble with your magic."

Her voice was muffled from holding a hand over her mouth. "Definitely not."

"I understand that truth and you are strangers."

She took her hand away from her mouth and pondered what he had said. "That's a true statement."

"I'm planning on taking you tomorrow afternoon."

"I know."

"You probably know what time to be here." Yoshi and her cousins nodded.

Emiko and Kyoko bowed to Harvey, then reversed their direction, and bowed to Yoshi. Harvey blinked, and his mouth hung open. He motioned with an index finger for Yoshi to stay when the cousins headed for the front door. The two cousins waited at the front door as Harvey leaned down to Yoshi and whispered, "Emiko's not wearing panties."

"I know."

"Never?"

"Never."

He gazed at Emiko and Kyoko in the entryway. They were giggling. Yoshi waved at Harvey and walked into the night with her cousins.

Harvey sauntered through the house as if looking for someone, then walked out on the deck where he stood in a light rain until his hair stuck to his forehead. He went back inside and sat on the sofa. He felt all alone until he saw her. He smiled. He stood, walked toward the end table where she stood, and blew her a kiss. "I forgot about you. I'm glad you're here to keep me company, Minnie."

Later, lying in bed, he realized how easily he had accepted as perfectly normal the crazy things he had been part of since he met Yoshi. He also surmised, that with three full-blown witches instead of one, he was sure to end up in court again or worse.

CHAPTER 10

The sun peeked between cotton-candy clouds as Harvey pulled into a parking lot across from the entrance to the fairgrounds. He heard excited talk from Emiko and Kyoko in the back seat. They were pointing at a grove of maple trees. He took a closer look, and on the other side of the trees, saw a tent with the sides rolled up. Inside were tables and people. He looked at the tent, at the two Kitsune, and at the tent again. "Bingo." The cousins' heads bobbed up and down. Harvey led the way. "If that's what you want, that's where we go."

They found open seats in the second row from the front amidst players who had three or four bingo cards spread in front of them. A woman, dressed like a Gypsy, called numbers in a tired voice while players ran their fingers over their cards. A deputy sheriff, who appeared to have emigrated from the wild west, sat in the corner with his hands wrapped around a coffee cup as if to keep them warm. Harvey thought both the deputy and the Gypsy woman would be more alert if they realized they had, in their midst, three real witches who would make a Gypsy seem like a convent student. Yoshi's cousins laughed.

Harvey glanced at Emiko. "You said you couldn't read minds in a crowd."

"The people were listening for numbers."

Yoshi opened the bag in front of her kimono and pulled

out a bottle of sake. Harvey grabbed the bottle and stuck it back in her bag. "You can't do that here. Wait until we leave the fair." She pursed her lips and glared at him.

An older man behind them yelled, "Bingo," and was called to the front to have his card checked by the Gypsy. At the same time, a woman left her seat in the front row to sell cards for the next game. Harvey bought a card for each of the Kitsune, causing the cousins to bounce with excitement.

Emiko dropped her card. "Oh," she said. She stood and bent to pick it up with her back toward the deputy. The deputy did a double-take, and his cup fell to the ground, splattering coffee on his pants. The Gypsy announced a game of straight bingo. When she called the first number. Emiko covered a number with a plastic button. After three more numbers were called, she yelled, "Bingo."

The Gypsy leaned forward and peered at Emiko. "Are you sure?"

"Yes, I'm positive."

The Gypsy glanced toward the deputy, then back at Emiko. "Bring your card here, and we'll check it."

Emiko carried the card to the Gypsy who checked the numbers called against the card. "Amazing," the woman said. "I've never seen it happen before, but the young lady has won with the minimum numbers required." The Gypsy gave her five bills. "Congratulations--you've won a hundred dollars."

Emiko stuffed the bills into her purse as she returned to her seat. A bill fluttered to the ground. When she bent over to pick it up the deputy's whole body jerked, and he almost fell out of his chair. Emiko smiled at him and returned to her seat. Yoshi congratulated her. Harvey rolled his eyes. Kyoko tapped Emiko on the arm, then touched her own chest.

The Gypsy started calling numbers again. After the fourth number, Kyoko yelled, "Bingo." The crowd was silent as she dashed to the front of the tent with her card.

Taking her time checking the numbers, the Gypsy inspected the card, hesitated, then peered at the deputy. He shrugged. She handed the card to him. He held it up to a light along with two other cards. He shrugged again and handed the card back to the Gypsy. She held the microphone up to her mouth. "The card is a winner." Kyoko collected one hundred dollars and pranced back to her seat. The deputy leaned forward, his body tense. When she made it to the table without dropping anything, he leaned back in his chair and wiped his brow with a red handkerchief.

The Gypsy covered her mouth with her hand and whispered to the deputy. He swung his head around to face Harvey and the Kitsune. Harvey left his seat and waved for his companions to follow him. "That's enough bingo for today. Let's go on some rides." Yoshi folded her arms and glared at him. Harvey and the two cousins hurried out of the tent with Yoshi following ten paces behind, leaving a deputy, a Gypsy, and a bunch of poor losers staring after them.

They strolled down the midway, through a cloud of popcorn aroma mixed with sweet scents, until they came to a shooting gallery. Yoshi's eyes brightened, and she raised a hand to stop her cousins. She eyed the stuffed animal prizes hanging over the counter. Harvey stepped between her and the stand. "I also read minds."

Yoshi pursed her lips and her eyes became slits. She pointed two fingers at him but yanked her hand down and stomped down the midway. The others followed. After Harvey steered the Kitsune away from a penny-pitch and a ring-toss, they came to the rides. Emiko stopped in front of the Rocket to The Moon. "I want to go to the moon."

"I do too," Yoshi said. Kyoko ignored the others and moved next to Harvey.

Harvey stared at Yoshi. "You aren't really going to the moon, are you?"

"No. I was there once, and it was dull. But I've never been on this ride."

"Make sure you pay for it and restrain yourself".

"Are you insinuating I'll do something that won't please you?"

"No. I just want to make sure you stay on this planet."

Yoshi's eyes narrowed and she fidgeted with her fingers.

Emiko grabbed Yoshi's arm and led her toward the entrance to the ride. She pulled a bill out of her purse and gave it to the young man operating the ride. "These are difficult to get into." She pulled her skirt up and raised a leg to climb onto the rocket, causing the operator to drop a handful of coins. They scattered on the ramp, and by the time he regained his composure, most of the coins had rolled between the cracks onto the ground below. His eyes were still glazed when he moved controls causing the riders to scream as the rocket swung back and forth.

Kyoko pulled on Harvey's sleeve while toying with a pigtail. "Mr. Long, would you ride the Tilt-a-Whirl with me?"

He thought how nice it would be to get his mind off of Emiko's antics and spend time with Kyoko. "Sure. It's nice to hear your voice. It's nearly as cute as you are."

"*Arigato.* That means 'thank you' in Japanese."

When they arrived at the Tilt-a-Whirl, Harvey spied the deputy standing near an ice cream stand, watching them. Harvey approached the ticket booth with Kyoko and made a display of paying for the tickets. After she ran to a red bucket and climbed in, he joined her and dropped the safety bar in front of them. A gasoline engine started.

"Whee," Kyoko shouted as the bucket whipped

around. She leaned over and laid her head on Harvey's chest. He put an arm around her. As the bucket whirled and twirled, she snuggled up closer, wrapped her arms around his waist, and raised her face upward. He felt her warm breath on his neck.

When the ride ended, Kyoko still held onto him with her face pressed to his neck. "The ride's over," he said. "You can look now."

She raised her head and twisted a pigtail. "I feel safe with you." Harvey pulled her close.

"Mr. Long, can we ride one more time? Please?"

"Maybe later. The others are probably wondering where we are."

She turned her face up to his, pulled on a pigtail with one hand, and toyed with his ear with the other. "I'm afraid to sleep in a strange place. May I stay with you tonight?"

He lifted the safety bar. "Probably not. You'll be safe with Yoshi. Let's go."

"I'd like a Coke first," she said as they stepped back onto the midway.

Harvey smiled. "You remind me of my daughter the first time I took her to the fair. She was about your size when she was nine." Kyoko giggled, wrapped her arms around the upper part of his leg, and leaned against him. He stopped. "You are so cute." He patted the top of her head. "Have you been to the U.S. before?"

"No."

"Where did you learn to speak such perfect English?"

She looked at him and shrugged. "I don't know."

"Well, you do a good job of it. You're fun to be with."

She snuggled closer to him. "*Arigato*."

Harvey bought a Coke for each of them at a stand which pumped a popcorn smell into the air, then they continued walking down the midway until Kyoko stopped and pulled on his arm. She pointed to a barn on the other side of the main street. "I'd like to see the horses."

"We ought to find the others first. We'll go see the horses after we find Yoshi and Emiko." Kyoko gazed up at him with her mouth open, then pouted, and pulled her hand away.

They located Yoshi and Emiko sitting at a picnic table cluttered with cheap stuffed bears, pandas, and other animals similar to those given as prizes at the game stands he and Kyoko had just passed. A bottle of sake was stuck up in the middle of the table as if it were a decoration. Yoshi and Emiko drank from paper cups as they offered stuffed animals to children passing by.

At the same time as Harvey and Kyoko sat, the deputy marched down the midway and up the to the table with his hands on his hips "I want to talk to you."

Yoshi glared at him. "Why do you want to talk to me?"

"I don't want to talk to you."

"I distinctly heard you say you wanted to talk to me."

He pointed at Kyoko and Emiko who were ignoring him. "Not to you--to those two."

Yoshi spread her arms. "Why didn't you say that?"

"I just did."

"A little late, don't you think?"

The deputy waved his hands. "Whatever. I want to talk to them."

"Is that your job, bothering young women? Instead of molesting us, why aren't you out catching crooks?"

"I don't want to molest you."

"You just want to molest those two?" Yoshi stood and faced him. "What's the matter? Am I too old to molest?"

"No. I think you're young enough."

Yoshi moved closer and looked up into his eyes with her hands on her hips. "What is it you think I'm young enough for. Are you some sort of a lecher?"

"I want to know how you did that in the bingo tent."

"Did what?"

"How you won twice in a row."

"I didn't win anything."

He pointed at Emiko and Kyoko. "Not you--them."

"Was it illegal for them to win?"

"It had to be, the way they did it."

"I thought you didn't know how they did it."

"I don't know how they did it, but I'm sure they took two hundred dollars from the game by some sort of trickery."

Yoshi sat at the table. She poured sake from the bottle into her paper cup and held her finger up for the deputy to wait a moment. She took a drink, then turned her body to glare at him. "If they hadn't won the two hundred dollars, what would you have done with the money?"

"Someone else would have won it."

"So, you didn't lose anything."

He pointed at the almost empty sake bottle. "What's in the bottle?"

Yoshi peered at the bottle as if to see what he was talking about, and the sake disappeared. "Nothing."

He looked around as if he'd see where the sake went. "What was in the bottle?"

"Did you read me my rights on self-incrimination? Remember the Miranda Decision? Anyway, what bottle?"

The deputy reached around her to grab the bottle. The bottle slid away. He tried to grab it, but it slid further away. He lunged for the bottle. It dropped on its side and rolled off the table. The deputy bent down to retrieve the bottle, but it vanished. He straightened up. "How'd you do that?"

"When you said you wanted to talk, you really meant it. You're talking my head off." As soon as Yoshi said that, her head vanished.

Harvey jumped up and confronted the deputy. "Now look what you've done." The deputy backed away, slapping himself on the cheek. The two cousins waved goodbye, but the deputy didn't wave back. He had turned and was running full speed down the midway.

Harvey looked at Yoshi, whose head had reappeared. "I thought you told me you wouldn't get me into trouble with your magic."

"I didn't get you into trouble. I kept you out of it."

"I'm sorry. I was talking without thinking."

"You're right," she said. "You haven't been thinking, and it's going to get you in a whole bunch of trouble. I want to talk to you."

"Go ahead, as long as you don't talk my head off."

"When we get to your home, before you have a drink, so your head's still clear, or I should say if I can get it to clear up, you and I are going to have a private conversation." She flicked a hand toward her cousins. "I don't want to think about it anymore with those two around."

They left the fair without seeing the horses. Harvey drove the two cousins to a house across from the cemetery. They waved as Harvey drove away with Yoshi. When he and Yoshi walked into his house, he said, "Talk."

She waved toward the deck. "This is important. On second thought, perhaps you'd better have a drink before I tell you. You have a bottle of wine?"

Yoshi set her glass on the rail and focused her eyes on the pond. "Where did you and Kyoko go while Emiko and I were riding the Rocket to the Moon?"

"We rode the Tilt-a-Whirl, drank a Coke, and went to find you. Why?"

Yoshi faced Harvey. "Cute, isn't she?"

"Yes, very."

He was about to sip his wine when Yoshi said, "Did she touch you?"

He peered at her over the top of his glass. "What do you mean?"

"Did she touch you when you rode the Tilt-a-Whirl?"

He set his glass on the rail. "Yes. She was scared. She put her head on my chest and wrapped her arms around me."

"And what did you do?"

"I put my arm around her to settle her down. What's your point?"

"Then she made an excuse to be invited to stay with you tonight because she felt secure around you. Right?"

"Something like that. She's just a frightened little girl."

"Fox feathers. She's Emiko's older sister, over two hundred years old. If you had agreed to let her stay with you, she'd be in your bed as soon as you fell asleep and in your skivvies minutes later."

Harvey sat up straight. "Why didn't you tell me all this before I put my life in danger?"

"I figured I'd be around you most of the day, but you surprised me by running away with old hot pants."

"You're saying I'd be a dead man." He drank his wine in one gulp and held out his glass.

Yoshi grabbed the bottle and filled his glass. "I want to make sure nobody else gets in your skivvies while Megumi's gone. If anybody lays you to rest, it'll be me."

"You certainly have a way with words, Yoshi."

"You're safe. I wouldn't want to kill the man who'll fulfill my dream. Now that I've said my piece, you can give me a ride home after one more glass of wine."

Harvey poured her wine and leaned back in his chair.

"What you say is so hard to believe. Kyoko looks and acts like she's thirteen years old."

"That's her modus operandi. She generally looks for guys who like to screw young girls. Sometimes, in fact most of the time, she just gets a bang out of getting a bang."

Harvey was quiet as he drove Yoshi to the house across from the cemetery. While driving away, he glanced at the rearview mirror and saw her cross the street.

CHAPTER 11

Monday morning after class, Dean Pigeon came to Harvey's classroom door and wiggled his finger. Harvey took it to be a signal that the dean wanted to talk. The dean wiggled his finger again, and Harvey followed him out a side door to the table where Meg had wanted to hold class. Harvey thought how much more enjoyable it would be to hold his marketing class there instead of sitting with a finger-wiggling dean.

Harvey sat, and Pigeon leaned against the end of the table, causing him to tower over Harvey. "Miss Sakuma is gone, and that's fine with me because she seems to have cast some sort of spell, causing you to become a party to strange goings on. Now I see you've been hobnobbing with another Asian woman, an older one. She had on one of those robes they wear. Do you know her well?"

"I wouldn't call it well."

"I hope not. She may have been involved in the Hope Jewelry Store robbery."

"I've been sort of busy lately," Harvey said, "and I haven't kept up with the news, so I don't know what you're talking about."

"I'm talking about three Orientals who stole thousands of dollars worth of jewelry in a broad-daylight robbery, Saturday afternoon. Of course, the manager brought it on himself. One's not supposed to put valuable jewelry on the counter in front of Americans, much less foreigners. He laid out expensive diamond necklaces and bracelets for them. Right in front of his eyes, the women and the jewelry vanished just like that." Pigeon snapped a finger in Harvey's face.

Harvey jumped back. "What do you mean, vanished?" knowing full well what the dean meant.

Pigeon snapped a finger in front of Harvey again. "Vanished, disappeared. One of the women indicated she'd like to see an item in the case, and the jeweler reached down to pull it out. When he raised his eyes, he discovered the women had vanished along with forty thousand dollars worth of diamond jewelry and a necklace with a large ruby for a centerpiece."

"That sounds rather implausible. He's not a drinking man, is he?"

"I assume he was entirely sober, but I understand he was shaking like a leaf when he told his story to the police."

Harvey leaned back and shook his head. "I find that tale hard to believe. I suspect he may have been hitting the bottle or possibly made the story up to collect insurance."

"I don't buy that. He's a God-fearing member of our church." Pigeon waddled away, headed to the door of the building, wiggling the same finger as before.

Harvey remained seated. "I believe I'll sit here a few moments. I could use the fresh air while I think about what an improbable thing to happen right here in Lansing."

Pigeon turned to look at Harvey. "By the way, the Lansing police may want to question you. I told them you might know those people."

Harvey put his open hands out toward the dean. "Why'd you do that?"

"I felt it was my duty as a law-abiding citizen."

Harvey was happy to see Pigeon disappear into the building. He sat for a few minutes, wondering what he would tell the police and how to keep them from locating Yoshi or even knowing who she was. He decided to get rid of those thoughts by going home and losing himself on the computer and was surprised to find he had received an e-mail from Meg.

I've had no good fortune locating Kitsune. They hide from mortals, so perhaps that's a good sign. Tonight, the annual festival of Kitsune-okuri is held. A priest will lead villagers who carry straw foxes to a fox lair on the mountain and have a ceremony where they bury the straw foxes. The purpose is to rid themselves of Kitsune. I won't join them. I don't want to get rid of Kitsune, just that part of me.

I miss my towering mortal lover. Nobody in Japan is as tall as you. I love you more than all the people I have ever known. I'll be home Friday and look forward to a happy orgy.

As Americans call their girlfriends here,
Your moose, Megumi Sakuma

Harvey read the e-mail three times and circled Friday on his calendar, then lay back in his Lazy-Boy chair and fell asleep. The phone rang. It was Yoshi, and she sounded excited. "I'm going to take my two cousins to the Historical Center, and I want you to come along and explain Michigan history to us."

Harvey's immediate thought was that it would be best not to join them because of the possible consequences but decided it would be better to go with them rather than let them run loose. "I'll meet you there. What time?"

"At two, Wednesday afternoon. We have to go to New York on business and won't return until tomorrow night."

"What kind of business?"

"I'll call you for a ride home when we return."

"Yoshi, if you three can fly to New York and back, why can't you get from the airport to your place?"

"We're not going there. We're coming to see you."

"What form of business are you conducting in New York?"

"*Sayonara.*"

Harvey lay back, closed his eyes, and thought what he would tell the police if they called, but before he had a chance to concoct a story, the phone rang. "Mr. Long, this is Sergeant Justin Owens, Lansing Police Department. Officer Bev Ford and I wish to question you about some people involved in an incident that took place in town Saturday. Could we come to your house?"

"Sure. How long will it take?"

"That depends on you, sir. We'll be there fifteen minutes from whatever it is right now."

One hour later, two cops arrived the front door. Owens introduced himself and Officer Ford. "Can we come in?"

"Yes, you may. What's this regarding?"

"Mr. Long, are you familiar with four Asian women about four feet tall?"

"No."

"We have credible information that you've been closely associated with at least two of them these past two weeks."

"Only closely associated with one woman, and she's over five feet tall."

"Please give me her name and address, sir."

"Her name is Megumi Sakuma. She's in Japan and has been there for the past three days. What is this regarding?"

"Can you tell me how to verify what you said?"

"Call the airport. They also have credible information."

Officer Owens glanced at Officer Ford. "Remind me to check that out." She nodded. He turned back to Harvey. "What about the one known as Susha?"

Harvey laughed. "I don't think she was Asian unless it

was Mongolian. I have no idea where she is, but if you locate her, tell her I don't want her cleaning my house. By the way, she was at least five feet tall."

"Why did you say was?"

"I don't know how tall she is now or even if she is."

"If she is what?"

"Whatever she was then."

"Is that why you said was?"

"Yes."

Owens thought for a moment, then turned to Officer Ford. "Write that down." Then he faced Harvey. "Who do you know who is four feet tall?"

"I know a bunch of kids about that height. Do you want to know their names?"

"I'm talking about full-sized adults."

"If they're only four feet tall, they're not full-sized."

Owens glanced at Ford. "You ask him."

"Mr. Long, do you know any adult women who are only four feet tall, and in particular, any Asian women?"

"Yes, ma'am. I know Yoshiko."

"What's her last name, and where can we locate her?"

"I don't know her last name. I heard she left town, and I don't know where you can locate her. Is there any other valuable information I can give you?"

"If you see this Yoshiko woman, tell her Lansing's finest wants to talk to her."

"I promise."

Owens nudged Ford. "What did he just promise?"

"He said he'd tell her you want to talk to her if and when he sees her."

Owens tipped his hat to Harvey and pointed at Ford. "Write that down and explain it to me at the station. . . . Tell him the stuff we're supposed to tell people we question."

She turned to Harvey. "If you think of any other information that will help us with this case, please call the police department. Thank you again for your help, Mr. Long."

As the two cops headed down the walk, Harvey thought how fortunate the three Kitsune had gone to meet their fence in New York, and how satisfied he was with his newfound ability to talk without saying anything.

The following night at eight, Harvey received a phone call. "This is the Information Desk at Lansing Airport. Three Japanese women flew in from New York and want you to give them a ride to their sponsor's home."

"Why are you calling instead of them?"

"They don't have money for a phone call--and they don't speak English."

"If they don't speak English, how'd you get the information from them?"

"The older one wrote it out."

Half an hour later, Harvey stopped at the loading zone in front of the terminal, thinking the Kitsune would be there, enjoying the warm and calm twilight time. No Kitsune there. He left the wagon running and hurried inside. They weren't in the front lobby, so he went to the Information Desk--they weren't there. At the ticket counter, the airline had no record of three Japanese women on the flight from New York. He decided to look in the place he should have checked first, the cocktail lounge. They were sitting on stools, barely able to see over the bar, drinking and laughing. Emiko sat sideways on her stool and had collected an audience of six men.

Harvey was relieved to see none of the Kitsune were wearing diamond jewelry. He pointed at the door. "Let's go. I'm parked in a no-parking zone."

Kyoko and Emiko picked up large purses that appeared

to have little in them. A box wrapped in brown paper stuck out of the top of Yoshi's. When the three jumped down from the stools, the bartender waved at Harvey. "Thanks for getting them out of here. I hope you like your present."

When they arrived where the Olds was parked, an airport security guard was writing a ticket. She placed it under the wagon's windshield wiper. Harvey was surprised when a sudden gust of wind blew it away. The guard viewed the calm night and wrote another. She lifted the wiper, folded the ticket under it, and gently placed it back on the windshield. Harvey wasn't surprised this time when a gust sent it flying.

"Michigan weather," the guard said. She pulled out her pad to write another ticket and a gust of wind blew her cap off.

Harvey drove away as she chased her cap across short-term parking. He looked at Emiko in the rearview mirror. "How'd you like New York?"

"It really is a big airport."

"What about the city?"

"Biggest airport I ever saw."

"What did you think about the city?"

"We conducted our business in the airport," Yoshi said.

They didn't talk again until they were in Harvey's living room with glasses of wine. Yoshi held hers up. "To my friend, taxi, benefactor, and future son-in-law." After they drank, Yoshi pulled the box from her purse and set it on the coffee table. "For you." Harvey opened the box and pulled out a ten-inch-tall, yellow, plastic model of a nude Statue of Liberty with a ruby where her bellybutton was supposed to be.

He held it up and inspected the multi-facet ruby. "Thank you. What's the occasion?"

Yoshi and Emiko spoke in unison, "We like you." Kyoko nodded enthusiastically.

After another glass of wine, Harvey dropped the three off across from the cemetery. Yoshi and Emiko hugged him. Kyoko winked and brushed a hand across his fly. He drove away wondering how anyone as cute as Kyoko could be so devious and so deadly. By the time he arrived at the house, he had two questions on his mind: *Where do I hide when things start going wrong at the museum, and where does one display a yellow, plastic, naked Statue of Liberty with a hot ruby for a bellybutton?*

CHAPTER 12

A white pine, the official tree of the State of Michigan, planted inside the Historical Center lobby, grew fifty feet tall through an opening in the roof. On an ordinary day, children threw coins into the pond that surrounded the base of the tree, the centerpiece that attracted admiring glances from visitors who filled the restaurant and gift shop or wandered through two floors of exhibits. This day was not ordinary. People emptied into the lobby to witness a different kind of attraction.

A pigtailed Kitsune peeled off her clothing and waded into a pool surrounding the tree. Kyoko laughed as she splashed water by kicking her feet, swinging her bra in a circle in time with each kick. Although she acted like and had the face of a child, it must have been obvious to the crowd, she was a fully formed, adult woman. The crowd grew, and men cheered as Kyoko splashed around and picked up coins from the pool. The petite woman, with the centerfold body, ignored the crowd but leered at Harvey when she noticed him watching.

A young couple surveyed the scene, the man with eyes open wide. "We got more luck than the kids who threw the coins in," he said to Harvey.

The woman with him pulled her arm away from his. "The longer you watch her, the less luck you'll have with me."

"Uuuhh." The man's body shuddered as he ogled Kyoko. "What did you say?"

"I said goodbye." The woman took one last glance at him and pushed her way through the crowd. He didn't seem to notice when she left.

Harvey shifted his gaze from Kyoko's performance to see the reaction of the other two Kitsune. Yoshi smiled. Emiko winked and strolled to the pool, swaying as she did. She removed her blouse and dangled it from her finger tips as she stepped to the edge of the pool, bare-breasted. She slipped off her skirt and threw it onto a bench along with her blouse, then strutted around the edge of the pool and waded in, waving and blowing kisses to the crowd.

Harvey filled his eyes with the view of nymph-like Kyoko and marveled at Emiko's body before easing his way over to stand next to Yoshi. "I want you to make them stop that right now."

"What your mouth says, and what you mind thinks don't match."

"What?"

"You're enjoying the show as much as the other men."

"Probably more than I should, but I'm worried what the security people will do."

"Look around, and what you see will erase your fears." Harvey did so and counted three uniformed guards in the audience, who appeared to be content to watch rather than interfere with the day's main attraction.

After the two had gathered all the silver coins, they climbed out of the pool, stashed their loot in Kyoko's bra, and held hands as they bowed to applause from the crowd. They exited through a glass door and donned their clothes, Kyoko without her bra, and Emiko without any undies as usual. They hurried directly to Harvey where they each grabbed an arm and snuggled up to him. He received glances of envy from many men as he hustled his coven away from the lobby, fearful security personnel might haul him away for stopping the show. He escorted the three Kitsune to an elevator.

After the door closed, coins jingled as they were dropped into one of his jacket pockets at the same time a bra was being stuffed into the other. He didn't mind carrying their loot as long as he couldn't be seen by the security force.

On the second floor, the Kitsune didn't seem interested in viewing exhibits containing models of early settler cabins and mementos of life in the wilderness. Harvey nudged Yoshi's arm. "Don't you guys care to see what life was like hundreds of years ago?"

"We know what it was like."

Harvey slapped his forehead. "Of course. Let's go to the next floor up. I keep forgetting you're older than the state."

Yoshi scowled.

After a quiet elevator ride, the third floor exhibits of early furniture and appliances didn't impress the Kitsune either, but Yoshi's interest underwent a dramatic change when they entered a room containing artifacts from World War II. Her scowl disappeared, replaced by a huge grin, and her eyes opened wide when she spied an olive drab 1941 Command Car and a Willys Jeep. She ran to the Command Car and climbed into the driver's seat.

"What are you doing?" Harvey yelled. She stuck her tongue out at him, then pointed two fingers at the engine and jerked them back and forth twice. After a coughing fit, the engine came to life.

An excited Emiko hopped into the Jeep next to the Command Car and imitated Yoshi's actions. The Jeep engine came to life, causing visitors to scatter except for two teens who whistled and gave her high fives.

Yoshi hollered, *"Banzai,"* as she drove the Command Car off its stand. Stainless steel pedestals, anchoring velvet covered chains, clattered to the tile. Looking much like children playing jump-rope, visitors hopped over chains that glided across the floor. The murmur of conversation was replaced by the roar of engines reverberating through the room, similar to the Indy 500 with the volume turned on high.

"Wait for me," Emiko yelled as she maneuvered the Jeep around the pedestals. People jumped out of the way, leaving a path for her as she squealed her tires and sped forward. The two Kitsune honked their horns. People screamed and cursed as they cleared a way for the vehicles that careened by. Harvey stood speechless as the roar of engines, the screech of spinning tires, and the stench of exhaust filled the room.

Kyoko crossed her arms and frowned as she watched the fun the other two were having. She stomped her foot. "What about me? Don't leave me alone." She pouted as she surveyed the room, but her pout disappeared and wide-eyed excitement took over as she ran to a white 1953 Corvette, perched on a tilted platform. She sprung over the barrier and settled herself in the driver's seat before Harvey realized what was happening. She used her magic to start an engine that purred in contrast to the roaring of the military vehicles.

"No, you can't do that," Harvey yelled.

Kyoko gunned the engine and laughed when she heard the sound of power. Harvey ran to the Corvette and dove headfirst into the passenger side just before she honked the horn and burst through a chain fence to chase the two army vehicles, scattering pieces of her broken grill along the way. Harvey rolled over to an upright position and saw they were catching the slower moving Command Car and Jeep. "I'm going to win this race," Kyoko screamed.

The three vehicles sped through an open hangar door into the aircraft display area. The Jeep and Command Car screeched to a stop on the tile in front of a olive-drab, four-engine B-24 bomber and flattened a sign that indicated the plane was built in Willow Run. Kyoko stopped but not in time. Her Corvette slid on the tile and crashed into the rear of Emiko's Jeep, crunching the Corvette's hood and showering spectators with fiberglass fragments. She swung her arms about in obvious disgust, until over to the right, her gaze locked onto a twin-boom, aluminum Lockheed P-38 fighter plane. Her face glistened as she swung a leg out of the Corvette.

Harvey grabbed her other leg and hung on. Kyoko slid back in. "That's all right--I can catch those two with one wheel tied behind my back."

"No you can't," Emiko yelled as she and Yoshi poised for a race. "We can run over things you have to go around, and we can go up or down stairs." The noise of military engines running at high RPMs, and the smell of rubber spinning on tile greeted stunned onlookers who arrived on the third floor from a crowded elevator.

Kyoko pushed her accelerator petal to the floor, causing a roaring noise that bounced back and forth between the walls. Harvey held his head in his hands. "Stop this right now. We'll be in jail for the rest of our lives."

Kyoko let up on the gas pedal, and the sound diminished. "Maybe you--not me."

"I thought you were scared of speed. Remember the Tilt-a-Whirl?"

"I was only prepping you for seduction, and I'm gonna get you someday." She reached over and touched him.

He jumped. "Don't do that. Do I have to wear a chastity belt when I'm around you?"

She put the Corvette in a lower gear and gunned it. "It won't do you any good."

The Jeep and the Command Car both slid to a halt when a security guard raced to the front of the vehicles. "Stop this immediately," he screamed. "Visitors aren't allowed to drive those. They're for display only." His eyes opened wide when Yoshi let up on her clutch and headed directly at him, filling the room with the roar of the ancient engine. He jumped out of her path just in time not to get run over. He shook his head in disgust, pointed a finger at her, and yelled, "You are barred from visiting the center again for a period of six months.

She flipped him off as she raced past him, yelling, "Good luck, rent-a-cop."

Emiko followed as they drove through a display of fifty-year-old appliances, sideswiping washers, ranges, and refrigerators, and scattering people while shouting in Japanese. An old man jumped out of the way. "This isn't an authentic Pacific War exhibition." he hollered. "Japs didn't have Jeeps."

Emiko veered the Jeep out of the appliance room, across the hall, and into the library. The Command Car followed, its engine racing in low gear, while the Corvette trailed close behind. The high-pitched whine rattled windows throughout the building. Both military vehicles careened down an aisle between rows of bookshelves, toppling books onto the floor and making a bumpy path for the Corvette. A librarian ran after them, waving her arms and shouting. "Keep the noise down, or I'll have to ask you to leave."

When Emiko saw the Corvette closing in, she headed for the stairs and bounced down until the Jeep became lodged in a landing halfway down to the second floor. She pounded on the windshield and rattled off oaths in Japanese, then climbed out just before Yoshi smacked the Command Car into the back end of the Jeep. Yoshi jumped out and ran down to where Emiko was criticizing the inferior quality of American Jeeps. A group of high school students watched with mouths agape as the Kitsune ran down the stairs to the first floor.

Kyoko drove the Corvette into the freight elevator and

rode it down while Harvey did his best to hide below the dash. When the operator announced, "First floor," the door opened and the Corvette roared out, scattering visitors as it headed to where Yoshi and Emiko sat on a bench eating ice cream bars.

"Hop in, losers," Kyoko yelled. Yoshi and Emiko tossed the remainder of their bars to a group of middle-school students and climbed in on top of Harvey.

Kyoko gunned the engine as if she believed the full glass automatic doors would open in front of the speeding car. The doors didn't open soon enough. She lay her head back and roared with laughter as the doors fell forward to the front steps sending splinters of glass in all directions. She stomped on the accelerator, and the Corvette sped across the sidewalk, made a hard right, skidding around ninety degrees to race south on Walnut, a one-way street going north. Many fists were raised, and curses hurled at the Corvette's occupants as oncoming cars swerved onto the sidewalks, scattering pedestrians.

Near the General Motors plant, Emiko spied a rock band playing. "Let's go where the music is," she yelled. Kyoko made a left turn and drove the car to a lot overlooking the Grand River. The Kitsune raised their hands above their heads and screamed as the car crashed through the fence at the edge of the lot and flew off the bank into the river. The speed kept the car moving until it floated into deep water, where it sank. The heads of three Kitsune and Harvey popped to the surface, coughing and spitting water.

Captain Mason, navigating the river in a sixty-foot replica of a Mississippi River steamboat, must have heard the sirens coming from the vicinity of the Historical Center, but he couldn't have known they were related to the people struggling to keep their heads above the surface of the river. He steered the boat up to them, and passengers pulled them aboard.

Harvey and the three Kitsune dried off with towels furnished by a deck hand. Captain Mason, a short young man with blond hair peeking out from under his captain's hat, leaned out of the wheel house on the upper deck. "Welcome aboard the *River Princess*. You okay?"

Harvey waved at the captain. "Thanks to you."

"I'm sure I'll get my reward in heaven."

Harvey saluted him. "We appreciate the free ride."

"Nothing doing. The mayor may be watching, and he'll want at least half fare."

"Tell him I'll buy him a drink someday."

"Tell you what," Mason said. "You buy me the drink, and if I find out he was watching, I'll buy him one someday."

Harvey was distracted from the conversation when he saw Emiko and Yoshi walk around the main cabin to a bar at the stern. He and Kyoko followed them until Kyoko made a right turn to climb a ladder to the upper deck. Harvey stopped. He thought about tailing her but decided the other two could cause more trouble at the bar. He went to the stern where Yoshi and Emiko had placed drink orders with the bartender.

Harvey paid for their wine and ordered one for himself, then the three of them sat along the rail, drinking as the boat cruised down the river. He breathed a sigh of relief that the hectic Corvette ride was over, and he relaxed like a fare-paying passenger as the boat passed beneath the Michigan Avenue bridge, cruising toward the dam.

Emiko and Yoshi seemed to be content that their wild ride was over. Harvey was sure they wouldn't cause any more trouble, so he decided to check on Kyoko. "Don't move from here," he said. "Don't do anything that will get me into more trouble. I'll be back to buy you another glass of wine in a few minutes." That promise brought nods and smiles, so he knew the rest of the trip would be serene.

Harvey climbed the ladder to the upper deck and spied Kyoko talking to the captain as he steered the boat down the river. With a sigh of relief, Harvey sat on a bench near the stern, sipped his wine, and watched couples stroll along the riverwalk. He edged close to the bow and hid behind a three foot high partition surrounding the wheel house, so he could eavesdrop on the conversation between Kyoko and Captain Mason. As the boat passed the Civic Center, couples on the riverwalk waved. Kyoko bounced with excitement and waved back. "May I blow the whistle?"

Mason touched a rope hanging from the overhead. "Just give that a couple of pulls." She giggled as she moved close to him, wrapped an arm around his waist, and gave the rope two quick pulls. The sound it made resembled the whistle of a steam locomotive, reverberating off buildings on both sides of the river. The couples waved again.

Captain Mason smiled when Kyoko rewarded him with a kiss on the cheek. She pulled on one of her pigtails. "Thank you, sir, and thank you for saving me. I was sure I would drown until you came to the rescue. In Japan, it is said, when a man saves a woman, she belongs to him for the rest of her life, so I guess I'm yours to do with as you'd like."

He waved at two men fishing from a rowboat. "It may be true in Japan, honey, but not here. My wife isn't the kind of woman who'd buy that story."

"Is your wife on the boat?"

"No. She doesn't ride with me."

Kyoko pointed to the rear of the wheel house. "Why do you have a bed up here?"

Mason spun the wheel to steer the *River Princess* around a floating log before he answered her. "It's not a bed-- it's a padded bench for visitors to the captain's bridge."

Kyoko grabbed the back of her neck with both hands.

"Oh, I have a muscle spasm. I must have strained it while climbing onto the boat." She dropped down onto the bench, out of sight. Harvey's body tensed.

Mason shrugged. "Just rest there till the pain's gone."

"That won't help. I need you to massage my neck."

Harvey wiped sweat from his forehead and set his drink down, ready to stand and go forward, but he hesitated when the captain said, "I'd like to help you, honey, but I can't leave the wheel. I have to watch where I'm going."

"Please help me," Kyoko pleaded from below the partition. "Please."

Mason kept his eyes focused on the river. "Sorry, honey--can't do it."

Harvey relaxed and leaned back but changed his mind and stood when he decided, as long as the situation was under control topside, he'd better check the two below to see if they were behaving. He tiptoed across the deck and stepped down the ladder. At the stern, he saw the bartender had served Yoshi and Emiko another glass of wine. Yoshi pointed at Harvey. "He'll pay for them."

Harvey rolled his eyes. *I'll be paying for the rest of my life, for what's happened today, if the authorities ever catch-up with me.*

The bartender held out a hand. "That'll be nine dollars."

Harvey handed the man a twenty dollar bill. "Give me a glass too and keep the change." That brought a big smile and a generous glass of wine.

Harvey picked up his glass, sniffed the wine bouquet, and was happy with it. He and the two Kitsune strolled to the other side of the stern where an old upright piano sat. Emiko squealed with joy. "I love to play piano--I'll play a song for you." She set her drink on top of the piano, sat on the bench, and hit a few chords. She gazed at Harvey. "I'll sing you a song called 'Furasato.' In America it would be something like 'Hometown' or 'Countryside.'" She played and gazed at Harvey as she sang. When the song was over, Emiko received applause from the passengers. She bowed to them, causing an older woman standing behind her to place a hand over her escort's eyes.

"I love your voice," a young woman in the audience said. "Please sing another."

Emiko gave the okay sign. "This was a popular song in Japan many years ago. In English it's called 'China Night.'" Passengers gathered around the piano to listen. Harvey relaxed. Everything was under control as Emiko played and sang, swaying from side to side. He was so engrossed in listening and watching her, he didn't notice when her wine glass slid down the piano toward the bow. But he did notice when the bench she was sitting on slid in the same direction.

Screaming and yelling erupted when the bow of the boat dropped as if going down a steep hill while the stern rose majestically into the air. Piano, stool with Emiko still on it, bar, bartender, Harvey, Yoshi, the audience, and their drinks joined together in a forward slide, some stopping when they reached the main cabin, and others not until they slid onto the rocks that broke the fall of the water cascading over the dam.

Nobody seemed to be hurt, but the peace and quiet along the Grand River was broken by the screams of the passengers, the sound of a paddlewheel spinning high in the air, and a rock band in the distance playing YMCA. Harvey guessed what caused the wreck of the River Princess when, from the direction of the wheel house, came an occasional, "Uuh, aah."

CHAPTER 13

"Everyone will stand to honor His Honor, Ronnie J. Haysid, Junior."

Emiko, Kyoko, Yoshi, and Harvey rose at the bailiff's decree and watched the judge enter the courtroom, shuffling like a farmer following a plow and scowling as if his wife weren't shouldering a fair share of the yoke. He sat at the bench and fixed his scowl on the three Kitsune and Harvey. "Are these our criminals of the day, bailiff?"

"Yes, your honor."

"I thought they might be the ones. Tell those broads they're supposed to stand to show respect for me when I enter the courtroom."

"They are standing, your honor."

"Are they midgets, or are they standing in a hole? We don't have a hole in our courtroom floor, do we?"

"No, your honor. They must be midgets."

"What about the littlest one, the one with the pony tail? She looks juvenilish."

"Evidently, she's the worst of the lot, your honor."

"Then she should be persecuted as an adult. What is it they done?"

"If I read all they've done, we'll be here until dark. I have four pages of charges. Do you wish to hear them all?"

"Read some of the major ones, and maybe we can put

them away for a few years. Then my replacement can try them for the rest of their crimes after I retire."

"Yes, your honor. These women commandered three vehicles in the Historical Center, on Pine Street, Lansing, Michigan, drove through the building, wrecked two of them after they destroyed the appiance exhibit and the library. Then they stole the other, our beautiful red and white Corvette, drove it the wrong way on a one-way street, and sailed it smack dab into the Grand River. After that, they sunk the *River Princess* and left the debris hanging over the dam."

"You'd better have them sit down. This could take a while. What did the guilty-looking guy do? Is he a lawyer or an accomplice?"

"I'm not sure. He wasn't with them during the jewelry store robbery, but he was listed on the charges I read, so he must be guilty of something."

"You ain't said nothing about a robbery."

"It's on page three of the charges, your honor."

"All right," the judge said, "Git on."

"Get on what?"

"Git on to what you're supposed to do next. Call a witness or give evidence--do something."

"The first witness is Chief of Security at the Michigan Historical Center And Library built in 1992 and dedicated by the then governor, your brother, Grover P. Haysid, who appointed you."

The judge expressed approval at the introduction by giving his first smile of the day. "Seems like you ought to give the witness's name."

"Jeffrey Haysid."

Jeffrey, a younger version of the judge, stepped onto the stand. "Hi, Bo."

The judge gave Jeffrey a friendly wave. "You ain't

supposed to act like you know me."

"Sorry, Bo."

After Jeffrey was sworn in, Judge Haysid waved a hand at him. "We'll start with the museum. Tell me exactly what these here culprits did there."

"Well, one of them there three women took off her clothes next to the pond in the middle of the lobby. It was awesome. I became suspicious that something was going to happen, so I decided to watch her and see what she was up to. I watched real close as she stood there bare naked, just in case she might engage in some form of criminal activity."

The judge leaned forward. "It's good to know you take your job so seriously, Bo. Which one of the three was it?"

"The cute one with the ponytail, except she had pigtails yesterday. But that ain't all. The other one, the one with her legs spread apart, done the same thing. She stripped and went to frolicking along the edge of the pool."

Judge Haysid leered at Emiko. She glared at him and moved her knees together. He shifted his gaze to Kyoko, and she smiled. "Tell me more about what that one done," he said.

"Me and two guards, assisting in the surveyance, watched her wade into the pond to steal the coins children throwed in--the ones we use for picnics. It was awesome."

"All right, git on."

"Right. After they took the elevator upstairs and went in the room that had all the--"

"Hold it. I mean git on with the story about her being bare naked in the pond."

"Right. She kept on splashing around in the water like she was a movie star. When she came up with a handful of coins, she strolled to where she kept a pile of them. Her body glistened in the spotlight. Awesome."

The judge leaned forward. "Tell me more, so I can get a

better picture in my mind of what she was a-doing."

"Well, I can tell you one thing. She may look like a teenager from here, but she's built like a you know what, and I suspect she knows how it's supposed to be used, from the way she strutted it around."

The judge hit his gavel on the bench. "The witness is excused. Court's in recess while I talk to the young lady in question to determine if she knows right from wrong and if she's old enough--to be tried as an adult, that is. Bailiff, escort her to my chambers."

Kyoko jumped to her feet, hurried to where the bailiff was standing, and waved at the other Kitsune as she followed the bailiff out of the courtroom, twirling her ponytail.

Yoshi leaned toward Harvey. "I'll bet you twenty *yen* she's found not guilty."

"That's if they're doing what you think they're doing in there."

"I don't have to think. I know what they're doing. I just don't know in what order they're doing it."

Thirty minutes later, when Kyoko, the judge, and the bailiff walked back into the courtroom, all wore smiley faces. The judge hit his gavel with such enthusiasm, the bailiff jumped. "As a result of my interview with Miss Kyoko, I find she is definitely old enough, and she also knows the right way from the wrong. I feel it's in the best interest of all concerned that charges against her, whatever they are, be dismissed, and she be released with the stipulation that she realizes what takes place in a judge's chambers is considered confidential. It ain't to be discussed with nobody." He rapped his gavel on the bench with his new found enthusiasm. "Two hour recess for lunch." He got up from his chair and left the courtroom, whistling "Zippidy-Doo-Dah.

After the recess, Judge Haysid returned to the bench, giving a couple of healthy belches before speaking. "Now let's take testimony about the sinking of the *River Princess*. It astounds me that a couple of foreign, female midgets can commandeer and sink a riverboat full of our Americans."

"Unfortunately," the bailiff said, "you dismissed all charges against the one who was responsible for running the riverboat over the dam."

"Do you mean to tell me that innocent little woman, I entertained in my chambers, was guilty of-- Why are you waving your hands at me, bailiff?"

"I believe the word you meant to use is interviewed."

"Thank you. Do you mean to tell me that innocent little woman, I interviewed in my chambers, was guilty of running that boat over the dam?"

"Yes, sir, except there's nobody to testify against her."

"Where's the captain of the boat?"

"He's in failing health, your honor. When he was retrieved from the wreckage, he had already started wasting away from some unknown malady. He refused to eat or sleep, and if it keeps up, he'll probably be dead in a month."

Yoshi leaned over to Harvey. "Eighty-nine days. He's already used up one."

Harvey rolled his eyes. "And the judge?"

"Ninety days."

"And the bailiff?"

"Ninety days, plus or minus fifteen minutes."

"At this rate," Harvey said, "she'll reduce Lansing's population by ten percent before she goes back to Japan."

"Remember that and don't become a statistic."

The judge glared at Yoshi. "Why are you talking while this court's in session?"

"I ain't heard anything I was interested in listening to."

"Young lady, if you pardon the expression, keep it up, and I'll find you in contempt of this court."

"I'm already in contempt of this court without your having to find it."

"Finding someone in contempt is a legal expression and not literal. If you're going to be a good defendant, you'll have to learn the proper language of the law."

"How's this for proper language? Screw you, judge."

The judge sat up straight in his chair and pointed a finger at Yoshi. "What was that you said?"

Kyoko raised a hand. "May I add something relative to her comment about screwing you?"

Judge Haysid glowered at Kyoko as if she'd stabbed him with a knife. "No. You was already excused. Go." He pointed at the door. He turned his attention to Yoshi. "I forgive you for what you just now said."

Yoshi left the bench and hurried to the exit. A policeman put an arm across the door in front of her. "Where do you think you're going?"

"Home. He excused me after Kyoko and I talked about screwing him."

"Let her go," the judge said. "We'll try her in absentia."

Yoshi jerked her thumb at Kyoko as she walked out the door. "For the record, did you entertain, I mean did you interview her in absentia?"

The judge banged his gavel. "Let her go, bailiff. She's obviously innocent. We still have two others we can find guilty." The governor's picture on the wall rattled when Yoshi slammed the door on the way out of the room.

Emiko stood and glared at the judge. "I'd like to screw you too."

"Let her go with the others," the judge said. "We still

have one." He glared at Harvey. "You try anything, and I'll put you away for the rest of your life, maybe even longer."

As Emiko scurried out the exit, she mooned the judge, then looked back at him. "That's longer than you'll be around." Governor Haysid's picture clattered to the floor when she slammed the door.

Judge Haysid jumped when the picture hit the floor. He peered at his notes and tore a couple of pages from the pad. "Bailiff, I declare a five minute-break from the proceedings while I review the case of the ringleader of this group of midgets to see how we can make him pay dearly for what they done to our Historical Center."

Harvey put his head in his hands. *I wonder if I'm trying to be what I'm not meant to be. Was it a mistake to get involved with Meg and the baggage she carries with her? She has, in two weeks, maneuvered me out of the doldrums and helped me regain much of what I've missed in myself these last few years, but after what's happened to the riverboat captain and what's going to happen to the bailiff and the judge, I wonder how much time I have left.*

The judge banged his gavel on the bench and jarred Harvey out of his daydream. He glared at Harvey. "I don't know what your part was in all this skullduggery, but we never had these problems until you and your accomplices got together to terrorize the city. I suspect that you are their leader, and as such, you will have to pay for the crimes of those who created havoc in the museum, on the *River Princess*, and in this courtroom. How do you plead?"

"I plead not guilty, your honor. How can I be held liable for the deeds of others, including a child I'm guardian of?"

The judge sat up straight. "Who are you guardian of?"

"The thirteen-year-old you interviewed in your chambers. As a juvenile she shouldn't have been in this court, much less allowed to be interviewed by you and the bailiff without me or an attorney being present to protect her rights. As her guardian, I feel obligated to question her to find out what happened in your chambers, then determine if her rights have been violated."

"Are you insinuating that something improper took place in my chambers?"

"Oh, no, your honor. I'm sure you demonstrated nothing but the highest moral standards. If fact, there would be no need for me to initiate an investigation if you were to dismiss all charges against each of the three women and me. If that were to happen, there would be no reason to request a determination of what took place between you, the bailiff, and a thirteen-year-old while you had her in your chambers."

"I understand your concern. To show you that justice in this county is fair, I will do as you suggest. In recognition of the high standards you have demonstrated by serving as guardian of a young visitor to our country, all charges are hereby dismissed."

Harvey bowed. "Thank you, sir. Enjoy your summer."

As he hurried out the door, Harvey heard Judge Haysid say to the bailiff. "I'm glad this day is over. I suddenly feel very tired. I need a rest."

"Me too."

CHAPTER 14

Meg ran out of the airport secured area and into Harvey's arms, bringing with her the fragrance of Jasmine. They hugged for a long time without talking, then he held her face in his hands and kissed her. "Welcome home."

She reached into her purse and pulled out a package, the size of a Kleenex box, and handed it to him. She leaned back and smiled. "Open it."

As she stood back and eyed him, Harvey lifted the lid. Inside were two wooden dolls that resembled miniature bowling pins with heads that pivoted around. One was painted as a woman, and the other as a man, both in formal Japanese dress. She opened her arms and wrapped them around him, almost knocking them from his hands. "They're traditional wedding dolls. Did you stay out of trouble while I was gone?"

"That sure was a quick change of subject. I'll tell you about it later."

She put her hands on her waist and glared at him. "You are not supposed to get in trouble unless I am with you."

"I didn't know your mother's cousins would be here to replace you."

She jabbed a finger at him. "Are you saying that while I was gone, those two witches replaced me?"

Harvey put his palms out to defend himself. "They replaced you as company for your mother."

"That had better be the only way they replaced me, or you'll be hopping around from now on."

He motioned for her to follow him to baggage claim. "Do I have to spend the rest of my life being careful of what I say and do, to ensure I don't spend it as a toad?"

"Yes. . . . No, not really. I use that expression because it's one you understand."

"There are many other expressions I understand that don't send shivers through my bones."

"You wouldn't have that problem if your bones weren't so close to the surface."

He pulled her baggage from the conveyor. "What happened to the woman, who a few minutes ago, gave me that hug of a lifetime?"

"When I did that, I didn't know you had been dilly-dallying around with that horny pigtailed witch. Now, tell me what happened?"

Without talking, they walked to the Olds in a light rain, where he tossed Meg's luggage into the trunk and opened her door. After he paid his parking fee and pulled away from the gate, Meg jabbed him in the shoulder with a thumb. "You haven't answered my question."

"I'm innocent."

"When people say they're innocent, it means they did something wrong."

He kept his gaze on the road but felt the barbs coming at him. "I thought she was thirteen or so, and we rode together at the fair."

"You rode together?"

"No, no. We rode on the same ride at the same time, the Tilt-a-Whirl. She said she was scared and huddled up to me."

Meg leaned away from Harvey and glared at him. "Did she kiss you?"

134

"No."

"Did she touch you?"

"Yes."

Meg appeared startled. "Where?"

"What do you mean, where?"

She hit him on his arm with the back of her hand. "You know what I mean."

"No, not there. She put her arms around me."

"It's a good thing she didn't touch you there, or I'd tilt you, so you'd never whirl again. That's my territory."

"What's your territory?"

He jumped when she pointed it out to him. Then she poked him on the arm again. "Stop the car."

He glanced at her and kept driving.

"Stop the car."

Harvey pulled over to the side of the road and stopped. She slid over, put her arms around him, and gave him a long kiss. "It's my fault. I didn't train you properly on how to act before I left you alone. I forgive you this time." She stuck a finger in front of his face. "But next time I leave you for more than an hour, you'll be held responsible for knowing the rules to observe when you're around Kitsune."

Meg snuggled up to him as he drove back onto the road, and they rode in silence. As the wagon pulled onto his street, Harvey nudged Meg. "You want to know what else happened while you were gone?"

"I don't think so. Is it something I might read about in the newspaper?"

"Some of it, but the rest may not be in the paper for ninety days."

"Kyoko?"

"Yes."

"How many?"

"Three that I know of."

"They probably deserved it. She usually works the lechers over. That's why she does her teen thing."

"I think one of them wasn't a bad guy."

"Sometimes she likes a challenge, or perhaps she was just horny. She's like that most of the time."

He drove into the garage and sat in the car waiting for the overhead door to close.

She pounced on him. "Like I am."

Fifteen minutes later, Harvey sat up. "That could have waited until we got to a bed, or at least inside. Now, my bones will ache for a week."

"I thought about doing it when we stopped alongside of the road but decided to act like a lady and wait until we were in the house."

"In the garage is not in the house."

"Quit being petty and tell me what else happened while I was gone."

"Why don't you just read my mind?"

"It's getting to be more work than I want to do. Tell me what happened?"

"I thought you didn't want to hear about it."

"I didn't then. Something more important I wanted. Now you've satisfied that want, so I can listen to your lies about what happened without wanting to drag you off to bed-- but it does sound like a good idea. Let's go."

In bed, Harvey told her about the jewelry store robbery, the winning experience at bingo, the full Tilt-a-Whirl story, what he figured caused the boat to go over the dam, and his stint as a defense lawyer at the trial.

"So you avoided serving time by using your communication skills."

136

"I had three good teachers."

"As another part of your education, I hope you've learned not to trust them. Kitsune all have their tricks, even my mother. It's inbred in them to get men in the sack, always with the same results."

"You mother warned me at least three times while you were gone."

"To stay away from Kitsune?"

"No. If anybody other than you would get in my skivvies, it'd be her."

Meg sat up. "She didn't try, did she?"

Harvey frowned. "You don't even trust her, do you?"

"No. And you haven't answered my question."

"She never tried. She only warned me to stay away from Kyoko."

"So, why did you need a warning?"

"I didn't need a warning."

"But you let her fondle you on the Tilt-a-Whirl."

"She just hugged me."

"That's too much. Let her do that again, and you know what'll happen?"

Harvey made a hopping motion with his hand.

She wrapped herself around him. "Conversation done. Now I want action."

"Hey, I'm forty--give me a rest break--I'm still stiff from that action in the garage. I want to hear what you learned in Japan this time."

She untwined from him. "Oh, all right. The concern I had when I left was if loving you would make you waste away and die. I'm no longer worried about that."

He stared at the ceiling. "It gives me great comfort to know you're not worried."

"I reasoned that you're still alive with no traces of

wasting away, other than the fact that you appeared to be wasted away when I met you."

"You sound like your mother."

"Well, it's true. It's part of your charm."

"Did you learn how much of you is Kitsune and how much is human?"

"No. I'm the only half-Kitsune around, and I didn't have any luck finding a whole one who could explain the difference. But as long as I've lost much of my magical power, I expect I've also lost the power of the curse and any ability I may have had to kill you."

"That makes me feel warm all over. Doesn't your mother have any insight into what you can and can't do?"

"She wouldn't violate my trust by telling me things she doesn't know for sure, for the same reason she holds off trying to seduce you. Her reluctance in what she says or how she acts, stems from respect or motherly love."

He swung around and put his feet on the floor. "I notice you don't have much of that reluctance in what you say or what you do with me."

She grabbed him by the arms and pulled him backwards. "But only with you. Come on, Boneyard, let's do it."

After they finished doing it, Harvey heard Kyoko's voice. "Emiko, what does reluctance mean? I'm not familiar with the word." Meg pulled the covers to their necks. Emiko and Kyoko stood in the bedroom doorway, smiling.

Emiko looked at the two in bed. "I've heard the word, but I don't believe it applies to us. We've never been reluctant in our services to men. What interests me most about what's going on here is the form of calisthenics we just witnessed."

Kyoko put on a huge grin. "Personally, I've never seen anything like it."

Meg raised her head. "You may not have seen it, but if you had as many things sticking out of you as you've had stuck into you, you'd look like a porcupine."

"Are you insinuating that I've done what you just did?"

"Not insinuating. It's a matter of fact, and with thousands of men."

Emiko nudged Kyoko. "Are you going to let her get away with a gross understatement like that? I believe tens of thousands would be more accurate."

"A hundred thousand would be closer to the actual number. But that's all right, as you know, I'm rather modest." She leered at Harvey. "When I get my chance to engage in that form of exercise with a man from this neighborhood, I'll make sure I do it in front of a mirror."

Harvey pulled the sheet up higher. Meg poked a finger at Kyoko. "If I catch you within three feet of my man again, you'll have more than seven years bad luck."

"From what I've seen tonight it may be worth it."

"It would be your last time," Meg said. "Now, go away and let us sleep."

Kyoko nudged Emiko. "I wouldn't be thinking of sleep if I were in bed with him, but I guess mortal women get tired more easily than we do."

The two cousins didn't move from the doorway. Meg sat up in bed. "Get out of here right now."

"Emiko," Kyoko said, "can a fake Kitsune boss two genuine Kitsune around?"

A voice boomed from the living room. "Out, you two, right now." Yoshi stomped toward her cousins. "She may not be able to control you, but I can. Do something like this one more time, and I'll change you into gerbils, and the only form of exercise you'll get for the rest of your lives will be turning a squirrel cage in some child's room." Harvey raised his head higher to watch the two intruders bow and back out the door. Yoshi followed them and continued berating them.

After quiet took over, Harvey heard a knock on the bedroom door, and Yoshi's voice came through, calmer than it had been earlier. "I want to see my daughter, whom I have missed greatly, and I apologize for the behavior of my two cousins. I believe they had too much wine." Yoshi entered, sat on the edge of the bed, and hugged her daughter. "Why didn't you chase them out?"

"I tried, but it didn't work."

"I'll stay a while to make sure they behave." She held Meg's hand. "I'm not sure I took the best care of your man while you were gone, but he hasn't wasted away any more than usual." She glanced at Harvey. "I've told you before--I like your lean look."

"He does look sort of starved," Meg said, "but if you think he's skinny with clothes on, you ought to see him naked." She pretended to pull the sheet off.

Harvey grabbed the sheet and pulled it up underneath his chin. "Will you two please quit making critical comments about my trim body?"

Meg poked him in the ribs. "You just barely have a body and no trim at all."

"Well, it's the only body I have, and you sure seemed pleased with it a few minutes ago. You'll have to get used to it if we're going to live together."

Meg put her finger on the end of his nose and pushed on it with each word. "Those-are-not-live-together-dolls-I gave-you. They-are-wedding-dolls."

He placed a finger on her nose, and pushed. "Yes, ma'am." She grabbed his finger, and bit it. "Ow," he said. "After you're finished exercising your cannibalistic tendencies, we have to decide if you're going to go back to school, get a job, or follow me around to keep me on the straight and narrow."

She put her finger on his nose. "I don't know about the straight, but you're so narrow now you're like a cardboard cutout. When you stand sideways in class, your students think you left the room. And I'm on a student visa, which means we have no choice. I'll be shipped back to Japan if I don't go to school." Her eyes opened wide. "Unless we get married first."

"You're going back to school." He looked at Yoshi. "Do you have anything to add to that, now that we're ready to let you participate in the conversation?"

"I believe going to school's the right decision, but you have another to make. My cousins came here at my request. Even though they got out of line tonight, other than a few minor misunderstandings, they haven't wandered too far from the straight and narrow during their stay. I'd like to say goodbye to them on friendly terms. They're our relatives and will be there for us if we need them." She focused her attention on Meg. "With the loss of your power, there may come a time someday when we'll require their help."

Harvey raised his head. "If you call what those two have done these past few days straight and narrow, you can call me fatso." He turned his head toward Meg. "What do you think about the friendly terms bit?" After Meg gave her approval, he said to Yoshi. "It's a deal. Friendly terms it is."

"Good. If we treat them to dinner at a nice place, I'm sure they'll behave." Meg and Harvey both closed their eyes. Yoshi grinned. "You're both so sleepy you can't keep your eyes open." She hugged Meg, patted Harvey on the cheek, and left the room.

Harvey sat up. "I wasn't thinking about taking those two witches to a nice place. I don't believe we can trust them. There are no serious bones in their bodies, and I'm going to have to get back to a serious life if I want to continue teaching."

"What do the bones in their bodies have to do with your teaching?"

"I can't teach from jail. . . . Okay, I'll buy into your mother's idea, but we have a whole bunch of planning to do."

Meg cocked her head. "How much planning is needed to have dinner for five?"

"With three witches on their last night in town, I'm not sure. Just enough to make it through the night without our ending up in court again."

"I don't foresee them causing big problems as long as we have Mama with us."

"Sure, just like in the Historical Center."

CHAPTER 15

Harvey tilted his head back to talk to Yoshi, seated with her cousins, in the back seat of the Olds. "Do you have ghosts and haunted houses in Japan?"

"Yes, but they're no match for us."

"I believe you."

He drove between century-old sugar maples and parked in front of a three-story brick mansion. Vines grew across broken windows in remnants of white frames that hung loose. A weathered sign that read "The Old Haunted Inn" squeaked on one chain as it swung in the breeze. Rusty chairs peeked above weeds dominating the lawn.

"Look," Emiko said and motioned with her finger toward a gable on the third floor. "That would be a great place for a ghost to appear at twilight." Within seconds, a white sheet appeared at the window with two dark circles for eyes. The sheet waved. Harvey saw the apparition and guessed it was part of the building's decor.

They entered the inn through an open door which hung on one hinge. Inside, a coffin opened to reveal a skaggy old woman in white. She sat up and cackled, "Welcome to my home," then dropped back inside. The lid banged shut.

A slender woman with long, black hair, wearing a floor-length, black, velvet dress and matching bonnet, slunk out of a closet. She led Harvey's party across a creaky floor to a table

143

set for six, covered with water rings and blemishes. Two bulbs on the wrought-iron chandelier above the table were not lit, and cobwebs crisscrossed between two empty sockets, leaving a lone bulb to give off a dim light. The woman seated Yoshi at the head of the table, and the two cousins across from Meg and Harvey. Meg touched a cobweb dangling from the chandelier. "Is this real?"

Harvey shook his head. "I'm sure it's a fake." After he spoke, a spider slid down the silken strand into a vase of dead flowers in the center of the table. Harvey scrutinized the three Kitsune. "Who did that?" They all shrugged their innocence. The spider reversed direction and disappeared up into a cocoon. Soon, from inside the cocoon, a television set flickered, and a tiny voice sang, "Off we go into the old light fixture, climbing high in a cocoon."

Meg bounced up and down, laughing so hard she couldn't deny what she'd done when Harvey pointed at her and said, "You're worse than they are."

She managed to control her laughter enough to lean against him and whisper, "I'm also better than they are." She stuck the tip of her tongue in his ear.

Distant screams came from somewhere beneath the floor. Harvey shuddered. The others smiled. Meg raised a finger. "That was not me."

"Probably for the first time tonight," Harvey said.

A server, with her head painted to resemble a bleached skull, with long gobs of shiny black hair, glided to the table with a stuffed black cat cradled in her arms. "I'm Esmerelda. Would you like an appetizer?"

Harvey glanced at the Kitsune, and they signaled agreement. "Esmerelda," he said, "we'd like a bottle of Merlot before we order."

Esmerelda jumped back and screamed when her cat

jumped from her arms and ran across the floor, leaped onto a bar at the end of the room, and sat as still as the stuffed animal it was supposed to be. Esmerelda regained her composure but stared at the cat as she walked to the bar to place her order. Harvey watched for laughter as a sign of guilt but saw none. All four of his coven of witches shrugged to proclaim innocence. He rolled his eyes and thought if it didn't get any worse, they were in good shape. He decided to continue monitoring them.

Esmerelda brought the wine. Yoshi poured, then proposed a toast. "To Kyoko and Emiko, for keeping me company while my daughter was gone." She raised her glass, and they all drank. Harvey gave a little jerk. He set his glass down and jumped again. Across from him, Kyoko played with one of her pigtails. Meg peered under the table, then motioned for Harvey to stand. She traded seats with him so he was across from Emiko. Two minutes later he jumped again. Meg glared at Emiko. Emiko smirked.

Harvey ordered another bottle of wine. On the way to the table with the wine, the cat hissed at Esmerelda. She set the bottle on the table and headed back to the bar, steering clear of her former stuffed toy.

An older woman sitting at a nearby table talked loud enough to be heard at Harvey's table. "First they bombed Pearl Harbor, then they tried to destroy the American auto industry by flooding the country with cheap cars. Now we have to put up with their antics in our restaurants." A skinny man, sitting next to her, nodded.

Emiko excused herself and hurried to a restroom that had a witch's hat painted on the door. Moments later a petite witch came out through the door and waltzed to the table where Esmerelda was serving barbecued ribs to the loud woman. "I've never seen the entertainment you have this evening," the woman said. "I don't know how you do it. I love your cat. And look at that." She pointed at Emiko. "I've never seen that witch before. She's so realistic."

Esmerelda blinked her eyes. "I haven't seen her either."

The witch reached over, pulled a rib from the woman's plate. "This is my first day. I've been eating bumble bees, spiders, and monkey tails for fifty years, and I'm hungry for something exotic." She chewed on the morcel a bit, then spit on the floor. "Uuh, monkey ribs."

The skinny man laughed. "That's great." The witch glanced at him, threw the bone on the woman's plate, and wiped her greasy hands on the shoulders of his suit coat. "What do you think you're doing?" the man yelled, "That's not funny. I want to talk to the manager."

The witch flipped him off. "I am the manager." Then she strolled through the room, singing "Memories Are Made of This." "I hope you're enjoying our show tonight," she said at the end of the song. "You must come again sometime."

Yoshi excused herself and went into the ladies' room. Moments later, a green-faced ghoul, swinging a rope with a noose at the end, trotted out and tossed it around the head of the witch, who was now strolling among the customers singing "Witchcraft" in Japanese. The ghoul led the witch back to the table where the angry man was wiping his coat with a napkin. She bowed to him. "The management apologizes. There will be no charge for your meals tonight." Then she led the witch out the front door. None of the diners seemed to make a connection between the ghoul and witch and Yoshi and Emiko who returned through a side door, sat at their table, and resumed drinking their wine.

"I didn't see a thing," Harvey said. He checked his watch. "Don't you think it's about time to eat?" He was surprised when they all agreed. He raised a hand to get Esmerelda's attention, and she brought menus to the table.

Harvey noticed the second bottle of Merlot had gotten empty in a hurry, so he ordered another. Before Esmerelda left to get it, Meg said, "Your cat seems to have settled down. You can probably pick him up again."

"I'm never going to pick that cat or any other cat up again. In fact, I don't care if I ever see another cat, real or stuffed, for the rest of my life. That one seems confused as to which it is."

When Esmerelda left, Meg put her hands on her cheeks. "Now I'm ashamed of myself for what I did."

As Esmerelda crossed in front of the bar, the cat jumped into her arms. She screamed and tried to push it off, but it wouldn't budge. She ran into the kitchen. Yoshi pointed two fingers at Emiko. "Enough is too much." Emiko slumped down in her seat and gave Yoshi a fake grin.

Minutes later, Esmerelda returned with the cat on her arm, alive but asleep. "It must love me," she said as she served the Merlot. "Are you ready to order?"

Harvey nodded. "We've decided to have a large plate of hors d'oeuvres."

For a few minutes after their order was served, the Old Haunted Inn was like any other restaurant where people ate and engaged in quiet conversation. A young couple in formal wear strolled through the dining area toward French doors at the side of the room, holding hands and gazing into each other's eyes as they passed the table where Harvey and his coven sat. The man bumped Meg's arm and spilled her wine. He neither apologized nor looked at her but kept his eyes on his lady friend. When he held out his hand to open the door for her, a toad jumped from his hand into her cleavage.

"Why'd you do that?" she screamed.

"I didn't do that."

"You certainly did."

"I did not throw that frog between your boobs."

She grabbed the top of her dress which appeared to have a life of its own. "Don't you know the difference between a toad and a frog? Frogs are green. This thing is gray."

"Let me see." He pulled back on the bosom of her dress and peeked in. "You're right. I'll get him." He thrust his hand down the front of her dress up to his elbow.

Two tables away from Harvey's group, a middle-aged woman whispered to her escort, "Why's he have to put his hand down so far?"

"Maybe he's trying to find out what comes next."

The woman smiled. "I suggest you wait until we're in the car before you try it."

The young lady opened the door, and at the same time, grabbed the middle of her dress and jiggled it. As she disappeared outside, her voice was heard: "Uuh, uuhhh."

Her beau's enthusiasm surely was evident to the dining room patrons. "Here, I think I can locate him this time."

A moment later, her voice resonated, "Beast."

Harvey frowned at Meg who was laughing at the action taking place outside the French doors. She read the accusation and pointed at Yoshi. Yoshi grinned.

Harvey and his coven finished their meal and left the Old Haunted Inn with Harvey whistling "I Don't Have A Ghost of A Chance With You" as he drove away. When they arrived at the house across from the cemetery, Harvey and Meg climbed out of the Olds along with Yoshi and her cousins. He stepped to the side while Meg hugged Kyoko and Emiko.

"When will you two be leaving for Japan?" Meg said.

Kyoko shrugged her shoulders. "I don't know. We've enjoyed our vacation here, but there's something I want to do before we leave." She fingered a pigtail as she glanced at Harvey. Emiko stepped between Kyoko and Meg.

"We want to go to New York to see more than just the airport," Emiko said. "Maybe we'll even take a side trip to Washington, D.C."

Harvey smiled at her. "You think the president could use advice from older, wiser Kitsune?"

"Actually, I'd prefer to see the vice president."

"I'm sure he'll be happy to listen to you, but why him instead of the president?"

"He's cuter."

Yoshi pointed at Harvey and Meg. "I'll stay here to keep these lovebirds company until your tour is over, then I may go back to Japan with you."

After he parked in the garage, Harvey sat with his arms wrapped around the steering wheel. "Why did Emiko step between you and Kyoko back there?"

"Did you see how Kyoko was fingering a pigtail?"

"Yes?"

"She has a subconscious quirk. She fingers a pigtail when she's thinking about caressing something about the same size. She did that while looking at you. Emiko saw her do it and stepped between us to avoid a confrontation between Kyoko and me."

Harvey looked over at Meg as he grabbed the door handle. "Fortunately we won't have to put up with Kyoko much longer. Your mama told me she and Emiko will head back to Japan after they return from New York."

CHAPTER 16

On Monday, Harvey and Meg walked into the Marketing Department office and were greeted by a smile from Sophie. "Good morning. What can I do for you?"

"Miss Sakuma would like to reenroll," Harvey said.

"I believe she needs the dean's approval after taking an administrative drop. He's in now." She peeked through Dean Pigeon's open door. "Mr. Long is here with Miss Sakuma to see about reenrolling her."

"Send them in."

Harvey and Meg held hands as they entered Pigeon's office. The dean glanced at their hands and rubbed the side of his face where the sliding hair pieces had been anchored. "Sophie will handle the paperwork right now if that fits your schedule. I'm happy to have you with us again, Miss Sakuma-- I expect it will make life better for all of us." Harvey pumped the dean's hand, and Meg bowed.

Sophie prepared the paperwork, Harvey reached out and held both of Meg's hands. "I'll meet you for lunch at the Downtown Deli at noon." He squeezed her hands, then left to teach his morning class.

Harvey watched Meg prance into the deli. She grabbed one of his hands, pulled him to his feet, and gave him a bear hug. "Both Dean Pigeon and Sophie now know this is a serious relationship. They treated me like a lady, and once again I'm a student. So once again you'll stand flustered in front of your marketing class as I walk down the hall. I'll burst into the room with a flourish. Maybe I'll hire a band to play 'Ruffles And Flourishes' in honor of the occasion."

"Maybe I made a mistake in hooking up with you."

"Maybe we can hook up again."

Harvey rolled his eyes.

He picked up chicken salad sandwiches as Meg got two glasses of water, and they met at a little table next to the window. Harvey removed the sandwiches from the tray, set one in front of Meg, and the other at his place. "It's possible they treated you like a lady because they know the problems you can cause if they don't do so."

"I don't think so. I believe their actions were genuine."

"Perhaps they enjoy the excitement that follows wherever you go."

"Is that what attracted you, dear?"

"I like everything about you."

She placed both hands on the table to keep from knocking it over when she stretched out to kiss him. Giggles came from three of his students at a nearby table.

After they finished lunch, without further displays of ardor, Meg returned to the business office to find out how to make up classes she had missed, and Harvey headed to the teachers' lounge to prepare for his marketing class.

Three minutes after he began the lecture in his afternoon class, a clack, clack echoed down the hall, Meg made her entrance, accompanied by what sounded like the Marine Band playing "Ruffles And Flourishes." Even when she marched across the front of the room in step with the music, Harvey didn't show stress. She sat, and the music stopped. She raised her hand once, causing him to stutter, but his voice returned to normal when he realized she had a legitimate question about something she had missed while absent.

When class was over, they talked while walking down the hall. "You need some make-up sessions," he said. "I'll give you private tutoring."

Meg's eyes opened wide.

Harvey waved a hand at her. "Make-up, not make-out."

"Still sounds exciting."

That evening, Meg cooked a Japanese dish that Harvey could tell was going to be tasty from the aroma that drifted through the house. She brought two bowls out to the deck and sat one in front of him. "I won't tell you what kind of meat the original recipe called for. It's not for sale in this country."

"Fox?"

She pursed her lips and glared at him.

"Excuse me." Harvey took a bite and patted his stomach. After they finished the meal in silence, he said, "That was very good. Lamb, wasn't it?"

Meg was not smiling when she said, "Yes." She opened her mouth. about to say something else, when the doorbell rang. Harvey breathed out, glad to escape what she was about to say.

He heard Rosie's voice. "Hello--anybody home?" With Ted following like an obedient puppy, she appeared at the door to the deck. "I should have known you'd be out here on such a beautiful day."

Harvey stood and gave her a hug. "I haven't seen you for weeks. Where've you been?"

"If you'd stay home sometimes, you'd know. We spent the weekend on Mackinaw Island. I wanted to make it our honeymoon." She elbowed Ted. "But what's his name here says we should wait."

Harvey faced Rosie's boyfriend. "Listen to her. So soon you discover the price you pay for love."

"Yes."

"That's one of the few times I've heard you talk."

"Like you say, Mr. Long, the price you pay for love."

"Ted, now that you're sleeping with my daughter on a regular basis, I believe it's time for you to address me in a fashion different than Mr. Long."

"Dad?"

"Why don't you start by just calling me Harvey. Do you intend to marry Rosie?"

"Yes, but not soon. I want to earn my degree and get a good job first."

Meg raised a hand. "We'll support you until you get your job and then we can have a double wedding." Harvey lowered his head and frowned at her with raised eyebrows.

Rosie grinned. "Yeah. I never thought of that. It'll be a giant affair. We'll invite Dad's students, and I'll invite my friends. And Meg, who would you invite?"

Harvey held up a finger, then another, then another. "Foxes and witches and goblins and gremlins and--" Fire blazed in Meg's eyes, and she pointed two dainty fingers at him. He backed up with palms extended. "Don't do it. I apologize."

She glared at him and lowered her fingers, then switched her attention to Rosie. "Mama's the only relative I'll invite."

"I don't believe we should schedule the ceremony for at least three weeks," Rosie said. "Too much planning and inviting to do, but my schedule's free in August."

Harvey held his hands up. "Hold it. Can't Ted and I share in this discussion?"

"What's to be discussed?" Rosie said. "We know who's marrying whom." She squinted and pointed at Ted.

"You'd better not take his side."

Harvey laughed. "What happened to the lovey-dovey stuff that was taking place between you two?"

Rosie gave her dad a plastic smile. "I just want to remind him who's boss. I still love him." She blew Ted a kiss.

Harvey turned to Ted. "I think she's been taking lessons from Meg." As soon as he said that, he realized he shouldn't have. He added, "Which is the way it should be. Learn from those older and wiser than you." Meg didn't smile, so he continued trying to escape the hole he'd dug. "At least she said she still loves you." Meg glared at him.

"Mr. Long," Ted said, "I definitely don't want to be supported by you or anybody else, and I won't graduate until Spring of next year."

"I agree with you. I don't need to support anyone else, especially with my employment situation at the college being as tenuous as it is right now."

Conversation stopped. Lillian Doerner had crossed the dividing line between the lawns, wearing her white bikini. She pranced across Harvey's lawn and up the stairs. Meg stood and faced Lillian with her hands on her hips. Lillian stopped halfway up the steps and waved the fingers of one hand. "Beautiful day, isn't it?" She reversed her direction, went back down the steps, and marched in a straight line back to the Doerner property.

Meg faced Harvey with her hands still on her hips. "You worm. If I ever catch you hanging around that hussie again, there won't be a wedding, there'll be a funeral. And if I catch you one more time playing footsie with that juvenile, two-hundred-year-old second cousin of mine, I'll make sure a slow death precedes it."

"What brought this on? I haven't been hanging around Lillian, and if you're rehashing what happened at the Haunted

Inn, remember, it was your cousin's foot doing it to me."

"You didn't move away from what her foot was doing."

"Because I was stunned at what her foot was doing."

"You were enjoying what her foot was doing."

"I moved, didn't I?"

"Sure. When you were told to. Even then you knew you'd get the same treatment from her sister."

Harvey tapped Ted on the shoulder. "See what happens as soon as they think they have you trapped?"

"I see."

Rosie thumped Ted on the back of his head. "I told you not to take his side. Do it again, and we'll have a double funeral." She crossed her arms and looked at Meg. "What manner of slow death are you contemplating for my father?" She touched Ted's arm. "If it has anything to do with fire, I have another piece of fuel I can toss on."

"Great idea," Meg said. "or I could turn them into toads. Then we could have toad legs for dinner. No, that wouldn't work. They'd have to pull themselves down the aisle on skateboards, and that would slow the ceremony down."

Rosie held up her hand. "I believe you mean frog legs."

"Oh. . . . Hey, Mama gave me an idea. I could turn them into gerbils and let them exercise their hormones by gaping at women from a cage."

The two men shook their heads in unison.

"Yeah," Rosie said. "Another idea--we could put those two vixens you mentioned in a cage next to them, so they could ogle to their heart's content."

"I'd appreciate it if you used a term other than vixen," Meg said.

"Excuse me. You know my heart's in the right place."

"You're so right. It's the beauty of the thought behind the spoken word that counts."

Rosie reached up and touched her temple. "Beautiful minds have beautiful thoughts."

"Maybe we should forget the wedding," Harvey said.

Meg glared at him. "If you think you're getting out of marrying me, you have another think coming. I intend for you to promise to love, honor, and obey."

"Didn't they remove the word 'obey' a few years ago?"

"I put it back in."

Rosie faced Meg and smiled. "I like you more all the time. Dad's so fortunate that you came along to enrich his life."

"Thank you. I'm so fortunate to have found him." She stepped over to Harvey, pulled his head down, and kissed him. Then she stepped back and surveyed him, put her arms around him, and laid her head on his chest.

Rosie watched. She walked to Ted and gave him the same treatment, then she went to Meg and hugged her. "It's nice that you live with my father. I'm learning so much about relationships from you."

"What happened to your relationship with your father?" Harvey said.

"Be quiet when I'm talking to your fiancée, or I'll have her turn you into a frog."

"Toad," Meg said.

Harvey raised his hand with his thumb and little finger sticking up in the air to signify drinking. "Would you like a glass of wine, Ted?"

Ted, Rosie, and Meg said, "Yes."

Harvey walked into the house and returned with four glasses and two bottles of Merlot. He pulled the cork from the first one and held the bottle up. "We should plant our own grapes and make our own wine." He pulled the bottle down. "No, I don't think so. The way we've been drinking lately, we wouldn't give it time to ferment. We ought to slack off some."

He filled the glasses and handed one to each of them.

Rosie held her glass high. "Ted and I have to leave after this. We need to make up some classes we missed."

"Meg does too," Harvey said. "In fact, I'll began her make-up sessions tonight."

Meg gave Harvey a huge grin. "Really?"

"Make-up, dear, not make-out. Remember?"

"We have to go," Rosie said. She grabbed Ted's hand and led him to the door.

After waving goodbye, Meg turned toward Harvey. "Rather than tutoring, let's try that making up thing. I understand it precipitates fine love making."

"Do you ever think of anything else?"

"Of course. There's wine and ahh, keeping you away from other women who would like to do it with you."

"Do what with me?"

"What I like to do, but nobody else had better."

"Why do you keep harping at me on the subject of what other women would like to do with me when I'm only interested in doing it with you?"

"Because a bunch of them, who like their meat close to the bone, hang around you."

"It's not their meat. It's mine."

"Ours."

He sighed. "At least there's one woman you won't have to worry about, soon."

"Who's that?"

"Kyoko. She won't cause any more problems for us."

CHAPTER 17

Harvey handed Meg a glass of wine across the kitchen table. She waved it off. "Neither with breakfast nor before."

He slid a newspaper to her. "You may change your mind when you see this." He handed her the front page of the *Journal*. She read the lead story: *An anonymous source in Washington D.C. announced that the vice president had a scare yesterday when he received an unauthorized visit by two young Asian women. FBI, CIA, and Homeland Security have been summoned to determine how two possible terrorists managed to slip through massive security.*

Reliable sources quote the vice president: "I suspected something was amiss when I felt a not unpleasant sensation beneath my desk. I let the sensation continue to give me time to analyze it before opening my eyes. When I did so, I noticed two women sitting on the front side of my desk. The younger one was pulling on one of her pigtails."

By the time Homeland Security personnel arrived, the women had disappeared, as had the sensation, leaving behind a tiny sandal with a thong. A thorough inspection determined that the thong was probably designed to go between a big toe and four others. The sandal is being held under security for analysis to determine if athlete's foot germ warfare was perpetrated.

After reading the article, Meg tossed the paper to the other side of the table. "I'm not surprised. They're typical

Kitsune. Mama was never like that when she was young, and since coming to America, she's acted even more human."

Harvey sipped his coffee, then set his cup on the table. Meg ate some of her cereal but stopped when he said, "I've wondered about the difference between your mother and her cousins. I didn't know if it was because of their age difference."

"It's not about age. She's appalled at what they do to people, perhaps because I'm half human, or maybe because of how she felt about my father. I fell in love with you just like she did with him. That's why I'm afraid I'll cause you harm."

"It's been two weeks, and I feel fine--unlike the boat captain, the judge, and the bailiff."

"How do you know how they feel?"

"It was in the local section of today's paper. I'll read it: *A high-ranking county health official stated today that department personnel are mystified by a rare malady that has affected three local men with similar symptoms: loss of weight and energy for no apparent reason.*"

Meg pushed the remainder of cereal away. "Your health department never discovered a connection to Kyoko? Didn't they ask the men, with whom they'd had been associating."

"Here's what the paper says: *Upon questioning, none of them mentioned any association with a common food, drink, or person that could have caused the condition. None of them have children, but all have wives who are furious with the ineffectiveness of the health department.*"

"And listen to this: *It was learned by the* Journal *that the wife of the* River Princess *captain has contacted a group of lawyers to initiate suit against those she holds responsible for her husband's condition. The list of defendants includes the City of Lansing, the Grand River Authority, the Acme Riverboat Company, the Chamber of Commerce, the Army Corps of Engineers, the Environmental Protection Agency, the Michigan*

*Bureau of Boat Licensing, and the Humane Society. In an
exclusive interview Mrs. Mason said, "It's a good thing my
husband didn't drift into the lake. Now we'll have a body to use
as evidence after he kicks off. Making money is not my object. I
just want the public to realize boat-riding is serious business."*

"Poor woman," Meg said. "Even though she's not
interested in getting rich from her husband's misfortune, it
sounds like the money will go a long way toward healing her
hurt. I expect the vice president doesn't realize how lucky he
was only to end up with a not unpleasant sensation." She
walked to the window and stared outside. "I'm still worried
about what I may have done to you."

Harvey got up from the table and put his arm around
her. "Don't be. I feel better than I've felt for years, and it all
began the first night I made love to you."

"But I'm only half-Kitsune, so maybe it takes longer."
He held her close, and they remained that way, standing next to
a kitchen table that held a bowl of cereal, an empty coffee cup,
and a glass of untouched wine. The front doorbell rang. Harvey
answered it. Yoshi strode in and hugged him. "My daughter is
no more Kitsune than you are." She let go of him, hurried to the
kitchen, and hugged Meg. "What did I just tell Harvey?"

"I have no idea."

"Why not?"

Meg put her head on Yoshi's shoulder. "I don't know."

Yoshi brushed Meg's hair with her hand. "Because
you're not even enough like me to read minds through a wall.
Harvey hasn't changed from the first time I met him. You have.
You can hardly read minds anymore, and when you use magic,
it's cheap stuff. I don't think you can even turn a man into a
toad. Try to do it to Harvey."

Meg shook her head rapidly. "No."

"I don't believe you have the power to do it. Go ahead-

-try it. If by some chance you succeed, I'll bring him back to his bony self."

Meg shook her head even faster. "No, Mama."

"All right, I'll do it, and you try to bring him back."

Meg held her mother's hands. "Please, no."

"See, you don't even think like you used to," Yoshi said. "You're like a wimpy human."

"That's what I want to be." They held each other. Harvey, who had been watching and listening, came over to them, and the three of them hugged in a circle.

"What's Harvey thinking?" Yoshi said to Meg.

"It's not clear, but it has to do with making me happy."

"And what am I thinking?"

Meg closed her eyes. "I don't know."

"See, baby, you're losing it."

Meg looked at Yoshi with her first smile in a while. "You haven't called me baby for over a hundred years."

"That's what you're turning into, a baby human."

"I hope so."

"Oh, shit," Yoshi said.

Meg frowned at her mother. "Mamasan!"

Yoshi walked to the door. "They're back."

When Yoshi opened the front door, Harvey heard Emiko say, "Yoshiko, watch your language. You're starting to cuss like a teen."

"It was appropriate. What are you doing back here? I thought you were going to Japan after your highly successful trip to Washington."

"We enjoy it here."

"It's easy pickings," Kyoko said. "They like me here."

Yoshi leaned toward Kyoko. "They didn't like you that much at the Capitol, I see."

"Too much security."

"We've beefed up security here too."

Kyoko shrugged. "What can a half-Kitsune do, even with the help of an old one who acts more and more human every day?"

Yoshi laughed. "Don't you realize you're already to the point where you'd rather chase a man than a rabbit?"

"What are you talking about?"

"Why do you think I'm becoming more human? Because I decided to? No. Because I haven't had a good run on four legs since I've been here. I don't know if I can ever go back to scrounging for rabbits, mice, and moles--they don't even sound appetizing anymore. You make fun of me changing, but that's exactly what's happening to you." Harvey grinned where he stood in the kitchen.

Kyoko waved a hand at Yoshi. "I know what you want. You want me to leave here, so I can't make out with your future son-in-law. I won't leave until I get in his drawers."

Yoshi laughed.

"What's so funny?"

"You can't see it, can you? The longer you stay, the more you'll like it; and the more easy pickings you get, the more you'll want. You two are on your way to becoming human. Sure, I'm losing my powers by staying here, but if you think that's funny, wait until your own magic starts fading. Goodbye." Harvey, eavesdropping from the kitchen, jumped when one of Yoshi's cousins slammed the door on the way out.

A moment later Yoshi walked back to where he and Meg stood. Harvey hugged her. "You done good, Yoshi."

"Remember," she said, "like my friend Amadeus said, 'It ain't over till the fat lady sings.'" The doorbell rang. Harvey and Meg peeked around the corner as Yoshi walked to the front door. She opened the door. "What now?"

Emiko folded her arms in front of her. "We were thinking about what you said and want you to know we appreciate your knowledge and experience. I want to stay the way I am, and Kyoko does too. We'll party here a while, maybe a week, then go back to Japan. Meanwhile, we'd both like to stay on good terms with you."

"Good," Yoshi said. "I'd like to remain friends with you too." Her cousins bowed and left after a more delicate closing of the door. Yoshi walked back to the kitchen. "Now that we have a success to toast, I'll take that glass of wine." They walked out to the deck and were talking about how well the confrontation had ended when Yoshi put a finger to her lips. "Shh. Don't believe a word of it."

"What now?" Harvey said.

"They're not people. They're female foxes. Foxes are wily--they connive--they lie. They're planning something--I don't know what, but it has to do with you two and it's not nicey, nicey."

"Why'd we drink a toast to success?"

"I wanted them to hear it, so they'd think they'd tricked us. Now I can't hear their thoughts, which means they can't hear ours, so we can do some planning."

"Why don't we just stay away from them?"

Meg leaned against the rail to gaze at the pond, then faced Harvey. "That won't work. Our best bet is to stay close to them, so we can see what they're up to."

Yoshi nodded. "I'm sure my little speech about losing their magic power got through to them, and they'll leave after a bit more time here. But you're right. We should keep them in sight in the meantime just in case."

"What about you?" Harvey said to Yoshi. "Do you want to be a wimpy human?"

"I think so, and eventually I'll come close. I'm not the

foxy type any more."

Meg's eyes shined and she glanced at Yoshi. "You mean you'll be staying here?"

"Not here in the house but here in the city. One of the human characteristics I've adopted is I like being around you. I never had a great desire to be near my kits. I've even forgotten the names of most of them, but I do want to be near you two."

"How many brothers and sisters do I have?"

Yoshi didn't answer for a moment. She took a drink of wine, then faced Meg. "None. Half brothers and sisters, a bunch, probably forty or fifty litters. I never kept track. None of them can give me what I so dearly want."

Harvey laughed. "I'll help you get what you want, but I hope I never meet any of your other offspring. Your cousins do enough damage. How'd you keep track of them?"

"We ran together and worked the same towns."

"I have a difficult time imagining you as a fox."

"Me too."

Meg opened her eyes wide and waved her index finger. "As long as we have to keep those two in sight, we ought to plan activities for them before they decide on an agenda of their own that will get us in trouble."

"You're right," Yoshi said, "but wherever we go, it may be a wild scene, and we don't want them to soil Harvey's reputation any more than he's managed to do on his own."

Meg raised her finger again. "I know the place--the Winkin' Pup. They can't hurt his reputation there, and nothing we can do will damage theirs."

Harvey put an arm over her shoulder. "You just want to play with that pup again."

Meg smiled. "He was cute, wasn't he? But no. I'll try to be on my good behavior."

"Try? You'll try? Do you know what 'I'll try' means?

When we get married, and the preacher asks if I promise to love, honor, and be true to you, I'll say, 'I'll try.'"

"Okay, smarty pants. I will be on my good behavior."

"I've seen your good behavior before, and I don't know if I want to see it again."

Meg turned her back to Harvey and faced her mother. "Mama, remember the conversation we had earlier about little furry animals?"

CHAPTER 18

The winkin' pup still wore the smile Meg gave him as he sat on his platform over the bar, blinking one eye at a full house of Wednesday night patrons while a band blasted out a rock song for the benefit of a wiggling, giggling mass of humanity. Harvey figured he, Meg, Yoshi, and the Kitsune cousins would appear to be a group of ordinary revelers as they strolled in and took seats at a round table close to the bar.

Jamie crossed her hands over her halter and observed the five revelers from her serving station. "My God," she said as she kept her eyes focused on them. Three women sitting at the bar next to Jamie must have sensed the tension. They observed her actions.

Harvey recognized Jamie's concern and placed one of his hands over Meg's. "She remembers us."

Jamie's face wrinkled from closing her eyes tight when Meg pointed at her. Nothing happened. Jamie opened her eyes and sighed. Meg breathed audibly, and her shoulders sagged. Yoshi placed her hand on Meg's "What are you trying to do?"

"I reduced Jamie's breasts the last time we were here, and I feel terrible about doing that to her. I want to restore them, but I don't have enough power left."

"I'll do it for you, baby."

Jamie watched from next to the bar as Yoshi pointed two fingers at her. She closed her eyes again and cupped her hands over her breasts. The bartender evidently realized something was bothering his server. He placed his hand on her shoulder. In unison the three women stared with wide eyes and mouths open when Jamie's breasts expanded and tried to escape the confines of her halter.

Harvey observed the change in Jamie's halter and turned to Meg. "I'm glad you made them big again."

Meg crossed her arms. "I'll bet you are. But Mama did it. I've lost my power."

"I think it was nice of you to return what she had."

"I've wanted to ever since I reduced them."

Jamie smiled and hurried to the table. "Thank you," she said to Yoshi, then spoke to Meg. "I forgive you for what you did last time you were here. I don't know how you two do this thing, but I thank you for putting me back together."

"You're welcome. I apologize for what I did to you."

The band took a break, and the place became relatively quiet. Jamie, Harvey, Yoshi, and Meg focused their attention on the bar where one of the three women who had witnessed the restoration, grabbed the bartender's arm. "Do that to me."

"Do what to you?"

"Like you did Jamie. Come on, touch me like you did her." She put her hands on her breasts. "Come on--touch me. I saw what happened when you touched her."

"You saw that too? I thought I was seeing things."

"You were. Her things got so big you couldn't help but see them." The woman ripped off two buttons in her hurry to get her blouse open. "I know you made them grow, so come on, touch me. Do it."

"If you say so." He touched her. Nothing happened.

She grabbed his hand and shoved it inside her blouse. "Do it again. Rub them." With the evident purpose of making a patron happy, he placed both hands inside her bra and rubbed her breasts. They expanded. He held his hands in front of his face and stared at them. The woman squealed, grabbed underneath her breasts, and jiggled them. "Uhh. Great job." She pulled the bartender's head over and kissed him on the lips.

Harvey frowned at Yoshi. "What are you doing?"

"Why do you blame me when I didn't do anything?"

A loud voice from the bar caught Harvey's attention. A young man pushed his stein of beer away and stood. "That's enough for me. Let's get out of here."

The young woman, with him, grabbed his arm. "Just a minute. Don't be in such a hurry." She pushed him back onto his stool and continued to watch the action.

The two women, next to the one who had received the breast enhancement, unbuttoned their blouses and fought to get close to the bartender. One pushed her way to the front, grabbed his hands, and placed them on her breasts. "Do it." Excited conversation came from patrons sitting at the bar when her request was granted. The woman scurried around the end of the bar and hugged the bartender. Soon his hands were inside the bra of the third woman. She squealed with delight when the snaps on the back of her bra popped open from the added pressure put on them.

The young woman, down the line, pulled her t-shirt over her head and flung it behind her as she deserted her escort and hurried to the end of the bar where the other three were comparing their newly enlarged breasts. Emiko bounced up and down in her chair, laughing. Harvey tapped Yoshi's arm. "Make her stop." Yoshi pointed two fingers at Emiko--the laugh faded and was replaced by a blank stare. He placed a hand on Meg's arm. "Whew, we got that stopped just in time. Make sure your mother keeps a rein on her, or we'll be thrown out of here again." He was startled when he heard screams and a pounding noise coming from the direction of the bar.

The young woman stood bare-breasted behind the bar, while next to her, the bartender was pounding his fists on the bar and yelling, "No, no, no." He had been endowed with breasts that threatened to pop the buttons off his shirt.

Harvey thought it was Emiko's doing, but then he saw Kyoko shaking her fists and laughing. He nudged Yoshi. "Stop her." Yoshi pointed two fingers at Kyoko, causing her to fold her arms and sit still with a smile frozen on her face, then she glared at Emiko, who put her hands up in the surrender position. Next, Yoshi gave her two finger point at the bartender, and his shirt reverted to its flat state. He rubbed his chest, ran out from behind the bar, and shoved his way through the crowd, knocking two tables over before slamming the front door behind him.

The young woman picked her t-shirt off the floor, grabbed her escort's arm, and pulled on him. "Let's go."

He grinned. "My place?"

"Hell, no. I want to catch that bartender." She ran across the room, pulling her friend along. Other patrons, who saw what happened at the end of the bar, left their drinks and scurried out the door. People, who hadn't seen the breast enhancement show, looked around as if to determine what caused the flight, then joined the rush to the street.

Jamie had appeared to be in a trance as she watched the show. Now, she turned to Meg, "I'll get you anything you want, even if I have to go to a liquor store and buy it, but I don't expect I'll have to. I know when I look at the back bar, I'll see a bottle of red wine that wasn't there before you came."

"Thank you, Jamie. Please give us five glasses of wine from that bottle."

"Yes, ma'am." Jamie hurried to the bar, ducked under the opening, and grabbed the bottle of Merlot off the back bar. She ran to Harvey's table carrying the wine bottle and five glasses on a tray, set the tray in the middle of the table, then joined the band in their retreat out the front door. The women at the bar were still checking their enhanced breasts and adjusting their tops to better show them off and didn't seem to notice the clatter of breaking glass and banging noises that echoed through the bar as departing patrons knocked tables and chairs over on their mad dash to the exits.

From a door next to the bar, a skinny little man had watched his server, the band, and his customers push and shove their way out of his place of business. The last of his patrons hurried out the door, leaving only Harvey's group and three happy women in the place. One of the women grabbed the little man's arm. "You're lucky to have such a wonderful bartender."

"If he's so wonderful, where is he, and what happened to all my customers?"

"I expect he's answered a new calling. Look what he did for me." She opened her blouse and shoved her boobs in his face. Being short enough to get an excellent view, he inspected them thoroughly. "Nice. I'd like to spend more time with you, but I have to find out what drove my patrons away." The woman tucked her gifts into her blouse but not all the way.

The manager glanced around the almost empty room and spied Harvey. He ran to the table and grabbed the wine bottle. "Out, right now," he yelled.

Meg stood. "I accomplished what I wanted. Let's go." Yoshi, Harvey, and Emiko followed her toward the door. Harvey noticed Kyoko wasn't with them. He looked back and saw her standing face to face with the manager, so close they were almost touching.

Harvey didn't hear what the little man said to Kyoko but heard her say, "Old enough." The man smiled. She waved to Harvey as he and the others headed out the door.

Late that night Meg and Harvey sat on the deck, listening to the croaking of frogs, an occasional splash, and the flutter of wings from swallows as they zoomed past. She put a hand on Harvey's. "I'm going to leave you for a while. Can you behave yourself for an hour or two?"

"Where're you going?"

"To the den. I'm worried about Kyoko."

Harvey leaned back in his chair. "Kyoko?"

"I'm concerned. I want to be sure she's come home."

He leaned forward. "I'll go with you."

"No, I have to go alone."

"I want to go with you. I've never seen her place."

"You don't want to see it."

"Sure I do."

She stood and peered down at him. "No. I don't want you going there."

"Why not?"

"You wouldn't understand."

Harvey rose from his chair. "There have been a lot of things about you and your family nobody else would understand, but have you ever seen me back off?"

"No, but you--"

"I'll drive you."

"I can run."

"Let me drive you."

She stared over the pond and then at him. "All right, but remember, I warned you."

Twenty minutes later, Harvey drove by the wrought iron fence surrounding the South Town Cemetery. "Stop at the gate," Meg said. Harvey parked the Olds, and they strolled through the open gate, across a wooden footbridge, and into the darkness. He wondered what would come next.

They crossed to the back edge of the cemetery where

the land made an abrupt rise to a peak. High on the slope, he spotted a cave below a rock outcropping. As he followed Meg along a narrow path up the slope, Harvey heard a rustle of leaves to his left and saw two gray forms streak down the hill in the dim light. He nudged Meg. "Did you see that?"

She stopped and grimaced. "We spooked them."

"You knew about them?"

"Of course; Mama and Emiko."

"That was them?"

"I knew you wouldn't understand."

"Wow."

Meg placed her hand on her forehead. "I wish I hadn't brought you. They're foxes. They just look like people when they're around you."

He put an arm around her shoulder. "I'm sorry--I apologize for being dumb."

"You're not dumb. You're just now seeing what they really are."

"Why'd they run away?"

"Because I brought you."

"Will they return?"

"Not until you're gone."

"I want to see their den."

She wiped her eyes. "It's nothing to see; just a niche beneath the rock. Go home."

"I'll wait in the car."

"Go home. . . . Please."

Harvey put two fingers under her chin and kissed her. "I'm in love with the most exotic, the most exciting woman in the world. Would you consent to marry a common, ordinary, everyday guy like me?"

"Yes."

"How will you get home?"

"I can run like a fox."

He made his way back between the tombstones and trees they had passed on the way to the den. When he arrived at his house, he brewed a cup of coffee and sat at the table, staring at the cup. *I wonder if this really happened.* He checked the kitchen clock. It was almost midnight. *I have class in the morning. She'll wake me when she comes home.* He went to bed and left the light on in the foyer.

Harvey didn't hear the door open or see the light go out but awoke when he felt the warm body slip in next to him and arms slide around him. He wrapped his arms around her and whispered, "Hi, sweetheart." She snuggled up closer. "Did you find Kyoko?" he said. She answered by fondling him.

"Meg. . . . Meg?" She didn't answer. He reached over and turned the bed lamp on. Kyoko smiled up at him. He tried to push her away, but she threw a warm leg over him and wrapped her arms around him tight as a straight jacket. He pulled on her arms but couldn't loosen her grip. "I don't want to hurt you, but I want you out of my bed, now."

"No you don't. I can tell you want me here."

He pushed on her. "I didn't know it was you."

She slid one of her hands across his cheek and fondled his ear. "Before I go, I want to make you forget you ever met my half-breed cousin." She slipped her other hand down between his legs and nuzzled her face in his neck at the same time. "I'll make you forget everything in the world except me."

Harvey broke her grip and hopped out of bed. He faced her and thrust his hand toward the door. "Out, right now."

She ogled him. "I can see you like having me here."

He grabbed his robe from a chair, put it on, and turned back to the bed. The covers were askew, but it was empty.

Meg's voice came from the doorway. "Are you finished?"

CHAPTER 19

Harvey didn't go back to bed right away. He paced the house and the deck for a while, then sat motionless on a chair in the living room until one in the morning. He went to bed but awoke many times during the night. What sleep he found, was troubled. He searched the house and the garage before he went to school. Meg didn't attend her morning or afternoon classes. In the late afternoon, he hurried to the house and called Rosie. "Come home--I need you."

"What happened?"

"I'll tell you when you get here."

"Tell me now."

"Meg's gone."

"Where?"

"I don't know--come home."

Rosie stepped onto the deck where her dad sat staring at the pond. She kissed him on the forehead and tapped on an almost full wine bottle that sat on the rail next to him. "Your problem can't be so bad--last time I found you like this, you had emptied the bottle."

He glanced up. "I finally realized wine is to enjoy, not to drown in."

"Are you enjoying?"

"No, but I'm not drowning, either."

Rosie pulled a chair next to him, until they faced the same direction. She put a hand on his. "What happened."

Harvey looked straight ahead and talked without looking at his daughter. "You know how Kyoko's always trying to get me in the sack. Last night Meg went to her mother's place. I fell asleep about midnight. I woke up and thought she had come home and wanted to snuggle." Harvey turned toward Rosie. "Kyoko had sneaked in bed with me."

"Did you find out soon enough?"

He turned his head away. "Yes. She cuddled different from what I was used to."

"And?"

"I couldn't get her to leave, so I got up to put my robe on. While doing so, Meg walked in, and Kyoko vanished. Meg walked out again, and I haven't seen or heard from her since." He lowered his head into his hands. "I don't know what to do."

"You don't have to do anything. She'll be back."

He jerked his head to face her. "How do you know?"

"She loves you."

"But she doesn't trust me."

"Sure, she does."

He stood next to the rail and faced the yard. "You've seen how she rags on me."

Rosie laughed. "Yeah. She and I rag on you and Ted all the time. That's part of how a woman says she's in love. Remember how I took her side last Thursday?"

He turned around. "When she said she'd turn me into a toad and cut off my legs, and you wanted to have a double funeral, with you throwing fuel on the fire? How could I possibly remember that?"

She stood, walked to him, and hugged him. "I love you, you old bag of bones."

"So that's the way it works, huh? I feel better now,

knowing I'll have to put up with that stuff from both of you for the rest of my life."

She backed off and held Harvey at arms' length. "How's Yoshi taking it?"

"Don't know--haven't seen her."

"About time you did, isn't it? Meg could be staying at her place."

Harvey thought about that for a moment. "No, she wouldn't go there. Kyoko lives with Yoshi."

"How long's Kyoko going to be around? I thought those two were only staying here while Meg was in Japan."

"I don't know, but there'll be no peace for me as long as they're still in town."

"We could hire a hit man."

Harvey nixed that idea by shaking his head. "Take too much money and too much time. I think we should find a way to make her want to leave."

Rosie opened her hands and touched the tips of her fingers together. "Why don't you set a trap for her?"

"What kind of trap?"

"Get Yoshi in on it. You know how to reach her, don't you?" She pointed at the door to the house. "I have to go. I'm due at Central to get ready for class tomorrow morning. If you two come up with a really great idea, call me."

Ten minutes after Rosie left, Harvey started the Olds and headed to the South Town Cemetery. He parked the wagon a quarter-mile from where he had Sunday night and crossed the bridge in the failing light. He tiptoed to the base of the hill where the den was located, staying in the shadow of bushes and tombstones as much as possible, then climbed until he came to an outcropping of shale. He leaned against it. "Yoshi, I want to talk to you," he mouthed.

Within minutes he heard a rustle in the leaves to his

right, and Yoshi appeared. "You look strange, sitting alone in a cemetery. What are you doing here at this time of night?"

"Getting my rear end wet. Tell me--you read minds."

Yoshi laughed. "You did nothing wrong. That's how love works."

"That's exactly what Rosie told me. It's not the only reason I came to see you, though. I feel it's time to put a stop to Kyoko's obsession with me."

"I can't say I particularly blame her, but you're right. What are you thinking of doing, short of killing her? She's not in season, you know."

"I have no idea what to do."

Yoshi placed a fist under her chin and closed her eyes. After a moment of silence, she opened them. "I'll tell you something you may already know: Kyoko has a gigantic flaw-- she's vain--she not only thinks she's the cutest thing man ever saw, but she struts her tail around higher than any other vixen I've known. If we can devise a way to humiliate her, she'll head back to Japan right now. That would make me happy too. Let me think on that."

"Okay, get back to me if you come up with something."

"Stick around a minute." Yoshi put her finger to the side of her head and poked her brow a couple of times. "I've got it. Fifty years ago there was this movie about Charlie Chan, a detective who had a son named Peter. Kyoko was all gaga about Peter Chan and told everyone how she'd protect him from the other Kitsune, but then she learned he was Chinese. From then on, she wished she could seduce him. She called him a wolf. Foxes hate wolves, you know."

"I can believe that."

"Here's what we do: We get ourselves a wolf and change him to look like Peter Chan. We plant him near the cemetery bridge, and get Kyoko headed that way. She'll see

177

him and want to do her thing. When she gets going real good, if you know what I mean, I'll change him back to a wolf. That's when we pop up out of the ditch and howl with laughter."

"I'm glad you're around and on my side. I believe your cemetery bridge is a perfect place. Now that you mention it, what a romantic spot, with the moon shining between the trees, and the smell of roses along the side of the mausoleum. Your idea's perfect. I can even hear the water rippling over the rocks in the creek below. Maybe we can make a path of rose petals for her to follow on the way to Mr. Chan."

"Rose petals, no, but we need a wolf."

"The zoo has a bunch. Can you spring one?"

"You bet. One thing though: Meg should be in on this to make it more effective when I do changee, changee back to a wolf. I expect by tomorrow night she'll feel you've had enough time to learn your lesson, and she'll come back."

"What lesson?"

"Nothing in particular."

The next day, Harvey wondered if Rosie and Yoshi really knew what they were talking about on the subject of a woman's love because of the way Meg acted in his Marketing 110 classroom. She nodded at him as he stepped to the front of the room. He nodded in return. She didn't show emotion when he lost his way, and he didn't spend much time looking at her. At the break, she passed by him as he talked to another student. He searched for her outside the room but didn't locate her. She returned after the break. At the end of class, she said, "I'll see you at your place after school's out." Then she left.

Rain came down the rest of the afternoon, but the sun peeked through the clouds at five. Everything smelled clean and fresh when he came home to find Meg standing in the living room. She didn't come to him. Harvey followed her lead and didn't go to her. She gave no indication of her state of mind when she said, "The deck?"

"Yes. Wine?"

"No." She walked to the kitchen, grabbed a towel, and headed out to the deck.

"Something to eat?" he said.

"No." She wiped the glider dry, and they sat side by side but not touching. "I know you didn't have sex with her."

"How do you know? Because I'm not sick?"

"No--I've always known you'd never make love to anyone other than me."

"If you knew that, why'd you treat me like a lecher?"

"That's my job."

"Is it your job to make me feel more miserable than I've felt in all my years?"

She lowered her head. "That was the wrong thing for me to say. I apologize for saying that and for what I did to you. I'm so ashamed of myself." She started crying. "All I could see in my mind was that vixen in our bed."

He tried to establish eye contact, but she didn't look up. "Why'd you leave me?" he said.

"Because I couldn't face you or talk to you." She raised her head to the level of his. "I have to do something about her. I can't go on like this. I can't take it anymore, and I can't have you running from her forever."

"I understand how you feel. I can't take much more of her either. Your mother and I discussed that problem, and I believe we came up with a solution."

Meg shook her head. "No. It's my problem to solve my way--I don't want either of you involved--it would only cause trouble for the two I love."

"We're already involved. I went to see your mother and

told her about Kyoko's antics that night. I didn't see you there. Where were you?"

"I stayed with Jamie, from the Winkin' Pup. She understands what I'm going through. One of her best friends took off with her boyfriend. I trust her, and I believe she trusts me now. More and more, I'm beginning to realize I'm almost totally woman, not much different than she is. She plays with men but doesn't let them get serious with her--like I used to. But I've found the man I want--she hasn't." Meg reached over and put her hand on Harvey's leg.

He covered her hand with his. "I've found the woman I want, too."

"I also found I have another friend."

"Kept yourself busy, haven't you? Who else?"

"Sophie. I missed two classes yesterday. Remember how she helped me catch up on those I missed before? She did it again. She heard I wasn't in class, so she got the instructors' assignments and brought them to me this morning. I like her."

"Even when you know she's hot after my body?"

"Many women are hot after your body, but she's not anymore. My hand on your leg beat out your hands on her boobs. As they say in golf, she let me play through."

"I see. Now, listen while I talk. I started to tell you about a plan your mother and I are sure will work, with your permission and help." He described Yoshi's plan to get rid of Kyoko by humiliating her.

"Mama's right. I'll buy into it, but I can't be near Kyoko before it takes place." She slid next to him, put her head on his shoulder, and kissed him on the neck. "I love you."

"I love you too." He picked her up and carried her to the bedroom.

By the time they got there, she had his shirt off and was working on his belt buckle. She grinned. "Now is our chance to do that making-up thing."

Later, Harvey lay on his back and sighed. "You know, you're a diddle machine."

She sat up and peered at him. "A what?"

"A diddle machine. Push a button and you diddle."

She poked him in the belly. "I see you like to push that button a lot."

"Yeah, but I'm getting old."

"You're not getting old. You already are. You're like a used car too beat up to be fixed."

"It's just that Japanese cars perform better and last longer than American cars."

She giggled. "You perform just right. Now, if I can just get you to last longer."

"You know what your mother said about your lovemaking the night I met her?"

"I can imagine. She was trying to get me married off."

"She said making love with you wouldn't be practice-- I'd be in the finals."

Meg grinned. She put two fingers on his belly and rubbed them around in a circle. "You like it that way?"

"It makes my daughter happy, but it sure leaves me winded."

"Speaking of happy women, Jamie's really happy with her new job as interim manager. The manager who threw us out of the Winkin' Pup is sick."

"No energy? Can't eat?"

She put on her serious face. "Something else. Jamie said when she took him to the emergency room, the doctor told her they'd had a rash of similar cases this past week."

The doorbell rang, and Harvey climbed out of bed. "Always rings at the wrong time." He went to the front door, wearing only a pair of pants.

Yoshi spoke loud enough to be heard through the house. "I knew where you two would be--get out of bed right now--we have to find a wolf. I already told Kyoko I had a surprise for her tonight, so I know she'll be at the den waiting for word from me."

"Let's do it," Meg yelled from the bedroom.

"You just finished doing it. Let's go get a wolf."

CHAPTER 20

Yoshi turned toward Harvey from her position in the front seat. "We have a problem. I don't think young Chan's name was Peter. I was thinking of Peter Pan."

"Who cares, as long as he's the handsome number one son of Charlie Chan."

"Yeah, but Peter the wolf would have been cool. Another problem: Any wolf we choose will know I'm a fox."

"And he'll know I'm a human."

A giggle came from the back seat. "He won't have any idea what I am."

Yoshi spoke over her shoulder. "That settles it--you talk to him, baby."

Harvey drove past the gatehouse to the zoo and along a river lined with families picnicking and feeding scraps to ducks and geese. They passed snoozing big cats, standing elephants, and the recognizable stench and screeching of monkeys before they arrived at the pens where canines paced back and forth. Yoshi slapped a hand on the dash. "Stop."

Harvey slammed on the brakes. "What?"

Yoshi raised her right hand and pointed at four red foxes, gazing at the car through a wire fence. "Poor things."

Harvey pushed her hand down. "No, Yoshi. I know how you feel, but you can't do that."

"You don't know how I feel."

"You're right, but I can imagine. We don't want any undue excitement until after we get our wolf out of here." Yoshi kept her eyes focused on the penned-up foxes as Harvey parked. She put two fingers to her lips and blew a kiss to them as she walked with Harvey and Meg to the wolves' pen.

Harvey sat on a bench away from the pen, and Yoshi sat next to him. As Meg walked toward the wolves, Yoshi yelled, "Make sure you pick a handsome one, baby." Meg strolled along the pen until she saw a skinny wolf. She pointed at him. Yoshi waved the flat of her hands. "No. That's what you like. Pick one who thinks he's God's gift to females."

Meg pointed at a silver male preening himself.

Yoshi stood and walked to the pen. "That's the one."

"Teach him English, Mama."

Yoshi walked up close, took a wide stance, planted her feet firmly on the ground, and pointed two fingers at the lone wolf. "Stand back, baby. This is going to take a lot of power, and I don't want you hit by the sparks." She waved the fingers and snapped both of them with her thumbs, then hurried back to where Harvey sat.

The force of Yoshi's magic shoved the wolf back on his haunches. His eyes moved from left to right and back again. His ears perked up as if they had detected the bleat of a lamb. His head swung around, and he surveyed the park until his gaze came to rest on Meg walking toward him. She stepped to within five feet of the wolf and kneeled down to his level. "Hi, handsome." His body jerked, and he glanced in both directions before focusing his eyes on her. "First time you've understood words, isn't it?" she said. "Say something."

"Hi, Sweetie." His eyes opened wide. He stood on all four legs and glanced around the pen before he again fixed his gaze on Meg. "How come I can understand you? How come I can talk to you? I like you even if you're not a wolf, and if you don't mind the expression, even if you're a bit foxy."

"Thank you. You haven't seen anything yet. How'd you like to get out of that pen and run in a straight line for a change? And I bet you'd like to participate in some fine love making."

"Babe, you just mentioned two of my goals in life. What's the catch?"

"You've heard the saying, 'A wolf in sheep's clothing,' haven't you?"

His whole body shook along with his head. "No way-- not me--not with a sheep."

Two young boys, near the pen, listened to the conversation between Meg and the wolf, then ran past Harvey and Yoshi to where a woman waited. One of the boys pointed at Meg and yelled, "Mommy, Mommy, she's going to let a wolf out of his cage to participate in fine love making, but he doesn't want to do it with a sheep."

The woman glared at the boy. "Scott, when we get home, I'm going to wash your mouth out with soap."

Meg glanced at the woman, then toward the wolf. "You have another surprise coming. I'm going to transform you into human form. You'll be propositioned by a beautiful woman, not a sheep, and you'll make out with her on a moonlit night, beside a rippling brook."

"Will there be soft music?"

"Great idea. You can serenade her with your guitar."

"I'm your wolf. I don't know how to play the guitar, but I'm the expert you're looking for to make mad, passionate love in the moonlight."

"By then you'll know how to play the guitar. As far as making mad, passionate love in the moonlight, I knew you were the wolf for the job when I first saw you."

"I realize I was an obvious choice, but how'd you do

those things you did? And how are you gonna spring me out of here, change me into a human, teach me to play guitar, and guarantee all these wonderful things?"

"I'm a witch."

"Cool. When do we start?"

"Right now. But don't run away, or I'll turn you into a sheep." He shuddered. Meg raised her hand behind her head and made a cutting motion. Yoshi pointed two fingers at the gate and it cracked open. After the wolf slipped out, the gate closed, and he trotted along next to his new friend. Zoo visitors, walking nearby, paid no attention to them, possibly thinking it was a woman taking her dog for a stroll. Meg led the wolf to where Harvey and Yoshi waited. "Don't get all bent out of shape," she said. "One of my friends is a human and the other's a fox. They'll stay with us to ensure everything works out the way I said. By the way, what's your name?"

"Peter."

"You're kidding."

"My mother liked the name so much, she named the whole litter Peter."

Meg introduced Peter to Harvey, then pointed at Yoshi. "She's the witch who'll change you into a handsome devil and set you up with your date."

"I'm already a handsome devil."

"You chose the right wolf," Yoshi said.

Meg opened the front passenger door, and Peter hopped in. She joined Yoshi in back. As Harvey drove past the fox pen, he noticed there were no foxes in it. On the way to the cemetery, he heard a window go down and felt a rush of air. Peter had stuck his head out of the window and was waving his nose back and forth in the air flow. He pulled his head back in. "I've always wanted to do this." Then he stuck it out again.

When they stopped in front of the bridge, Peter hopped

through the window and ran toward the woods next to the cemetery. Yoshi did her two finger point, and Peter ran into an invisible wall. "Ouch." Peter rubbed his nose with a paw. "I just want to run in a straight line for a minute. I'll be back."

"You'd better," Meg said. "Remember the sheep thing."

Peter ran for five minutes and came back breathing hard. "Thanks--you don't know how good that felt."

Meg pointed a thumb at Yoshi. "She does. Thank her."

Yoshi made a bunch of hand signals and flipped her fingers in a circle around Peter's head. A metamorphosis took place, changing Peter from a wolf to number one son of Charlie Chan. The handsome young Chinese man stood tall and looked down at his new body. "Wowie."

Yoshi spoke loud enough for Peter to hear. "Baby, watch him until I return. If he tries anything, turn him into a toad--no, a sheep."

"How can you be sure Kyoko will show?" Harvey said.

"I know her dominant motivation." Yoshi reached behind her and when her hand came back it held a Spanish guitar. She handed the guitar to Peter. "You'll find you know how to play it." Peter studied the guitar as if he didn't know what to do with it. He cradled it under his right arm and strummed the chords C, F, and G-7. His eyes opened wide as he picked the strings and played "Home on the Range." Yoshi peered back over her shoulder as she scurried up the hill in the fading light. "Her favorite is 'Moonlight Serenade.'"

Peter closed his eyes and played a soft rendition of the Glen Miller tune. When he finished the song, he opened his eyes. "I'm really good."

Meg applauded. "You'll be a great lover for Kyoko. We'll be in the ditch on the side of the stream down where we parked the car, so we won't see the action. You can do your thing anywhere you want as long as it's up here on level ground. But while you're waiting for her to come down the hill, you should be sitting on the bench playing the guitar."

"'Moonlight Serenade.'"

"Yes. And you have another surprise coming. After your performance tonight, you'll no longer be cooped up in that pen. We'll set you free."

"Swell."

Yoshi ran down the hill and motioned for Meg and Harvey to follow her. The three of them left Peter on the bench and headed along the ditch toward where the Olds was parked. Halfway there, Yoshi grabbed Harvey's arm. "You stay in the ditch where she won't be able to read your thoughts. I want to be further away, so when I talk to Megumi, Kyoko won't hear me. Call me when you hear them at it, and I'll come back to turn him into a wolf at just the right time for a perfect climax." She giggled, then waved as she and Meg snaked their way between shrubs along the top of the ditch.

Kyoko trotted down the hill, wearing a full, flowered skirt and white blouse, her pigtails swinging. When she was close enough to hear a guitar playing her favorite love song, she slowed down and swayed to the music. She sauntered past Peter but kept her gaze on him. She stopped on the bridge and leaned on the rail, swinging her hips and twirling a pigtail round and round. Peter ambled to her side, playing his guitar and singing the words, "I sing you a song in the moonlight."

She walked over to him, took the guitar, and laid it on the bridge railing. Then she moved to him until their bodies touched. *Moshi, moshi.*

"And hello to you, beautiful." He placed his hands on her waist. "I'm a stranger here, and I was thinking how this night would be complete if I had a gorgeous woman like you to share it with." He put a finger under her chin and kissed her.

She fondled his ears. "Fate must have brought us together. Until I saw you here, I was alone. Now that we're together, I yearn to make love to you." She took him by the hand, and they strolled across the bridge to lush grass. She pulled him close, opened his shirt, and ran her hands around his waist. Her fingers slid up his back. "My name's Kyoko. What's yours?"

"Peter."

"Perfect." She reached a hand behind her back. When her hand reappeared, it held a blanket. She spread it on the ground. He lay on the blanket and gave her his hand to help her down beside him. By the time she was next to him, she had his pants down.

Harvey crept to the top of the ditch and became engrossed in watching the lovemaking. Then he remembered he needed Yoshi to change Peter back to a wolf. He crept along the ditch until he came to Yoshi. "They're at it." he whispered.

Harvey and Yoshi crawled back through the ditch in time to see Kyoko saunter away, singing her own words to the "Moonlight Serenade" melody. "That's what you get for being a lousy actor, Peter Chan." She swung her hips as she whistled the tune and disappeared into the darkness toward the den.

On the blanket, a naked Chinese man lay howling at the moon, "Oouuuw, Oouuuw, woof, woof, woof, Ooouuuuuww, Ooouuuuuww."

CHAPTER 21

The same moon that shined on the three-minute romance at the cemetery, hung over Yoshi and Meg as they leaned on the rail facing the pond. Harvey sat in a chair behind them. The night was silent except for boogie woogie piano music that drifted on the breeze from the direction of the Doerner house. Yoshi's voice added more sound. "Why didn't it work? We did everything right. The moon cooperated, water rippled in the stream, soft music filled the air, and we had two willing participants. What went wrong?"

"Maybe she heard you talking at the car," Harvey said.

"No."

"Perhaps she was just in a hurry."

Yoshi shook her head. "Definitely not. She's never performed that fast in her life. Quickies aren't her style. For most Kitsune, it's a job that has to be done, but Kyoko lives for that sort of thing and keeps it going hot and heavy as long as she can. She knew it was a trick. But how? We were far enough away. She couldn't hear us, and you were out of sight and out of thought for anyone as busy as she was."

Harvey eased his hand. "I bet I know what happened."

Two heads turned in slow motion and stopped when they faced him.

"She saw me when I peeked over the top of the ditch."

Meg scowled at Harvey. "You what?"

He put his hands together as if praying for forgiveness. "I peeked over the top."

"You stuck your head out?"

"Just a little. I wanted to see what they were doing."

"You knew what they were doing," Meg yelled.

"But I never watched anybody do it before."

She hovered over him and waved her arms about in a voice loud enough for the neighbors to hear. "Why didn't you rent a video? Or did you just want to see how Kyoko does it?"

"I already have a pretty good idea how she does it."

"What do you do, lie in bed at night and dream about how she does it?"

"Don't say that. You know it's not true."

"Why'd you have to pick that time to watch her do it?"

"I'm sorry."

She marched back to stand beside Yoshi. "Sorry about what? That she was doing it with Peter instead of you?"

"Sorry I messed it up. Now she knows what we were up to, and it may kill the chance for us to try something else."

Yoshi nudged her daughter with her elbow. "Be easy on him--he's just a man."

Meg strolled back to Harvey, sat on his lap, and put an arm around his neck. "That's the only redeeming quality I see that may make him useful some night."

"Every night, I suspect."

Meg smiled at her mother and kissed Harvey on the nose. "I forgive you."

"You two are witches," he said. "Mix up a potion to arrest her sex drive."

Yoshi took a slow drink of wine. "It would take a gallon just to slow hers to half-speed." She looked at Meg. "By the way, I changed Peter back into a wolf and set him free. I didn't want to take advantage of him more than we already have.

Being a canine, he's immune from the slow death men deserve."
She grinned at Harvey.

Meg nodded. "Good--I promised him his freedom."

"Yoshi," Harvey said, "if you hadn't made that remark
about what men deserve, I'd offer you a ride to the den."

Yoshi stuck her tongue out at him. "I'm not a man--I
can run." She turned and stomped off the deck, muttering, "You
probably just wanted to pick up a few pointers."

Meg grinned at Harvey. "Did you get any."

Harvey pretended he didn't hear either comment as he
watched a gray shadow dart between the pines on the side of
the pond. Meg interrupted his concentration. "She's putting on
a show for you. And I withdraw my comment--you don't need
any pointers." She buried her face in his neck and kissed it.
After a moment of silence, she lifted her head. "Tomorrow
night I'm going to Japan with Mama for the weekend."

He looked down at her. "Why again?"

"I have to. I can't talk to Kitsune, but Mama can. She's
thinks some of her other kits have had problems with Kyoko,
and they may give us advice on how to deal with her."

"Why do you have to go with her? You have school,
and you're just now catching up on some of the lessons you
missed last time."

"I can pick that stuff up in five minutes. I only took
your class to pester you until I got you in bed."

"So the truth comes out. You have Kitsune blood
galloping through your veins."

She grabbed his chin and pulled his head around to kiss
his lips. "Perhaps, but I fell in love with you, so I can pester
you before, during, and after."

"Then stay and keep doing it."

"Mama'd miss me. She'll be leaving herself someday,
and it'll be nice to spend time with her. We'll leave tonight and

be back on Sunday. My only problem is finding someone to watch over you."

Harvey shrugged. "I did all right before you came."

"Sure, but two horny Kitsune weren't running around Lansing back then."

"I thought about that, but I believe Emiko is on our side, as far as protecting me is concerned. She's never shown any inclination to try anything."

"Except with her foot."

"I'm sure that was in jest. Look, I can take care of myself, and Kyoko hasn't been successful so far."

"Why do you say, 'So far?'"

"That's just a manner of speech. Ask Emiko to take Kyoko to Toronto for the weekend. It's usually full of guys from Detroit looking for a good time."

"Detroit's population is declining fast enough without her help. But I guess you're right about not needing anybody to watch over you. You'll die if you do it with Kyoko, you'll get shot if you do it with that over-sexed biddy next door, and Sophie'll tell me if you try it with her. If you're able to overcome those odds and still get laid over the weekend, good riddance, and may your miserable body rot in peace."

"Amen," Rosie said from the doorway. "I'll help you dispose of the body."

Harvey patted his chest. "If my body's so miserable, why's it in such demand?"

As soon as he dropped his hands to his side, Meg poked his chest with a finger. "That, along with crop circles, is one of the world's unsolved mysteries."

Rosie strolled toward them with her hands on her hips. "What about Stonehenge and the rock heads on Easter Island?"

Harvey put his hand under Meg's chin and pulled until she faced him. "You were around then. Who built them?"

"Before my time, but you keep talking like that, and I'll send you back there to find out for yourself." She bit his ear.

"Ouch." Harvey looked at Rosie. "Why'd you come here other than to say nice things about me?"

"You were going to call me when you came up with a plan. Remember?"

"Yes, now that you remind me."

"What happened?"

Harvey described the debacle, accompanied by occasional sarcastic comments from Meg, and Meg told of her plan to get advice from Kitsune in Japan. During the half hour after that, they tried to concoct a plan to get rid of Kyoko, without success.

Rosie reached for Meg's hand and held it. "Gotta go. I'll miss you. I'll try to keep him in line for you, but I don't really think it'll be necessary--he's hooked." She put a finger first to her lips and then to Harvey's before she left.

Harvey drove Meg and Yoshi to the airport. After the plane took off, he left the terminal building and saw Lillian Doerner standing at the curb. "Would you like a ride," he said, "or is Arnold coming to pick you up?"

"Arnold's on his way, but if I had known you were here, I would have ridden with you. You weren't on the plane from Detroit, were you?"

"No. I was seeing Meg off for the weekend."

"Oh?"

That night, Harvey experienced mixed emotions when he viewed his bed. Meg wasn't in it, but nobody else was either. He had a good night's sleep.

Friday started out to be a normal day just like the old days before Kitsune. Harvey came home from school, nuked a frozen spaghetti dinner, and ambled onto the deck to eat, drink a glass of Merlot, and enjoy the peace and quiet. Two mature Canadian geese glided across the water with seven small replicas paddling between them. He had just finished his dinner and was enjoying the last of his wine when one of the adult geese circled around the little ones.

Harvey left his chair and stood at the rail, searching the pond to see what caused the goose to become protective of her young, but he saw nothing. After a minute of vigilance, both the watchful goose and Harvey resumed their relaxation. Again, the adult circled around, this time with evident reason. A man with his bathrobe flopping in the wind dashed across the lawn, resembling a bather gone mad. A flash of light shot out from the muzzle of a pistol he held in front of him. A bullet cracked past Harvey's head, and splinters from a wooden shutter closeby, showered him. He snapped to attention and leaped into the house just as another bullet shattered the door jam where his head had been a second earlier.

Harvey glanced back and saw an out-of-breath Arnold Doerner climbing the stairs holding a silver, thirty-eight, Smith & Wesson revolver in a raised position. "You're safe," Arnold said. "Those were just warning shots in case Lillian was cohabiting with you. I see she's not here, so you can relax." Harvey wasn't ready to relax. He stuck his head out the door just as Lillian's husband plopped into a deck chair, set the pistol on the rail, and picked up the wine bottle. "You have another glass?"

Harvey eased himself onto the deck. "I was enjoying a drink alone and have not been cohabiting with your wife. I have my own woman to cohabit with."

"Yeah, but I understand yours is out of town for the weekend. Naturally, when mine disappeared a while ago, I thought she might be making sure you weren't lonely." He held the bottle up. "Now, are you going to be a friendly neighbor and get me a glass?"

"I'll get you one if you promise not to shoot me."

"I may later but not right now." Harvey went to get a glass. From inside the house, he heard Arnold yell, "Not only could I use a drink, but a little peace and quiet would do wonders for my nerves. One doesn't often get it with a woman around. I expect you can understand that."

After Harvey grabbed a glass in the kitchen, he heard a whisper from the direction of his bedroom. "Don't let him know I'm here, or he'll cause trouble."

Looking through the bedroom door, Harvey saw Lillian perched on the edge of the bed, giggling as she struck a pose in her baby doll nightie. He cupped a hand in front of his mouth. "Go home. He has a gun."

"I know, but he won't shoot me. He never does."

"Get out of here."

Arnold bellowed from outside. "Did you find a glass, or do I have to come in there and help you?"

Harvey waved his hands at Lillian to leave, and hurried out to the deck, holding a glass high. "I have one."

Still puffing, Arnold took the glass and poured it half full of Merlot. "It's quite a distance from my house to yours. I'm getting too old to run that far."

"I hope to get older, but you seem determined to reduce my chance of attaining that goal."

"Not if you refrain from cohabiting with Lillian." He raised his glass. "A guy's gotta protect his family. Here's to yours. You have a family, don't you, other than those foreigners I see here sometimes?" He had just put the glass to his lips when a crashing noise came from inside the house followed by a feminine, "Oh." Arnold chugged the wine down, tossed the glass into the pond, and reached for his pistol.

Harvey was on his way down the steps when the first shot zinged over his head and buried itself in the ground in front of him. He raced around the house. Another bullet zipped past. He felt the shock wave. He dashed across the front yard at the same time Lillian made her exit through the front door. He almost ran into a porch post when mesmerized by the sight of her rounding the corner with her nightie flying high.

Harvey recovered his balance, sped into the house, and slammed the door behind him, hoping Arnold would use the rest of his ammo to shoot Lillian. Not so. A round zinged into the door, sending splinters onto the carpet. Harvey decided, enough's enough. He dropped into a chair in the living room and watched as Arnold charged in with his revolver at the ready position. Harvey leaned back in the chair and pointed a bony finger at him. "It's illegal to shoot a man in his home."

Arnold made an abrupt stop. "Why?"

"A man's home is his castle."

"Says who?"

"The law."

Arnold shoved his free hand at Harvey. "I never heard of that law."

"Ignorance of the law is no excuse."

Arnold dropped the revolver to his side. "Makes no difference, anyway. I only have one round left, and I'm going to check the house before I waste it on you." He went from room to room but soon came back and plopped on the sofa, breathing audibly. "You're safe. She's not here. . . . As long as that's over, why don't you get me another glass. Excellent wine, full bodied, just the way I like it."

Harvey took a deep breath and left the room, murmuring, "Your wine and your women."

Arnold, still breathing hard, trudged out to the deck, and Harvey followed with a glass. Arnold laid his Smith & Wesson revolver on the rail, poured himself some wine, and took a sip. He held the bottle up, cocked his head, and read the label. "Saint Gerard. Great wine. Great exercise. We ought to do this more often."

Ten minutes later, Arnold drank the last of his wine and gave a final grunt as he stood. He picked up his revolver, broke it open, and ejected his last shell. He folded it back together and spun the cylinder. "Got to clean this sucker now. Goodnight, my friend."

CHAPTER 22

Saturday morning, Harvey peered out the door to the deck. Nobody lurked there with a gun. He glanced at the Doerner house next door and viewed serenity. He donned his work gloves, mowed the lawn, trimmed around the pond, and weeded his only garden, three red flowers in a pot that Rosie had given him on his birthday. When finished, he sat on the deck with a glass of iced tea and surveyed the property he had just made more beautiful than it had been for many weeks.

The doorbell rang. Before Harvey could stand, a voice came from inside. "I know where you are." His gaze followed Emiko as she walked onto the deck, wearing red short shorts and a white sleeveless t-shirt with no bra. "I'm glad you like my outfit," she said.

"I admit I do, but I'm still not used to you guys reading my thoughts."

She cocked her head. "You have thoughts like you just did and still call me a guy?"

"That's just an expression. No, you don't look anything like a guy. Iced tea?"

"Now, if you could read my mind, like I can yours, you'd know the answer to that. In fact, you would've had it waiting for me when I arrived."

He stood. "Sugar?"

"No."

"Be right back."

When he returned with her glass of tea, Emiko was standing by the rail. He handed the tea to her. "Have a seat."

"I've been lying around the den all day doing nothing. I need to stand for a while."

Harvey looked at her, then away.

"Thank you." She gazed over the pond and took a drink of tea. "I have you at a disadvantage, so let's get off that subject and talk about why I came here." She turned to face him. "I'm worried about Kyoko."

"I should be the one worried about her."

"True, but I am too. I haven't seen her since the night at the cemetery bridge."

Harvey was about to sip his tea, but pulled the glass away from his mouth. "You were there?"

Harvey drank as Emiko spoke. "No, but I heard about it. I knew a plan was in the works but stayed out of it. I realize something had to be done sooner or later to slow her down, but she's my sister, and I worry how that may have affected her. I haven't seen her since."

Harvey set the glass on the deck beside the chair. "Where do you think she is?"

"Following the music."

"I don't understand."

"I thought you knew. We hear music when we get close to men. It gets louder and louder around those we want to get next to. Sooner or later we have to get rid of the sound."

"And there's only one way to do so."

"Yes."

"Do you hear the music now?"

She faced the pond again. "It's deafening."

Harvey moved his head side to side in slow motion. "Why am I safe around you?"

"I gave my word to Yoshiko."

"How will you get rid of the music?"

She set her glass on the deck rail. "I'll have to leave here and find someone else."

"That works?"

She kept her gaze on the pond. "Not completely."

"I'm sorry, Emiko. I enjoy your company."

"I know." She dumped the rest of her tea over the rail and turned toward Harvey. "I'd better go. I'll be back later tonight. I just wanted to tell you I'll stay outside your place in case Kyoko shows. I told Yoshiko I'd watch over you while they're gone." She left her glass on the rail and hurried toward the door without looking back.

"You're welcome to sleep on the sofa."

She stopped and faced him. "It would be better if I didn't. Kyoko can't read a fox's thoughts, but yours would give me away. I'll stay outside." She left.

Harvey didn't fall asleep for a hour after he went to bed. His mind raced with the realization of how complicated life had become. *It would have been impossible month ago to imagine what's happening now. That beautiful little woman's actually an animal stationed outside my house like a guard dog.*

Harvey wasn't sure how long he'd been asleep or what woke him, but he felt the presence of someone in the room. He reached for the light. "Leave it off," a voice said. "You know what I look like, and I know what you look like. That wasn't a nice trick you pulled on me at the bridge. I knew you were watching. Is that what you are, a watcher rather than a doer?"

Harvey let his hand rest next to the light switch. "Do you actually believe I'd give up life to have sex with you?"

"You don't have to give up anything. I can nullify the curse. Tell him, Emmy."

"Don't believe anything she says." Harvey lit the bed lamp and searched for the owner of the voice. Emiko looked like a model, sitting crossways in the window with her legs propped up, wearing the same outfit she wore that afternoon.

Kyoko frowned from where she sat cross-legged on top of the dresser. "Why don't you think the same of me as you do of my sister? You want me to leave, but you wish she'd stay, even though she doesn't know how to turn off the curse, like I do. You don't know how, do you, Emmy?"

"I don't think it can be done, but then it was never important enough for me to find out."

Kyoko pointed at Emiko. "I know your problem. You want him as much as I do. I'll tell you what--you can have him after I'm finished--I promise to leave him in good shape."

Harvey sat up in bed. "Kyoko,--"

"I know. You want me to leave, but she can stay. Okay, I give in because she's my sister, even if she isn't smart enough to know she can turn off the curse. I have to leave." Kyoko disappeared. Harvey knew why she had to go.

"She won't be back at least for a while," Emiko said. "I have to leave too."

"I'm sorry."

Harvey awoke tired the next day. He moped around, feeling like an old man. After twenty minutes of reliving what had happened the previous night, he decided to grade papers although he didn't feel like doing anything. Later that day, he glanced up from the dining room table when a young man entered through the front door without knocking. The man was covered with grime, and the odor of grease hung heavy on him. "Hi, Dad," the man said as he did a balancing act, removing his shoes without touching any of the furniture.

"That you, Jason?"

"Yeah, it's me." He lined up his shoes on a throw rug and walked to the dining room in white socks.

"What happened?"

He stood in front of his father. "Like, I got a job."

"Doing what?"

"Western Truck Rental, grease monkey."

Harvey stood. "Come out to the deck to tell me about it. You didn't quit school, did you?"

"No. That's why I work on Sundays. I just decided it was time to grow up."

Harvey leaned on the deck rail. "Why, all of a sudden, did you get that idea?"

"I thought I might have to in case you lost your job."

Harvey folded his arms and cocked his head. "What made you think that?"

"Rosie told me all those screwy things you've been doing. She thought they were funny, but I didn't. At first, I thought having a job might be necessary, but now I enjoy the work. I should have done it a long time ago."

"I won't lose my job, but I'm glad you've joined the working class. You've always been able to do almost anything. Do you expect you'll continue to do this for a living?"

"No. It's just for the money. . . . I'm still concerned about you and Rosie. Like, you're going off the deep end."

"I appreciate that, and I don't blame you for thinking that way. Tell you what: Get cleaned up, and I'll let you know what's happened around here. You may find some of it hard to believe, but I'll give it to you straight."

"Do you have some old clothes I can wear?"

"I'll throw some in the bathroom. Don't plug the drain with grease."

After Jason took a shower, they went to the Village Restaurant for dinner. Harvey told his son what had happened

203

since he first met Meg, including her Kitsune background and their trips to the Winkin' Pup. Jason laughed. Back at the house, Harvey talked about Kyoko's trail of sick and dying men in the Lansing area. "Most of them thought they were having sex with a teen."

Jason wrinkled his brow. "You going to stay involved in all this craziness?"

"I love Meg and want to take her away from it. She's my life now that you and Rosie are emerging adults."

"I haven't emerged very fast, but I'm on my way. I'll give Meg a fair shake, but don't be concerned if I'm skeptical at times." They shook hands, and Jason left. Harvey couldn't remember the last time he shook hands with his son.

He checked the clock to see if it was time to go to the airport to pick up Meg and Yoshi. A few minutes later, he looked again. Five minutes later, he went to the kitchen to see if the clock there agreed with the one in the living room. It did. He picked up a mystery novel he had read years ago and took it out to the deck with him. Soon he went inside to see if it was time to go. He drove to the airport and hurried inside. The monitor listed her flight on time, scheduled to arrive at seven-thirty. The clock showed seven.

He watched CNN, occasionally glancing at the ramp where they were to deplane. When their flight unloaded, Meg let her carryon bag slide as she greeted him with arms and lips. Yoshi showed approval by smiling. Harvey let go of Meg, hugged Yoshi, and went back to Meg for another embrace.

Harvey carried their two bags through the terminal and out to the wagon, loaded them in the back, and drove out of the parking area. As he pulled onto Grand River Avenue, Yoshi laughed out loud. Meg turned her head toward her mother in the back seat. "It's not funny."

Harvey glanced at Meg. "What's not funny?"

Yoshi leaned forward. "Hah. You're trying to figure out how to tell her what happened last night, and you're telling her by thinking how to say it."

"It's not funny," Meg said.

Harvey kept his eyes focused on the traffic. "What's not funny, and how do you know what I'm thinking if you can't read minds anymore?"

"Your backpedaling thoughts were so loud, a child could read them."

"I wasn't backpedaling. I was only trying to think of a way to convince you I'm innocent. She sat on my dresser. I did nothing except try to get rid of her."

Meg poked him on the shoulder. "You haven't been innocent since you were a babe in your mother's arms, and I sometimes wonder if you were then."

Harvey paid attention to his driving as he talked. "Do you expect me to believe you've spent time thinking about me, when I was still a babe in my mother's arms?"

"That was a slight exaggeration to make a point. To be more realistic, probably what happened was, while in your mother's arms, you were thinking about some babe."

Harvey stopped the Olds at a red-light and confronted Meg. "Why haven't you ragged on me about what I thought of Emiko's outfit?"

She stared back at him. "You're a man, but still I should talk to her about wearing that kind of clothing around you. Of course, if you weren't such a lecher, you wouldn't have had those lecherous thoughts about her."

"If you're so good at that mind reading thing, why don't you read all the wonderful thoughts I have about you?"

"There are times when they represent your number two redeeming quality."

"Harvey," Yoshi said, "would you really like to hear

what she's thinking while she's making those caustic comments about you? She can hardly wait to get you alone where she can tell you how much she's missed you. And that place is your bed, or any other bed, for that matter."

Meg glanced at Yoshi. "You're a great help. How can I train him with you around? She pointed at Harvey. There's no way you can keep me from knowing how the bullet hole got in the front door."

"You're going to complain about that little episode?"

"Little?"

"That was a slight exaggeration to make a point."

She poked him in on the arm. "Had to stab me with my own knife, didn't you?"

"At least I finally got one point."

"No points when you're hedging on discussing an altercation with the jealous husband of a sex fiend who's old enough to be your mother."

Harvey smiled. Meg bopped him on the back of his head. "Smart aleck."

After dropping Yoshi at the cemetery, Harvey drove to the house and pulled into the garage. He started to enter the house through the back door, but instead, followed Meg around to the front where she had stuck her little finger into the hole in the door. "It's a bit high and to the right. Next time, ask him to aim lower, so we can make a peep hole out of it." She looked back over her shoulder. "Or maybe you ought to kneel and lean to the left when you see he's getting ready to shoot you."

Meg disappeared into the house while he reached back to pick up her luggage. Once inside, he didn't see her in the living room. He checked to see if she was in the kitchen--she wasn't. He heard her voice come from the bedroom. He stuck his head through the open door.

She peeked over the top sheet. "Come on. Hurry."

CHAPTER 23

At breakfast, Harvey poured corn flakes into two bowls and sprinkled blueberries over them. Meg helped by pouring a cup of tea for him and one for herself. She sat across from him. "You never asked what we learned in Japan."

He poured milk over their cereal. "Nothing."

"How do you know?"

"You didn't say anything about it at the airport, in the Olds, or later on."

"I had something more important on my mind."

He took a bite and was quiet until he swallowed it. "So what's new?"

She picked a blueberry from her cereal and threw it at him. He opened his mouth and tried to catch it, but it hit him on the chin. She glared at him. "Is there something else you feel we should have done first?"

"I'd rather leave those decisions to you."

"One decision I've made is to go to the college with you this morning to see what I can do to make up the classes I've missed. Too bad I don't take all my classes from you."

"Why's that?"

She put their breakfast dishes in the dishwasher, then hiked her skirt up and swung her hips in a dance over to him. "I could make them up in bed." She sat on his lap and wrapped herself around him.

He spoke to the ear next to his lips. "Listen, sweetie--"

She leaned back and frowned. "Where do you get that sweetie bit? You sound like Peter the wolf."

Harvey laughed. "You called him handsome. You never call me that."

"You're not handsome--you're sexy."

"Which would you rather have me be?"

She wrapped her arms around him, pressed her body against his, and whispered to him. "Just like you are, sweetie."

He looked at his watch. "You're not going to like this, but I have to go to school."

She stood and glared at him. "Always excuses."

On the way to the college, Harvey told Meg about his visit with Jason. "He said he would accept you based on what he knows, or something like that."

"That's fine, depending on what he knows."

"Not a whole bunch about the real you."

"We'll have him over for dinner, so we can get better acquainted."

Harvey stopped the Olds at a light before turning onto the college grounds. "If we do, we should invite your mother."

"Makes sense."

He parked in a faculty lot and wrapped his arms around the steering wheel. "I'll set something up with Jason, maybe Wednesday night." He leaned over and kissed her.

She leaned against him with one of her hands on the door handle. "What if he doesn't approve of me?"

"First thing is, he will. Second thing, it makes no difference. I approve of you, and that's what matters." He grabbed the driver's door handle, leaned over, and gave her a kiss, a good long one, then opened his door and felt it bump into someone.

"Hey, watch what you're doing."

Harvey looked up and saw he'd bumped the dean. "Excuse me, Mr. Pigeon,"

Pigeon studied Meg's slender legs when she bent over to get something from the back seat. "Oh, that's all right," he said. "I realize you were busy doing something important and didn't see me." He rubbed his hand on his arm and waddled toward the school.

Meg and Harvey walked behind him but not fast enough to catch up. "We see him everywhere," she said. "You have a rubber band attaching the two of you together?"

Harvey blew her a kiss as she headed toward her marketing instructor's office, and he to the Business Department. He opened the door and it bumped into someone. Harvey hoped it wasn't Dean Pigeon again. "I'm sorry."

Craig Akers stepped back from the door, rubbing his arm. "You're dangerous."

Harvey laughed. "You don't know the half of it."

"I do too. I saw you in the parking lot."

"Oh, I'm thankful it was you this time."

Craig waved his hand for Harvey to follow him. "Hey, come out here and tell me some more lies."

Harvey sat next to Craig in the little lounge. "What kind of lies do you want to hear?"

"More of those about your cleaning lady." Harvey reared his head back and gave a laugh that could be heard down the hall. Craig stared at him. "That good looking woman you were making out with in the parking lot was called Susha when I met her. Megumi, Susha--whoever she is, she's a student of mine as well as yours. Are you trying to get fired?"

"That won't happen."

"What is she, a witch?"

Harvey waved a hand at Craig. "Come on. Don't tell me

you believe in witches."

"I didn't till I saw what she did to Pigeon at the picnic."

"What makes you think that was her doing?"

"I don't think." He gave a single nod. "I know. While everybody else was looking at his fly, I was watching her hands orchestrate what was happening. I finally connected it all together. She's the real thing, isn't she?"

Harvey glanced around, then at Craig. "Do I have your word you won't repeat what I say if I tell you the true story?"

"Hah. People'd think I flipped my lid."

Harvey told about his half-witch and her Kitsune mother. "She's a student of mine, and yes, we're going to be married. We haven't announced it, but we will soon. In fact, she and I made plans this morning to have our families meet and make a formal announcement. Pigeon knows about us, and I suspect he knows she's a witch, but he won't say anything or fire me. He's afraid to."

Craig tilted his head and cradled his chin in his hand. "And the other two?"

Harvey tried to look innocent. "What other two?"

"You know the ones I'm talking about."

"How do you know about them?"

"They've been hanging out at the Cappuccino House. At first I thought they were students, but I don't think so. They're witches, aren't they? What are they doing here?"

"I'll check them out and get back to you."

"I'd appreciate that." Craig waved a hand up and down the hall. "I like this place and wouldn't want bad things to happen here."

"I'm with you."

Harvey and Meg sat on the glider sipping Merlot and watching two mallards swimming with four little ones. When the setting sun bounced off the water to give the house a golden glow, he stood and shoved the glider sideways to get the reflected sun out of Meg's eyes, and when the glider was where he wanted, he sat next to her. He thought for a while, trying to decide how to tell her what Craig had said, but finally just blurted it out. "Kyoko and Emiko have been seen at the deli across from the college. Craig told me they're spending time with students."

Meg closed her eyes and shook her head. She put her head in her hands. "My presence here, more and more, is turning your good life into a hell."

Harvey slid next to her and put his arm around her. He placed a hand under her chin and lifted her head even with his. Warm tears dropped on his hand. "That's not true. You've changed my life from doldrums to excitement. This is just another problem we have to deal with. We can handle it. We'll get our families together and figure out what to do about it. We'll be getting together anyway." Meg buried her face in Harvey's neck, and he inhaled the familiar aroma of jasmine in her hair. He heard the deep voice of a bull frog somewhere around the pond. "Listen--he's giving his mating call."

Harvey expected an aggressive reaction from Meg because he mentioned mating, but when she finally spoke, it was to say. "We should invite Rosie to the approval meeting."

"It's not an approval meeting. It's so you and Jason can get better acquainted. You're worrying about nothing. I've noticed something this last couple of weeks. You lack confidence when it comes to being accepted. When we first met, you almost disappeared from my life because of that. You worry about Jason, and you take the blame for what other people do. I love you, and everyone else around here does too."

"What about Lillian?"

"She loves men."

Meg raised her head. "I'm glad you love me. You are my strength. Without you, I'm a stranger in another country."

"There you go again. Just what I was saying. You're not a stranger here. You're one of us. Listen to me, my love. I'm about to interfere in your territory. I've made a decision to do something that's always been exclusively your domain."

She tilted her head. "What's that?"

"To give my mating call."

"What took you so long?"

CHAPTER 24

Harvey watched Meg cut up vegetables and throw them into a bowl. "What are those? I've never seen anything even closely resembling them."

"They're vegetables."

"I figured as much. What kind?"

"You writing a book?"

"Where'd you learn that expression?"

"One of your students. I thought it was something you taught him."

"You're picking up a lot of bad habits."

"Must be from you. I haven't been with anybody else, and you never take me anywhere. All you ever do is bug me while I'm slaving over a hot stove."

"You're starting to talk like an American wife."

"I'm working at it."

"What else is for dinner?"

"Fish heads and rice."

"You're kidding, of course."

"Don't knock it till you try it."

"You seem to have learned a lot of great expressions from my students."

"Right on."

He turned away. "I get the idea you don't need help fixing dinner."

"Stay. I want you here. Otherwise I wouldn't have anybody to tell me how to do it right." She stepped over to him and put her head on his chest. "I'm sorry. Would you really consider marrying someone as mean to you as I am?"

"Ask me again after I taste the fish heads and rice." The doorbell rang. Harvey kissed the top of her head and walked out of the kitchen. "It has to be your mother. She's the only one who announces her arrival around here."

While he was hugging Yoshi at the front door, Harvey saw Jason pull up and park his beat-up Ford pickup truck out front. "Wait here a minute, and I'll introduce you to my son."

Jason walked up to the door, wearing pressed trousers, a white shirt, and tie. Harvey scrutinized him. "Come in and meet Yoshi, Meg's worldly-wise mother. Yoshi, this is Jason. He's guardian of the only logic in the family."

Jason's mouth spread into a smile. "Hi."

Yoshi acknowledged Jason with a sour look, "I'm glad to meet you, but excuse me--I have something I have to do."

Jason didn't seem to notice being cut-off short, and he waved as she walked away. "Nice meeting you."

Harvey watched Yoshi walk through the kitchen door and wondered why she had given such a cool reception to his son. He continued talking to Jason. "You really look neat."

"I took off work today--otherwise I would have smelled like grease. Who else is coming to dinner?"

"Rosie."

"Any relatives of Meg other than her mother?"

"No. Why do you ask?"

"Just wondered."

Rosie came in the front door, stopped in front of Jason and inspected him. She circled around him, then extended both hands. "I'm Rosie--who are you, handsome?" Jason laughed and hugged her. She kissed him on the cheek. "Why so pretty?"

"It's an important dinner."

"You've had important dinners before but never dressed up. How come so pretty?"

"You look nice too. Where's your boyfriend?"

"Up north helping his brother put insulation in their cottage, so they can use it in the winter."

"Kinda serious about him, aren't you?"

She smiled. "As long as he does what I tell him." She focused her eyes on her dad while pointing at Jason. "You're right. He's a different guy. He looks great and he talks." She nudged Jason on the arm. "You act like you're in love." She winked at him and walked into the kitchen.

Jason laughed. "No thank you."

Harvey grabbed his son's elbow. "Let's follow her, and I'll introduce you to the cook."

Meg put down the spoon she was using to stir the ingredients in a wok and extended her right hand to Jason. He ignored the hand and gave her a hug. "Nice to see you again."

Meg smiled. Yoshi scowled.

Meg served dinner by dipping a spoon into the wok and dishing the food into shallow bowls. She watched as they tasted the meal. When she saw smiles and nods, she joined them. The main course of shrimp stir-fry was followed by cheesecake and strawberries. After they finished dessert, the two families sat at the table and became better acquainted through light conversation as they drank green tea.

Meg didn't say much. She was all smiles as she listened to the excited chatter between Harvey, Rosie, and Jason. Yoshi didn't say anything and didn't smile. She tapped Meg on the arm and indicated with her thumb to follow her to the bedroom. "Excuse us a minute," Meg said. Then she and her mother left the table and went into the bedroom. Yoshi closed the door.

Minutes later, they returned to the kitchen where Harvey was putting dishes into the dishwasher. Meg glanced around the room. "Where's Jason?"

"He's on the deck with Rosie. Why?"

"Come in here a minute," Meg said. Harvey followed her to the bedroom while Yoshi finished clearing dishes from the table. Meg closed the door. "What do you think of the way Jason's acting?"

"I think it's wonderful--so different than I expected."

"Do you know why?"

Harvey stared at her. "He said he was going to give you and Yoshi a fair shake."

"That's not why--he's been seeing Kyoko and Emiko."

Harvey's shoulders slumped. "How? Where?"

"I don't know, but when he saw Mama at the door, his thoughts reverted to them, and he was thinking how to act, so he could get along better with Mama and me. You saw how he greeted me, didn't you?"

"Yes."

She held her index finger up. "What I mean is, do you know why he's being so cordial to everyone?"

"If what you say is true, it's because he wants to stay on good terms with you because of his relationship with your mother's cousins."

"You know it's true."

"You're right." He turned away. "I guess I just find it difficult to accept."

"I do too. . . . I wonder what the relationship is."

Ten minutes later, Harvey sat in the driver's seat of the Olds, staring straight ahead. "Jason, I've pondered how to say this but still don't know a right way, so I'll just say it." He turned his head to the right. "I understand you have a relationship with Kyoko and Emiko."

"Not true."

"Are you seeing either of them?"

Jason maintained a deadpan expression. "No."

"I don't believe you."

Jason shrugged. "Whatever."

"You know what'll happen if you have sex with one of them, don't you?"

"It doesn't seem to have harmed you."

"Look, son, those two only look like young girls. They're animals, and they're deadly."

"Huh. Like, you could have fooled me."

"I thought you hadn't been seeing them."

"I know what they look like."

Harvey folded his hands around the top of the steering wheel and gazed straight ahead. "You don't believe anything I say about them, do you?"

"Can't say as I do."

Harvey turned his head to look at his son, shaking it from side to side as he spoke. "Don't you believe the newspapers?"

Jason opened the car door and put his right foot on the ground. "The paper only said that some guys got sick. It didn't say how they got that way, and it didn't say they were dead or dying. You're exercising some kind of personal vendetta against those two girls. I don't know what your problem is, but it seems like you've set out to destroy their reputations while trying to convince the world that Meg's a saint. They're a hell of a lot more saintly than that witch you're tied up with or her stupid little mother." He stepped out and leaned down to look at Harvey. "Like, I have to go. See you later."

"Jason, listen to me--I don't want to lose you--stay."

"Goodbye, Dad." Jason slammed the door and

sauntered toward his pickup. Harvey watched as his son climbed in, started the engine, and drove away without ever looking back.

Meg and Harvey faced each other in living room chairs as he told her about his conversation with Jason. She shook her head again and again. "He's blind."

Harvey nodded. "I know, but the sad part is, I don't really blame him that much. Remember how I fell for Kyoko's line on the Tilt-a-Whirl? Those two don't look like animals, and in no way do they match people's conception of witches."

She jabbed a finger at him. "But you listened to Mama. He's not listening to you."

Harvey rested his elbows on his knees and placed his face in his hands. "I should have told him at least to wear a condom if he's going to mess around with them."

Her voice was soft. "Harvey, a condom won't help. It's not a disease. It's the curse that causes death. There's nothing he can do to protect himself except stay away from them."

Harvey made a karate chop with both hands. "That won't happen unless we can convince him of the danger."

Neither of them spoke for a minute. Meg broke the silence. "I forgot--you have a message. Somebody named Red called and said he had information for you about those two."

Harvey jerked his head up. "That would be Craig. What did he say?"

"He said to look at the ad on the lower right corner of page two of the entertainment section in the morning paper."

"That's all?"

She pointed at the sofa. "Yes. There it is."

Harvey opened the paper to an ad on page two for Dream Dolls, an adult theater on East Main. He read the large print out loud: "*Dream Dolls presents their newest attraction*

218

on stage, two Japanese dolls, Honsee and Sonsee." He studied the ad, but there were no photos. He put the paper down. "It's probably them."

Meg spread her hands apart and hunched her shoulders. "I wonder why. They don't need the money. What are they trying to accomplish? Emiko attracts men everywhere she goes. And why Kyoko? Guys stand in line for her service."

"I should check it out."

Meg folded her arms and stared at him. "Her service?"

"No, and not Emiko's either. I have my own combination service provider, exhibitionist, but I should find out as much as possible about this. Jason may be involved."

"Well, you go there alone--I can't go with you."

"You're right. You'd be the only woman in the audience. He reached over, put his hands on her cheeks, and kissed her. "I don't want to go alone. Perhaps I can get Craig to go with me, or maybe he should go alone. I wouldn't want them to know I was there."

"Remember, they can't read minds in a crowd. Just don't let them see you."

Harvey glanced at his watch. "I'll call Craig to see if he'll go with me." He grabbed the phone and talked to Craig. "Thanks for the information on Dream Dolls. Would you go with me tonight to see if Honsee and Sonsee are who we think they are?"

"I thought you'd ask. Yes--I'll be at your place by eight--first show's at eight-thirty."

A little after eight, the front doorbell rang. Meg opened the door and Craig walked in displaying a broad grin. "You look like Susha." Meg's jaw dropped. "I'm sorry, Meg. I didn't mean it that way. I want you to know I recognize you, except you're beautiful now." He stepped past her, to come face to face with Harvey, who wore baggy clothes with his hair combed straight down, sticking out from beneath a royal blue beret. He turned back toward Meg. "Where'd you find the French teen?"

Meg laughed. "He says he dressed like that so Honsee and Sonsee won't recognize him. I don't even think Susha'd hang around with anything like that."

Craig grabbed both of Meg's hands and held them. "You don't look anything like Susha, and you're much too beautiful to hang around anyone like that." He fixed his gaze on Harvey. "Would you consider marrying me instead of that?"

She bowed. "*Arigato*. Sorry, but I'm engaged to that."

Craig laughed. "I was shocked when I saw Susha at the picnic and heard she was engaged to Harvey. Now I'm shocked that someone as pretty as you would admit it was true."

Meg turned her head toward Harvey. "I like your friend."

Harvey walked to the door and opened it without looking back. "I'm much too sensitive to listen this drivel. I'm going to Dream Dolls, where sophisticated people of my stature gather to enrich their lives. They'll appreciate me."

CHAPTER 25

The sign in front of Dream Dolls was only the size of a realtor's FOR SALE sign, but on the roof of the converted gas station and garage painted black, flashing lights traveled around a giant neon screen depicting two bare-breasted dancers in G-strings. As Craig's SUV pulled into the lot at the side of the building, Harvey was relieved not to see Jason's truck parked there. The two professors strolled across the lot and into the heavy air of smoke and booze.

Harvey frowned as he paid the ten-dollar cover charge, then checked to see if Jason was one of the men sitting around little black tables in front of a stage. He wasn't. The red-curtained stage was ringed with red lights which joined forces with cigarette smoke to make a whirly effect on the ceiling. Craig and Harvey took a seat in the back, ordered a pitcher of beer from a buxom topless server, and waited for the show to begin. She brought their pitcher and glasses. "That'll be eight dollars." Harvey gave her a ten-dollar bill, and she dropped two dollars on the table.

Drums boomed out from a hole in front of the stage, adding rhythm to a growling cornet and a rinky-tink keyboard playing "Let Me Entertain You." Craig's and Harvey's beers were still untouched when the curtain parted, and a leg wearing a red lace stocking stuck out. The leg was followed by the rest of a Venus built-alike with arms. She bumped and ground her way across the stage dressed in a red blouse, skirt, and heels.

Venus did her routine, tossing clothing into the air until she wore only a thin bra and G-string. She took those off and threw them at two burly guys sitting at a front row table, then stepped down into the audience, carrying the only article she had left, a purse. Men dropped bills and coins into it. As she passed Harvey's and Craig's table, she picked up Harvey's two dollars, stuffed them in her purse, and lah-dee-dahed as she swung her way to the front. With a final bump, Venus disappeared into darkness at the right of the stage.

The next act was a skinny man with a pencil mustache who wandered back and forth on the stage, wearing a tuxedo, and telling dirty jokes which received a smattering of laughter. When members of the audience began talking during his performance, he waved a hand toward a stage wing and shouted, "And now direct from Tokyo, I present our two Japanese Dolls, Honsee and Sonsee."

A short, skaggy, old Asian woman using a mop as a cane staggered onto the stage to the sound of Oriental music played by an instrument being plucked one string at a time. She was followed by another hag carrying a bucket, who glanced around as if she were lost. Neither had teeth, and their heads were topped by dirty, stringy hair that partially hid wrinkled faces. They waltzed to the front, and when the music changed to "Love Potion Number Nine," one danced with her mop while the hag with the bucket tossed water on four men in leather jackets at a front row table. The four cursed and made menacing motions with their fists as Honsee and Sonsee continued their version of bumps and grinds across the stage.

"What the hell's going on?" someone backstage yelled. As if on cue, the two hags dropped their skirts at the same time, revealing pink panties hanging over huge rear-ends that swayed back and forth like tugboats in rough water. The voice came again. "Cut the music." The music stopped but started again within seconds. Honsee and Sonsee waltzed back across the front of the stage with a flailing of arms as they removed the sleeves from their white silk blouses and tossed the sleeves over their shoulders. "Cut that Goddamned music," the voice hollered. The music stopped, but seconds later, came back on louder. The Japanese Dolls continued dancing, swaying back and forth as they unbuttoned their blouses and threw them at an audience sitting in stunned silence. The offstage voice yelled again, "I told you to cut that Goddamned music."

"I did, but now it's stuck in the on position."

"Then pull the fucking plug."

The music stopped but started again, playing a Hawaiian tune. The dancers swayed with their backs to the audience, then unhooked their bras and tossed them over their shoulders. Boos and catcalls greeted them when they faced the crowd to display sagging breasts. The joke teller ran on stage, swung his fists at the dancers, and yelled, "Out." A beer can clattered at his feet, the beginning of an avalanche. He ran offstage as glasses, cans, ashtrays, and chairs flew toward him.

The music volume soared to new heights as Honsee and Sonsee swayed in place, protected from flying missiles by an invisible shield that surrounded them. A number of men headed for the exit but glanced back in time to see the dancers step out of their pink panties to reveal khaki-colored boxer shorts. The men increased the speed of their flight.

Harvey and Craig joined the crowd running to the exit as the Japanese Dolls danced down the steps, following the men with their arms spread wide. Somebody yelled, "Hey, you dumb broads." Harvey stopped to look, but Craig continued running for the door. The two burlies, who had caught the bra and G-string, raced to catch Honsee and Sonsee. Just before they got to the dancers, they ran into invisible shields and landed on their backs. Honsee and Sonsee waved at Harvey and blew kisses as puffs of pink smoke enveloped them. They floated to the ceiling and faded away, shouting, "*Sayonara*."

Except for the beret he dropped in his rush to vacate Dream Dolls, Harvey was still dressed as a French teen when he carried a plate of cookies to his living room, where Meg served tea. Craig sipped his in silence as Harvey told Meg what took place at the Honsee, Sonsee show. "It was not a fun evening by any stretch of the imagination."

Meg pointed at him. "That's what you get for frequenting that kind of place."

Harvey sat next to Meg and turned his face toward her. "I knew I was in the wrong place when those two cousins of yours headed our way. I could just imagine them getting strangle holds on us. When we made it to the car, Craig's face was so white I could see his features in the dark. He couldn't talk all the way here. It really was some show. I don't know how, but those two knew we were in the audience before they came on stage. They didn't see us outside. The place had no windows, and they weren't in the lot when we arrived."

Meg shrugged. "They couldn't have read your minds in all that noise. What I wonder is why they put on that act."

The doorbell rang, the door opened, and Yoshi stuck her head through the opening. "*Moshi, moshi.*"

"Hello, hello," Harvey said.

Yoshi stepped into the room and bowed to Harvey and Craig. "What are you doing here?" Meg said to her mother.

"I want to find out what happened at the porn club. I know something went on there tonight. Emiko and Kyoko came in cackling like a couple of hens. Emiko said they had been guests at the porn club, but she ignored my other questions. After a few more cackles, they lay down and went to sleep."

"What made you think we'd know the answer?"

"Kyoko was thinking about Harvey's friend." Craig slid down in his chair.

Harvey pointed at Yoshi. "Craig, this is Yoshi, Meg's mother." He waved a hand toward Craig. "You'll have to excuse him, Yoshi. He thought the two hags doing the striptease were going to grab him. He's still so nervous he can't talk."

Yoshi's head perked up. "Maybe they'll get him yet. They're here, and they're still cackling." The doorbell rang. Craig glanced around as if looking for a place to hide.

Harvey turned his head toward the door and whispered, "Come in, Kyoko. Come in, Emiko."

The door opened. Emiko, dressed in a white blouse a red micro-miniskirt, and Harvey's royal blue beret, did bumps and grinds into the living room as she sang, "Break the seal, pull the cork, and drink the wine down with the two newest stars in Lansing town." She waved a hand toward the door. "Welcome, Sonsee." A hook-nosed hag, dressed the same as Emiko, swung her way in, playing a ukulele. The hag stopped playing the uke, and both of them undid the top buttons of their blouses.

Yoshi put her palms out toward them. "Stop that." They buttoned the blouses up again.

Harvey studied the two for a moment as if he could get a clue to what they were thinking, then said, "The least we can do is buy you two stars a drink. What'll you have?"

Emiko danced between Harvey and Craig as Kyoko strummed the ukulele, then bowed to Harvey while they both sang, "W-i-n-e, wine." Craig's teacup fell on its side on the saucer, spilling the tea on his lap.

Harvey pulled a napkin from a drawer, threw it at Craig, then pulled a bottle of wine from the cabinet above the drawer and used a corkscrew to open it. He poured five glasses, emptying the bottle. "Come get your own. Too many for me to

225

serve." He sat on the sofa with Meg between him and Craig. Yoshi sat on a chair. Kyoko transformed into herself, and the two cousins sat cross-legged on the floor facing the sofa. Yoshi pointed two fingers, and a blanket floated down over their laps.

Emiko looked up at Craig. "Did you enjoy the show?"

"Which one?"

Harvey suppressed a laugh. Meg crossed her arms and glared at Craig. "You're no better than Harvey."

"Pardon me--at the club? No--not at the time."

Harvey pointed at Emiko."Did you enjoy your debut as a performer?"

Emiko beamed. "Exceedingly."

"How did you know we were in the audience?"

"We saw you in the parking lot."

"But there was nobody around."

"We were in the woods." She made a running motion with four fingers.

"Oh."

"There had to be a reason for your performance," Meg said. "You didn't do it just for these two. Why'd you do it?"

Kyoko wrinkled her face and puckered her lips. "I'll tell you why--that kind of place puts women down. We run past there and hear those men yelling and screaming like a bunch of maniacs at some poor girls trying to make a living."

Meg poked Harvey in the ribs. "See what we think of you guys?"

He poked her back. "Those guys, not me."

"Hah," Yoshi said to Kyoko. "You're just envious that those men pay to imagine doing what you do for free."

Kyoko pointed at Yoshi. "You used to do it--probably still do when nobody else is around."

Yoshi shrugged.

Meg pointed her hand palm-up at the cousins.

"Actually, I appreciate what you did. If you'd invited me, I may have gone along, but Harvey wouldn't have escaped."

Harvey grinned. "Maybe I wouldn't want to. But Craig still would've been shaken up. I'd love to have seen him in the arms of one of those old hags."

Kyoko sat up straight and tossed the blanket away from her lap. "I'm happy to know you feel that way." She leered at Craig, and he sunk down on the sofa.

Yoshi grabbed the blanket and threw it back onto Kyoko's lap. "Settle down, young lady--and I use both words, young and lady, loosely."

Harvey grinned at Craig. "Don't take us seriously, Red. Everything worked out fine just like it happened."

Kyoko winked at Craig. "Maybe next time." Craig sunk further down.

Meg glanced around the room. "It's so nice to be together, enjoying each other's company. I'm only half Kitsune, but I appreciate what these two did at Dream Dolls tonight. Although I want to join the human race, I have strong feelings for my heritage and pretty much feel as they do." Yoshi blew a kiss to her daughter.

"This is a family affair," Craig said. "Time for me to go." He pulled himself up from the sofa and sidestepped away from the others. Kyoko started to stand.

"Sit right back down, young lady," Yoshi said. Kyoko sat. Craig waved and walked out the front door. Kyoko crossed her arms and pouted.

Meg glanced at the cousins while pointing at Harvey. "I'm going to marry this man and become part of his family. I'm concerned about his son Jason. He's been spending time with you, and that puts him in peril. Tell me your thoughts."

Harvey sighed, relieved he didn't have to broach the subject.

Kyoko and Emiko glanced at each other while the rest sat still. Kyoko spoke first. "He's old enough to make his own decisions."

Emiko frowned at Kyoko, then faced Meg. "I understand your concern. Jason's a naive young man. He looks on us as being real women. I believe--"

"You're talking like that because you have a crush on his father," Kyoko said.

Emiko glared at Kyoko. "Shut up. Yoshi invited us here to help her, and I believe as difficult as it is to turn our backs on our heritage, that's what we should be doing. Jason's part of this family, and we should stick together to help one another, not think only of what we want."

Kyoko tossed the blanket aside and stood. She glared at the rest of the group, did an about face, and stomped out the door. Emiko followed her sister's lead. "I have to go. She's my sister." She tossed the beret to Harvey and left to join Kyoko.

After Emiko left, Meg turned to Harvey. "At least we know where their thoughts are. I believe Emiko will maintain a steadying influence on Kyoko."

Harvey stared at Meg with a blank expression, and it was a while before he said, "I sure hope so. Somebody has to, or Jason's in trouble."

CHAPTER 26

Harvey handed his students a pop quiz based on required reading. He guessed Meg hadn't done the reading after being up so late because of his porn club visit, yet she submitted a paper. After class he pulled hers from the stack:

You never take me anywhere. You and your friends frequent porn clubs and have a good time while I stay home and scrub floors. You take other women to county fairs, to museums, and for riverboat rides, but you never take me anywhere. You leave me home to wash diapers and take care of the baby while you galavant with someone else. I think you're trying to get rid of me by practicing an insidious form of neglect.

He left the classroom and bumped into Meg standing around the corner from the door. She started in on him where her paper left off. "You used to take me places. Now you take me for granted. I think I'll go back to Japan and leave you here with the baby. No. I believe it's time to take the toad route."

He stepped back. "What did I do to deserve this?"

She poked him in the chest. "You're mean to me."

He waved for her to follow, and they walked down the hall to sit at their favorite lounge. "Why all this now?"

"You never take me to the beach."

"You sweet thing, would you like to go to Lake Michigan on Saturday?"

"What's the matter with this afternoon?"

"I have to teach a class."

"Get a substitute. The students will be happy to have a change, especially if it's someone who's taking the day off to spend it with his most affectionate student."

He crossed his arms. "Why do you stay with me if I'm so mean to you?"

"I only stay with you because, occasionally, you recognize quality in one who brings you contentment, one who looks after your every need, one who adds romance to your life, one who's always been there when--"

"All right--all right." He stood and walked to the Management Department office. Meg stood outside the door as he entered and approached Sophie. "An emergency situation has come up, and I need a substitute teacher for my afternoon class. Can you make sure that's taken care of?"

Meg waved through the open door, and Sophie waved back. "I understand," Sophie said. "I'll see if I can get Craig Akers. He can tell the class about the personal experience the two of you had last night involving the hospitality industry."

"Thank you, Sophie. That'll give me such a feeling of comfort, I can spend the whole day without having to worry about whether my class is in good hands."

Three hours later, the two lovers were soaking up sunshine on the beach at Saugatuck. Meg patted Harvey's hand as he dozed on two towels laid end to end. "You are such a nice person to take time off from your job to surprise me with a day at the beach. Your thoughts and actions to enhance my happiness overwhelm me." She grabbed his hand, pulled his arm up at an angle, and gave the hand a squeeze.

"That's what love's all about, sweetheart." He pulled to get his arm down, but it wouldn't budge. He rolled his eyes and quit trying.

The gentle roll of surf had almost lulled Harvey asleep, when he heard a female call for help. He sat up and yanked on his hand, trying to free it. "Let go--someone needs help." He tried to rise, but Meg's grasp on his hand kept him from being able to stand. "Let go. She's drowning."

Meg didn't even glance at him. "Go back to sleep. That's Kyoko. She's trying to attract a man, and it's not going to be you." Harvey heard a thump, when to his right, a tanned young man jumped from the lifeguard tower onto the sand and raced through the surf. He swam toward thrashing arms a hundred yards off the beach as Harvey and others watched. Meg ignored the show. When the lifeguard reached the area where the splashing occurred, the water was calm. His feet rose into the air as he dove under. Soon his head popped up, then he disappeared again, only to come up to take another breath and dive once more.

Harvey tapped Meg's shoulder. "Are you sure? He keeps diving after her."

"She's fine. If you feel the need to worry about someone, worry about him."

The drama ended when Kyoko swam to shore. Not far behind her, the lifeguard's head stuck out of shallow water. Kyoko walked over, sat next to Harvey, and leered at him. Meg and Harvey watched as the lifeguard called to a young woman sitting on a blanket near the stand. She ran to him and threw him a towel. He wrapped it around his waist and passed by her without saying a word, then entered a shed near the road.

"Where's Emiko?" Meg said to Kyoko.

Kyoko pointed to a concession stand. "Over there."

Meg watched a man come out of the stand, drop the overhead service window, and sneak back in through the door. Then she glanced at Kyoko. "You have a good swim?"

Kyoko showed a lot of teeth in a smile. "Yes." But

soon her attention was drawn to the lifeguard as he left the shed to cross over to the parking lot. She blew him a kiss.

"What are you doing in Saugatuck?"

Kyoko didn't look at Meg. She was watching two men walk down the beach, checking out women on the way. "I thought it would be a fun place to spend the day."

"How'd you know we were here?"

"I heard you tell Yoshi. . . . Are you going back to Lansing tonight?"

"Yes--are you saying you'd like a ride?"

Kyoko spread her arms. "I don't know. I like the people here."

"Especially the guys."

A smile made Kyoko's face shine. "Yes, and they like me." She watched a young man, with sun-bleached hair, walk from the lot toward the empty lifeguard tower.

Emiko came through the concession stand door and sauntered up to Harvey and Meg, carrying a hotdog and a bottle of pop. Kyoko eyed the hotdog. "That looks good. I want one."

"This stand's closed." Emiko pointed to a stand two-hundred yards down the beach. "But there's another near the next lifeguard station."

Harvey sat up. "Aren't you guys afraid somebody will drown after you've disabled all the lifeguards?"

Kyoko raised a hand toward the lifeguard station she had caused to be vacated. The young man with sun-bleached hair was climbing to the top of the stand. Emiko handed her hotdog and bottle of pop to her sister. "No," Kyoko said. "Let's take a walk." She pointed down the beach where the other two men had gone. "Maybe they'll give us a ride home."

Meg sat up. "How'd you get here?"

"Hitchhiked. We got a ride from a couple of old men

from Kalamazoo."

"All the way here?"

"They weren't coming to Saugatuck but went out of their way for us."

Harvey glanced at Kyoko. "And I suppose you went out of your way for them."

She grinned. "Such evil thoughts you have."

The cousins trotted away as if they had a time limit to accomplish their mission. Meg dropped back down onto her blanket and faced Harvey. "They can ride back with us if we're still here after they've emptied the beach."

Harvey slid next to Meg. "I worry about what they're doing. I doubt if anybody will drown, but there won't be much food served on the beach today."

"And not many men to serve to anyway. If you really feel the need to worry about something, worry about what will happen if the authorities discover a connection between us and Michigan's decreasing population."

Kyoko and Emiko rode home with Harvey and Meg. After dropping them off at the cemetery, Harvey said to Meg, "I hope we have peace and quiet tomorrow."

"You must be getting old. You've wished that every day for the past week."

CHAPTER 27

At twilight, Meg and Harvey sat on the deck in a light rain. Holding an umbrella by her side, Rosie peered at them from inside the house, "What are you doing sitting in the rain?"

Harvey didn't even look her way. "We're drinking a quiet glass of wine."

"I can see that--you know what I mean. Why are you drinking in the rain?"

"You should have said what you meant."

"Smart aleck. Why did you say a quiet glass of wine? All wine is quiet."

He grinned at her over his shoulder. "Okay, it's a draw. Let's start all over."

"You're too much trouble. Meg, why are you drinking wine in the rain?"

"We're thirsty."

Rosie held her hands up in the air. "You're starting to sound like him."

Meg reached out to Rosie. "I apologize. I shouldn't have done that. We've had a hectic week. We're sitting out here in the rain, so nobody will join us to destroy the peace and quiet we seek. It's nice that you're here. It's somebody else we want to get away from."

Rosie left her umbrella inside and walked into the drizzle. "May I guess who?"

"I'll pour you a glass of wine if you guess right."

"I don't know who, but I bet her initials are Kyoko."

Meg started to stand, but Rosie waved. "I really don't want any wine. I want to talk. I understand Daddy had a wild time at Dream Dolls Monday night."

Harvey set his glass down. "How'd you hear about Dream Dolls?"

"Jason."

Harvey wiped the rain off his face. "Damn, that means he's been with one of them. Let's go inside--we have to talk."

They sat at kitchen table, and Rosie talked as her dad and Meg dried their faces with paper towels. "I told Jason that Kyoko and Emiko were witches. He believes that, but he won't believe they're animals. He has a crush on Emiko."

"Emiko?" Harvey said.

"Yes."

Meg put her hand on Harvey's arm. "He's probably safe. If it were Kyoko, she would have done him in by now."

Harvey's voice increased in pitch. "How can you say he's safe when he's just a step away from death? If I had given her the slightest invitation, Emiko would have hopped into my bed when you were gone, even though she gave her word."

"You're right. He's in serious trouble hanging around either of them."

The rain came down harder, loud enough to be heard pelting the roof. Meg faced Rosie. "We don't know how to get rid of them, and we can't convince Jason they're animals. I'm sure he'd stay away from them if he realized they really are."

Rosie nodded. "I know he would. He just has a crush on a pretty woman with a great personality, not on an animal masquerading as a person."

"We have to get through to him," Meg said. "but he doesn't believe us, and he doesn't trust Mama. We can't take him to their den. Even if he saw two foxes there, he wouldn't believe they were Kyoko and Emiko. We need help."

"Whose?" Harvey said.

Meg turned her face toward him. "Emiko's."

Harvey leaned forward with his mouth agape and stared at her. "Emiko? She's the one he has a crush on."

Meg nodded. "True, but she's the one to help us."

"How?"

Meg held her hands up. "I don't know, but first we talk to Mama. She has more insight about how those two think than we do. Right now, I wish I were Kitsune, so I'd know their thought patterns."

Harvey leaned back in his chair. "No thank you. I like you as you are."

Meg slid her chair close to Harvey's, put her hand on his knee, and peered into his troubled face. "I love you."

Harvey put a hand on hers. "We don't have much time. We may be too late already."

Meg squeezed his hand. "I'll go talk to Mama. Don't wait up for me."

"How can I not wait up for you?"

"If she's gone, I'll have to stay until she returns."

"I'll stay here with you, Daddy," Rosie said.

"No, I'm okay. Go back to school."

Meg wiped her eyes with her towel and faced Rosie. "Did you and Ted come to a decision regarding marriage?"

"We agreed it makes sense to wait until he graduates. When are you two going to get married?"

"We haven't discussed a date but know we should."

"It's about time," Rosie said.

Harvey put on a fake, serious face and nodded. "You're right. We've already known each other for two weeks."

Meg stood, hugged Rosie, and kissed Harvey on the

cheek, then she grabbed his hand, and they walked to the front door together. After a hug, she ran into the rain. Rosie met her father as he returned to the kitchen. "You sure you're all right?"

"I'm all right--really." She kissed his forehead, opened her umbrella, and left, blowing him a kiss as she walked away.

Harvey woke up numerous times during the night to hear the rain beating on the roof. When morning came, the sun shined through the window on the vacant spot where Meg was supposed to be. Concerned, he hurried into the living room and found her asleep on the sofa. He brought a blanket from the bedroom and draped it over her. She stretched an arm out and touched his cheek with her finger. "Emiko didn't come back to the den last night. Kyoko was there, so even though I sat up with Mama most of the night, we didn't talk."

Harvey carried her to their bed. "Why'd you sleep on the sofa?"

"I didn't want to wake you. You needed the sleep."

"I appreciate your understanding. I have to get ready for class now, but we can talk later." He showered and shaved, kissed her, and left.

During a break between classes, Harvey called Western Truck Rental. "I'm looking for my son, Jason."

"He doesn't come in till five."

"Please ask him to call his dad when he comes in."

"I'll leave him a message."

Harvey called Jason's dorm, but nobody answered.

After his last class of the day, Harvey drove home. Meg wasn't there. He checked his watch: a quarter to five. He waited another half-hour before calling Western Truck. "I'd like to speak to Jason Long," he said.

"He ain't in yet. I'll have him call when he gets here."

Five minutes later, Harvey was still sitting on the sofa next to the phone when Meg dragged in, slumped over. She dropped to the sofa and toyed with his fingers. "Emiko's still not home. Kyoko and Mama both say they have no idea where she is. Mama and I went away from the den for a while, so Kyoko couldn't hear our conversation about protecting Jason."

"What did you decide?"

"Just that we should talk to Emiko and see what she says, I guess. We made no decisions. Mama feels as we do that Emiko has enough compassion to stay away from Jason. But she's not around, and we have no idea what's become of her."

Harvey stretched his legs and rested his head on the back of the sofa. "I tried to reach Jason, but he hasn't showed at work. I did a lot of thinking today about things I should have done with both Jason and Rosie. So much of my life, I've been wrapped up in myself and what I wanted to do, I've shortchanged them. I can't help thinking, if I had done things differently, Jason and I would relate better."

Meg caressed Harvey's forehead. "You can't blame yourself for what your kids do. You raised them both, and Rosie adores you. Even if I didn't know you two were related, I could tell in a second."

"Daughters are different."

"Sometimes even brothers are as different as two species. Your children are still children." She placed a hand on his cheek and looked into his eyes. "Someday you'll look at Jason and realize he's grown up, just like when he decided to get a job."

"You're probably right, but I can't help but wonder if things would be this screwed up if I had done things differently." He reached over, held her hand, and she snuggled up to him. He looked down at her. "Do you think I should call the hospitals?"

"What are you going to tell them, that your girlfriend's mother's cousin didn't come home last night, and your son is an hour late for work?"

Harvey frowned, but a moment later, it became a smile. "Sometimes, you put stuff into its proper perspective. You're more than just a pretty face. You're an intelligent broad."

She smiled through the tears that slid down her cheeks and across her mouth. He pulled out his handkerchief and wiped her tears away, then reached over and wrapped his arms around her. They held each other in silence for a few moments. She wiped her eyes. "About time for fish heads and rice, isn't it?" They walked into the kitchen holding hands.

The phone rang. "You wanted me to call," Jason said.

"Where are you?"

"At work."

"I called and they said you weren't there."

"I was checking a damaged truck. Who'd you talk to?"

Harvey sighed. "Evidently, the wrong guy."

"What do you need? I have to get back to work."

"I want to apologize for being so short with you Monday. Can you come over tonight after work? I could use your company. It's been a tough few days."

"What about a little after nine?"

"Sounds good--see you then."

Harvey went into the kitchen where a smiling Meg waited. "I heard," she said. "This calls for a celebration. You get the wine and I'll fix you a special treat."

"Right." He headed into the living room and came back with two glasses of red wine. He set them on a counter and pulled her to him. "You smell like fish." Looking over her shoulder, he saw two red snapper lying on a cutting board next to their heads which had been chopped off. "Fish for dinner?"

"How'd you guess?" She wrapped the fish in plastic

and put them in the refrigerator. She picked up a pan, poured oil in it, scooped up the fish heads, and threw them into the pan. She put a lid on the pan, placed it on a burner next to boiling rice, and turned it on to medium.

After dinner, Harvey leaned back in his chair. "That's the first time in my life, what I ate, stared at me while I ate it. I always thought you were kidding me."

"You like?"

"It may take some getting used to, but not bad."

Meg's eyes opened wide. "You want to have it again?"

"Maybe someday when we invite Dean Pigeon and Pricilla over for dinner."

Her jaw dropped, but then she broke into a smile. "What about at our wedding reception? We could have a marlin head for a centerpiece with a circle of little heads dancing around it."

Harvey placed his hands together and swung them back and forth. "What about a pair of marlins dancing cheek to cheek for the centerpiece?"

Meg touched her glass to his. "You're strange."

"That's why we relate."

They sipped their wine. Meg put her glass down and waved off a refill. "I'm going to run down to find out if Emiko's showed and see how Mama's doing. I'll be back by ten. That'll give you time alone with Jason."

"Good idea. I was so elated about him being okay, I forgot about your family. I can give you a ride to the cemetery, if you'd like, and still have time to do my paperwork."

"I accept."

"That's a first."

She stood. "I must be getting old."

Harvey dropped her off at the bridge. After driving home, he graded quizzes in his office until he was interrupted by a phone call. "I can't make it tonight," Jason said. "Can we do it tomorrow?"

"Need a ride?"

"No. Something personal came up. I'll see you tomorrow, same time. Goodbye." Harvey set the phone down and drummed his fingers on the desktop. He checked the time: Eight-fifteen. Meg wasn't due for over an hour. The rain came again and pounded on the window. He couldn't concentrate on grading quizzes and was happy to hear the front door open.

Meg dragged herself into the house soaking wet. Harvey held her, getting his shirt, face, and arms wet. He backed away. "I'll get a towel to dry you off." She didn't speak, just stood dripping on the carpet as he headed to the bathroom. He returned with a face towel and handed it to her. "What are you doing here so early?"

She held the towel without using it. "Is Jason here?"

"No. He postponed until tomorrow."

"Emmy's back. Yoshi's with her."

"Problem?"

"Yes."

"Well?"

"She's pregnant."

Harvey leaned forward. "You're kidding."

Meg wiped her face with a sleeve. "We're pretty sure."

Harvey took the towel and used it to dry her face. "As a person?"

"Yes."

He stopped drying and set the towel on an end table. "I'm almost afraid to ask. Do you know who the father is?"

"Not Jason. That's what you wanted to know."

Harvey sat on the sofa and wiped his brow with his

hand. "Whew." He patted the cushion next to him.

She kneeled in front of him. "I'm too wet."

"I have a difficult time understanding how she could be pregnant." he said.

Meg reached up and poked him in the chest. "Remember me?"

He picked up the towel and dried her hair by rubbing her head as forceful as one would when giving a massage. "I knew that, but I understood it was rare."

"You remember what Mama said about those two becoming more human?"

"Sure, but that seems far-fetched."

"Another parallel. Mama fell in love with my father."

He tossed the towel toward the bathroom. "You're saying Emiko's in love?"

She nodded. "Probably."

"In a way, I'm relieved. With her being in love, it reduces Jason's chances of having sex with her. Your mom's staying with her--she knows what Emiko's going through."

"That's how they put the puzzle together--Mama knows all of those feelings. Emmy had no idea. She only knew she was sick and depressed. She had feelings she never had before, never even heard of."

"Who's the lucky man?"

"A student at State."

"And how is he?"

Tears came to Meg's eyes. "He's a patient in University Hospital."

Harvey wiped her tears away with his wet handkerchief. "How old?"

She got up from her knees and sat next to Harvey. "Twenty-three, I believe. He's in the graduate program at the medical school."

"Sad."

"We're not one hundred percent sure she's pregnant, but we know he's sick, and Emmy knows she did it to him."

"So that's where she was."

"Yes. She needs someone to be with her. That's why Mama's staying with her."

"Do you know the father's name?"

"Emmy wouldn't say. She's all mixed up. She didn't want to live knowing what she'd done, but she does, now that she believes she's carrying his baby."

Harvey held Meg's hand. "So what do you think?"

"It creates problems and it solves one."

"Which one does it solve?"

"Danger to Jason, or for that matter, to a lot of men."

"But there's still Kyoko. Was she there?"

"For a while, she was talking about going back to Japan. I think, with Emmy in that condition, she's worried what Mama said about becoming more human is true. She's concerned that what happened to Emmy may happen to her. But I don't think so--I don't believe she's capable of love."

"Isn't she staying with Emiko?"

"No. She left the den before I did."

"What time?"

"About eight."

Harvey walked away from Meg and stopped in the middle of the room. "Damn!"

Meg put a hand out to him. "What's the matter?"

He covered his face with both hands. "Jason called at eight-fifteen and said he wouldn't be able to make it tonight because something personal came up."

CHAPTER 28

Meg picked up her cereal bowl and put it in the dishwasher. "I'm going to the den. I want to see Emmy and maybe relieve Mama. Are you going to the college today?"

"I have to. I'm worried about Jason, but I can't sit around here and mope. I'll just have to wait till tonight to talk with him. He was probably with Kyoko last night, which means he's in trouble. Hopefully she had a change of heart and told him the truth." He faced away, then back. "No. Not much chance of that. Call and let me know if Kyoko came back to the den last night."

"I will. I don't feel like running. Drive me, please?"

Harvey dumped out the little bit of cereal left in his bowl and stuck the bowl in the dishwasher. "Let's go." He reached over and held Meg's hand while he drove. "Interesting. You seem to be closer to Emiko than ever before. I notice you've started calling her Emmy."

"Have I? I guess because of our new kinship. As far as I know, she's only the second Kitsune who's gotten pregnant by a human. Let's get off that subject now. Also, I don't want to be talking about wedding plans with all this taking place. By Monday, we should know what's going on. We'll talk about it then." She leaned over and kissed Harvey, then got out of the car, ran across the bridge, and up the hill.

Harvey watched until she was out of sight, then drove

to work, going directly to Dean Pigeon's office where he talked to Sophie. "I should be getting an urgent message from Megumi--have it delivered to me in the conference room."

A half-hour later the door opened, and a student aide handed him an envelope. He read it: *Kyoko came in late last night and left before I arrived this morning. She didn't talk to anyone before she left. Sorry, that's all I know.*

Meg was waiting for Harvey in the living room when he came home. He looked at her face and knew she carried bad news. "What happened?"

"Kyoko came back this afternoon. She crept into the den as if she didn't want to be seen. When Emmy asked her what she had done, Kyoko slid down in her burrow and shapeshifted to a fox. She wouldn't look at the others. Emmy yelled, 'You didn't.' Kyoko cowered down lower, trying to disappear beneath her bedding."

Meg reached for Harvey's hand and held it. "She'd been with Jason. I had to leave. I came right home. I'm so sorry."

Harvey walked out to the deck and stared over the pond. Minutes later, he sat with his hands over his face. He took them away, then put them back again. Meg leaned on the rail next to him, staring straight ahead. Harvey pulled his hands down and stood. He scowled. "If your mother hadn't asked those two to come here, this never would have happened."

Meg spun around. "It's not her fault--it's mine. If I hadn't told her I'd fallen for you, she wouldn't have come to see you." Meg rushed into the house. With no change of expression, Harvey stared at the door she'd disappeared through. He faced the pond. Minutes later, he shuffled toward the door. He wiped the scowl from his face, straightened his posture, and walked into the house, straight to his bedroom.

Meg sobbed as she opened a dresser drawer, grabbed

some undies, and tossed them into a suitcase. He took the undies out of the suitcase and tossed them back into the drawer. She took them out again and threw them at the suitcase. He picked them up and tossed them into the drawer. She turned to face him. "Let me go."

"Never." They held each other and cried.

She pulled away and faced a window, her words interrupted by sobs. "Look what I've done to you. I wish I'd never met you. I should have stayed with my own kind."

He placed a hand on her shoulder. "I wish I had been the father I should've been. My mother used to say, 'Wish in one hand and shit in the other and see which gets full first.'"

Meg jerked her body toward him. "If you're trying to be funny, it's the wrong time."

Harvey took one of her hands in his. "She'd say that when I'd wished for something I had no control over. We have no control over what's already happened or what other people have done. This is right now, and wishing won't change anything. I love you, I love Yoshi, and I love Jason. If a mistake was made, he made it. Nobody else is to blame, not you, Yoshi, or me. We don't even know if it's happened, so let's find out, then we'll figure out what to do."

She glared at him. "You do what you want, but I've made a decision I should have made long ago. I'm going to the police to have something done about my cousins."

"What can they do?"

"That's up to the police."

"Let's wait until we find out what's happened. Jason's supposed to be here soon."

Meg pulled her hand away from Harvey's. "Just a minute ago, you said we had to figure out what to do. I did that. I'm going to call the police first thing in the morning." She pointed at him. Don't you wait until morning. Go find your son." Harvey stared at her a moment and walked to the living room. He called Jason's dorm. There was no answer. He called Western Truck. Jason hadn't showed at work. He checked the hospitals. They had no inpatient or outpatient record of Jason. By the time he had exhausted places to look, it was eleven and Jason still hadn't arrived.

Harvey didn't sleep. He checked the time throughout the night, and at seven, called the hospitals again with the same results. He called Jason's number at the dorm--no answer. He called Western Truck--they hadn't heard from Jason. "Let's go to the police," he said. "I'll report Jason missing while you lodge a complaint about your cousins."

At the red-brick city police station, Meg stood back as Harvey approached a cop at the front desk. "We need to talk to Missing Persons, and I want to lodge a complaint against two people who are spreading a deadly malady in the area."

"I'll send you to Missing Persons," she said, "but you'll have to call Centers for Disease Control for the other."

"It's different than a disease. It's more of a crime."

"Tell them that at Missing Persons."

She sent them to the detective division, a room crammed with desks. A man in plain clothes led them to a large room full of ragged overstuffed chairs and beat-up coffee tables. Soon, two men wearing dark suits strode in, one about thirty, and the other a bit older. "What can we do for you folks?" the younger man said.

"My son is missing," Harvey touched Meg's arm with his thumb, "and she'd like to give you insight on a string of people who have contracted a malady that eventually will lead to their death. We believe that's what's happened to my son."

The man turned to Meg. "Are you a doctor?"

"No. It's not a disease, but there are similarities."

"Have you contacted any of the doctors who have those people as patients?"

"No."

The older man scowled. "What are you doing here? This is not a hospital."

Harvey thrust a finger toward the floor. "We came here because it's more of a crime than a sickness. It wouldn't do any good to go to a hospital. Doctors aren't familiar with the cause, and they probably wouldn't believe us if we were to tell them."

He smirked at Harvey. "Tell me--see if I believe you."

"Her two cousins are Kitsune, Japanese foxes that turn into beautiful women. They seduce men who then degenerate and die within three months. They've done that to a number of men in Lansing over the past two weeks, and we want to put a stop to it."

"Is that right."

Harvey glared at one of the men and then the other. "You guys think we're kooks. That's the problem we'll have if we try to convince doctors or hospital personnel."

"Have you tried?"

"Do you think they'll believe what I just told you?"

"I see what you mean. Tell you what we're gonna do. We'll give you a detective who'll work with you to see what you come up with on your son and on this malady, as you call it." He grabbed the younger detective's arm. "Let's go."

Harvey placed his hand on Meg's. "Good." But soon his expression changed from pleasant to sour when he watched the cops stroll down the hallway. The older one was circling his left ear with his index finger.

Minutes later, a young man who resembled a college student wearing a sport coat and tie, entered the room. Harvey was pleasantly surprised when the man said, "I'm Detective

Barry Finn, and I've been assigned to help you." Finn continued talking as he set up a recorder on the table in front of them. "As I understand it, you have two problems, a missing person, and a disease that's affecting local residents." Meg and Harvey nodded. "You have to speak," Finn said. "The recorder can't see you nod."

They both said, "Yes."

"Let's talk about the missing person first." Finn turned to Harvey. "Your son, I understand."

"That's right. His name's Jason Long."

"And you are?"

"Harvey Long."

"When did he disappear?"

"He was supposed to come to my house at nine last night, but he didn't show. I called his work number where he was scheduled to be at five, and he hadn't shown there either. I called his dorm at State and got no answer. I tried them all again this morning with the same results."

Finn looked at Harvey as he spoke. "Ordinarily, we don't list people as missing until twenty-four hours have elapsed, however I can give you some help in the meantime that may lead us to him. What do you think happened to him?"

"We believe he's been infected with a rare malady that has incapacitated him."

"Is that malady the other problem you're reporting."

"Yes."

"Let's start with your missing son. Did you talk to anyone at his dorm?"

"I called his room, but there was no answer."

"Someone else share the room?"

"During the fall and spring terms but not in summer."

"Let's go there." Finn picked up the recorder, and they left for the parking lot.

Harvey opened the front door of the unmarked Ford for Meg to get in. "She can fill you in on the malady on the way," he said. "You know where Potter Dorm is?"

"Yep. Graduated from State."

Meg spoke to Finn as he drove. "Mr. Finn, you may find this difficult to believe."

"I'll listen to what you say. And call me Barry."

"All right, Barry. My mother is a witch with magical powers, but my father was mortal, so I ended up a half-witch." Detective Finn peered at her out of the corner of his eyes.

Meg pointed at Finn's head. "You don't need to wear your cap in the car." Suddenly, the cap jumped off his head and landed beside him. His eyes opened wide as he glanced at the cap, then at her. "But you may as well wear it," she said. The hat flew back to his head.

"Hold it a minute." Finn pulled the car off the side of the street. "I don't think I should be driving while this kind of thing is happening."

"You should turn your flashers on," Meg said. He reached to turn them on, but they began blinking before his hand reached the lever. "Now you're thinking you won't tell anybody this happened, and you won't put it in your report."

"Anybody could figure that out, ma'am, but that's okay; you've convinced me. Perhaps you can do more later if my memory needs to be jogged. Now, tell me about this disease." He turned off his flashers, drove back onto the street, and continued on to Potter Dorm.

"Kitsune are Japanese foxes. They roam down from the mountains into villages and turn into beautiful women who seduce men, causing them to die within three months. In the meantime, the men loose energy, refuse to eat, and waste away. We believe that's what happened to Jason. You see, two Kitsune related to me are now living in Lansing. They just look like pretty, young girls. Jason knows them but doesn't believe they're witches or that they're a danger to him."

Finn parked in a circle drive in front of the dorm. "I understand why he might feel safe." The three of them climbed stairs to the second floor. Finn knocked on the door of room 202, but there was no answer. He put an ear against the door. "I don't hear anyone. Let's get a key."

After he checked out a key from the dorm office, Finn unlocked the door and pushed it open. Jason lay on a bed with his eyes open, staring at the ceiling. Harvey ran to him, put a hand on Jason's arm, and looked at his son's vacant stare. Jason tried to raise his head. "I'm sick."

Harvey placed a hand on Jason's forehead. "We need to get you to a hospital, but we have to know; did you have sex with Kyoko?" Jason's nod was faint.

"We need a stretcher," Finn said.

Harvey pushed the flat of his other hand at Finn. "I'll carry him. Hold his head up until I get him off the bed." Finn held Jason's head while Harvey lifted him, and they rode the elevator to the main floor. After Meg took the key back to the office, she went to the car where Jason was lying on the back seat with his head on Harvey's lap. Finn turned on the flashing lights and drove toward University Hospital. Harvey placed his hand on Jason's forehead, and tears filled his eyes as his mind raced: *I played with fire, and Jason's the one who got burned. My son is dying.*

When they arrived at the University Hospital, Meg looked back at Harvey. "This is where Emmy's friend is. I don't know his name, but he's a grad student here."

"Another one?" Finn said.

"Yes."

"We'll talk to his doctor."

In the emergency room, a nurse ran response tests on

Jason. "He's in some sort of a coma. Do you know what caused it?"

Finn flashed his badge. "Yes, ma'am, but you may have trouble believing it. Another young man with the same problem was brought here--" He turned toward Meg. "When?"

"Two, three days ago."

"I'm not familiar with the case," the nurse said. "Let me see what I can find out." She left and was back in five minutes. "I located him. The resident physician wants to talk to all of you. He said to have your young man admitted."

Harvey stepped forward. "May I stay with him? I'm his father."

"Yes, until he's admitted. Then the doctor wants to talk to all of you."

Jason didn't speak or move. He lay on the cart with his eyes open.

CHAPTER 29

A frail Doctor Ortiz led them to an empty room and peered over the top of his wire-rim half-glasses. "I don't know the cause of my patient's problem and cannot reveal information to you about his case, but I'd appreciate any light you can shed on it."

"I know what caused his condition," Meg said, "but I can't tell you what to do about it."

"You tell me the cause--I'll be able to treat it."

"I don't think so. What happened is he had sex with a Japanese fox that shapeshifted into a woman and when--"

Ortiz leaned toward Meg and squinted at her. "Thanks for your help." He turned and started toward the door.

Finn grabbed the doctor's shoulder. "Listen to her."

Ortiz glared at Finn. "Who are you?"

Finn waved his badge in front of the doctor's face. "Listen to what she's saying."

Ortiz puckered his lips. "Whatever you say." He turned to Meg. "Speak."

"Having sex with the fox causes men to waste away and die. That's what happened to your patient and to Jason Long, who we just brought in."

"With a fox? You're all crazy."

"They had sex with the women the foxes changed into."

The doctor crossed his arms and glowered at her. "I

know you believe what you're saying, miss, but--"

Meg pointed a finger at him. "Raise your arms over your head." The doctor gave Detective Finn an appealing look as if he would find relief there.

"Do what she says--raise your arms."

Doctor Ortiz remained still for a moment, then tried to raise his arms. They wouldn't budge. He strained and grunted, but they wouldn't leave his sides. Meg pointed at him again, and in a flash, his arms were held high. He jerked his head to look at Meg, then at Finn and back at her. She made a sweeping motion with her hand, causing a white metal table on wheels, next to the bed, to roll toward where he stood shaking. It stopped behind him. "Sit on the table," she said. When he refused, the table bumped him in the rear. He plopped on it and rode around the room with his arms in the air, looking as if he were going to cry.

Finn watched with wide open eyes. "You can be sure this won't be in my report."

A nurse walking down the hall saw the doctor riding the table. She stopped and poked a finger at him. "Doctor, you should be ashamed of yourself."

The table came to an abrupt halt when it got back to the starting point, and Ortiz lowered his arms. "You win. I'll listen to you until tomorrow if you wish." He jumped from the table and backed away from Meg, holding his palms out in front as if he feared she would attack him.

"Dozens of men in the Lansing area have the same malady," Meg said. "Two cousins of mine are responsible for their condition. What can you do to help these young men?"

"Nothing. I'd suggest Centers for Disease Control. Anything else you need?"

"Take care of my son until we get help," Harvey said.

Ortiz backed away from his tormentors. "I will.

Anything else? Anything at all."

Meg pointed at him. "Make sure you take good care of these two men."

Ortiz jumped back and raised his hands to shield himself. "Yes, ma'am." When nothing bad happened, he scurried out the door.

Harvey walked to Emergency to tell Jason goodbye. Jason mouthed, "Bye."

Harvey wiped his eyes with a handkerchief and joined the others in the hospital reception area. He faced Meg. "I remember your saying you had lost your magic. What do you call what you did with Doctor Ortiz?"

"Reserve power, I guess."

Finn, who was listening, glanced at Meg. "I'm sure you'll have no problem convincing Centers for Disease Control of the origin of this malady. They don't open till Monday, so I can take the rest of today to see how many have been infected."

Harvey raised a hand. "I'll work with you. I know of at least six more cases, and there are probably a couple dozen others we don't know about."

"Those two have been busy, haven't they?"

Harvey repeated to Finn what Yoshi had told him when he met her: "They go about it with vigor, and they do it well."

Meg and Harvey listened to Finn as he called other hospitals and located twenty-two more cases, not including Captain Mason, Judge Haysid, his bailiff, the Winkin' Pup manager, four young men from Saugatuck, and the two old men from Kalamazoo. Finn sighed. "It's been a long, exciting day, one I'll never forget."

Meg spoke up. "There's one more job for you, the toughest of all. I want you to meet the two who caused all this. You can't incarcerate them because they'd destroy your jail system, but I'd like them to know we're trying to undo what they have done. They may be ready to talk now, since both have regrets about their last conquests."

Finn shook his head over and over as they left the hospital. "Take me to them. Anything you can do to make my day complete."

"Great--now's a good time--they should be in the den."

After they climbed out of the police car and crossed the cemetery bridge, Meg tapped the top of a green bench. "You two stay here. I don't want you to spook them." Then she left.

Harvey sat on the bench next to Finn. "They can read minds and would know we're coming as soon as we got near them. I believe Meg can calm them down and get them here. Her mother, Yoshi, will probably be with them."

"Would Meg's mother like for her two cousins to leave the country?"

"Yes. Very much so. . . . Excuse me a minute. I have to call my daughter and let her know what's going on." Harvey crossed the bridge, talked on his phone for a few minutes, then rejoined Finn on the bench.

Meg came down the hill with the three Kitsune following her, Yoshi in front with her chin held high, Emiko slumped over, and Kyoko strutting. As they neared Detective Finn, Kyoko grabbed a pigtail and broke out in a smile. Meg waved the flat of a hand at her. "Settle down."

Finn directed the two Kitsune cousins to sit on the bench while he, Meg, and Harvey faced them. Yoshi stood off to the side as Meg said, "Our primary interest is to save the lives of two young men in University Hospital." Emiko sat up straight, but Kyoko displayed no emotion. "Detective Finn wants to verify that you've had sexual relations with the two sick students." The cousins both nodded.

"One other question," Finn said. "Are you considering returning to Japan, or do you want to stay in America?"

"I want to go back to Japan," Emiko said, "but not until I know if anything can be done for Larry. If nothing can be done, I don't know what my future will bring."

"Larry. Is that the name of your student friend."

"Yes."

They all stared at Kyoko. "I'll go with Emiko. She's my sister." Emiko smiled and patted Kyoko's hand.

Finn turned to Yoshi. "And you?"

"I'm not sure yet. I'll probably stay around long enough to make sure they know I want to be a grandmother." Meg smiled. Harvey rolled his eyes.

Finn leaned toward the cousins. "I don't know if anything can be done for your two young men. We have to check with Centers for Disease Control, but I don't have high hopes based on what I've learned today."

Meg raised a hand as if she were in school. "I have an idea for a possible antidote. I've been thinking about a story Mama told me she heard from an American sailor who had too much to drink at a party in Tokyo."

Yoshi grinned. "Many fit your description. Be more specific, please."

Meg turned toward her mother. "The one who said he had to be sober before going aboard ship, so he took another drink of sake mixed with orange juice. You asked him how more sake would sober him up."

"Now I know the one. Yes. He said, 'I cure the bite with the hair of the dog that bit me, I take a drink of what got me drunk--not straight but mixed with something that's good for me, and that helps me sober up.'"

Finn asked Meg. "How does that story relate to an antidote for the curse?"

257

"I understand a similar idea is used in vaccinations, and I believe that sometimes an infection can be cured by the germ that caused it. It's worth looking into. I'm sure Mama's cousins are willing to give blood to develop a serum to save these two young men."

Emiko waved a hand. "I'd like to do that."

Kyoko frowned. "You want to give your blood to them? They'll poke needles in you and take what's yours. . . . But I can do anything you can do."

Emiko put a hand on Kyoko's. "We're ready to help."

Finn nodded. "I don't know much about that sort of thing, but I'll check with CDC on Monday. In fact, I'll talk to one of our medical technicians today to see if it's feasible."

Harvey reached for one of Meg's hands and squeezed it, but in his mind, he was concerned. *Any cure that depends on the participation of those two, will contain inherent problems for which there may be no solution.*

CHAPTER 30

Monday morning, Detective Finn pulled the squad car in front of the new limestone CDC building, and they were escorted by a doorman to what resembled a doctor's waiting room with nobody waiting. Kyoko tapped Emiko on the shoulder as she ogled colorful wallpaper depicting horses competing in an English-style steeple chase. Emiko nodded with enthusiasm, evidently realizing what Kyoko was excited about. Harvey had no idea what they were contemplating, but knew they were up to no good.

Yoshi plopped down in an overstuffed chair and gave a contented sigh while Meg and Finn waited for a receptionist at the appointment window. Harvey stood to the side where he could watch Emiko and Kyoko to see what they were planning. The cousins seated themselves on upright chairs, and their heads began to bob up and down. Harvey followed their line of sight and saw that a brown horse, and a black one with a white blaze, had come to life and were running across the wallpaper, jumping hurdles, and water hazards. He grabbed Yoshi's arm and pointed at the wall. "Stop them."

Yoshi sat up. "Yes." The horses kept running.

Meg rushed over to where Yoshi sat watching the race. "Stop them, Mama."

"They're almost finished. I want to see who wins."

"Now, Mamasan."

"Oh, all right." The two horses came to a halt hovering over a water hazard.

The receptionist stood at the window. She shifted her eyes from the steeple chase to the cousins, then to Meg. "The doctor's ready to see you." She glanced at the two horses stopped in midair and pulled a shade down over the window before opening the door to the inner office.

"I'll stay here and keep a semblance of order," Harvey said as Meg went through the door. Finn took a chair where he had a front row seat when the race started again. Kyoko jumped up and down as the horses made the final hurdle and squealed with delight when her black horse won by a nose.

"You cheated," Emiko yelled. "You started early."

"All's fair in love and racing."

"But you cheat at both."

Harvey knew the main event wasn't over when he saw Yoshi's gaze fixed on the two horses poised at the starting gate. He tapped her on the shoulder. "What?" she yelled.

"Stop them."

"They are stopped."

"For how long?"

"I'll take care of them." As soon as she spoke, the horses took off running. Yoshi pointed at the wallpaper. With the whirring of spinning wheels, a red Ferrari roared onto the course, spewing chunks of sod onto the carpet as it raced past the horses, then circled around the back of a water hazard they were approaching. The horses fell into the hazard, splashing water on Finn. Then the Ferrari sped away. Finn sat with his mouth agape as Yoshi pulled a decorative handkerchief from his suit coat pocket to wipe the water off the arms of her kimono.

Harvey stood to knock on the door Meg had gone through to ask her to put a stop to the races. As he raised his fist to knock, it opened, and he almost hit the receptionist on the forehead. "Excuse me. I was trying to knock on the door."

"We're ready for those two," she said and slunk back through the door.

Harvey turned to see the horses climb out of the hazard and shake the water off, spraying Finn again. *I wonder if anybody can ever be ready for the madness generated by those two*. He waved for the cousins to follow him--they pouted but went along with his request. He took one last look at Yoshi. "Can you behave like a grownup while we're gone?"

She frowned. "That was the best way to stop the race." Just as the door closed behind him, Harvey heard a horse neigh.

Inside a white room with cabinets full of medical equipment, a young man with an Arnold Schwarzenegger build, stood next to Meg. He nodded at Harvey. "My name's Mark. Drawing blood is a simple task, so you and Ms. Sakuma can wait in the lounge if you'd like."

Harvey watched Emiko and Kyoko survey the room. "These two may not be as easy to handle as you think. They're. . . . Let's just say they're of a different culture."

"Look mister, I grew up in a tough Brooklyn neighborhood and had to subdue all sorts of types on my way through childhood. I can surely handle these two."

Although reassured by Mark's stern manner, Harvey didn't move. "We'll just stand here and won't bother you."

Mark switched his attention from Harvey to the two blood donors. Kyoko was blowing up a latex glove, and Emiko had her hand in a cabinet reaching for another. He jabbed a finger at Kyoko. "Put that down." Kyoko batted the glove and hit him in the face with it. By that time, Emiko had blown hers up and was batting it around like a balloon. Harvey's body tensed, and he held his breath but breathed out when Mark calmly picked up a scalpel from a cabinet and poked holes in the gloves, causing them to drop to the floor. Then he pointed the scalpel at two metal chairs. "Sit." Harvey relaxed after Emiko and Kyoko sat.

While Mark was organizing his blood drawing equipment, his back was turned away from Kyoko, who had picked up her glove and filled it with water. A stream of cold water hit the back of Mark's neck, and he jumped. He calmly strode to an open door on the other side of the room. "Doctor Clark, please come in here." An unsmiling woman entered the room to be greeted by squirts of water in the face, one from each of the cousins.

Doctor Clark snatched the latex water-guns from them. "Get them seated," she said. "I'll sit on them if I have to, while you draw their blood." She pushed the flat of her hand toward Harvey who was on his way to help. "Relax--we're in control."

The cousins followed Mark to the chairs without resisting. Doctor Clark hovered over Emiko to keep her in her seat while Mark tried to insert the needle into Kyoko's vein. Emiko covered her mouth with her hand and snickered, causing Doctor Clark to look around. Kyoko was rubbing her free hand across Mark's fly as he tried to get the needle into her vein. The bulge in his trousers grew, and Kyoko began to fondle it. He backed away and shrugged at the doctor.

Doctor Clark slapped Kyoko's hand and stomped over to where Harvey and Meg stood. "Take them away. They obviously are not interested in saving the lives of those young men." She turned to Mark. "You can leave. We're finished." Mark left the room, and Kyoko frowned.

Harvey stepped over to where Emiko sat with the remains of a smile, and kneeled in front of her. "Evidently you're more interested in having a good time than you are in saving the life of your baby's father." Emiko's smile disappeared, and she was quiet for a moment. She covered her mouth with her hand, and tears formed. "You'd better change your actions if you want to save his life," Harvey said. He motioned toward Kyoko. "And get her to settle down too."

Emiko began to whimper and nodded. Kyoko spun around and confronted her. "Just because you're turning into a human, doesn't mean I have to change."

"Then I'll do it alone," Emiko said. She turned to Doctor Clark. "Take my blood." Kyoko turned and faced the wall and said nothing. Emiko stared at Kyoko's back for a moment, then walked around her and looked at Kyoko's face. Emiko touched a tear on her sister's cheek. "You're crying. You've never cried in your whole life."

Kyoko strode over to where Doctor Clark stood and held her arm out, palm up. "Take my blood."

On their return to the waiting room, Harvey, Meg, and the two cousins encountered Yoshi asleep on a sofa, snoring, probably the reason Finn was nowhere to be seen. Meg woke her, and they all went outside where Finn was pacing back and forth. "Mission accomplished," Harvey said.

Nobody spoke as Finn drove the Kitsune to their home. After they climbed out of the car and headed into the cemetery, Harvey touched Meg's arm and pointed at the two cousins as they crossed the footbridge. Kyoko and Emiko were holding hands. "Amazing," Meg said.

Minutes later, Finn dropped Meg and Harvey off at their home, then drove away. While walking into the house, Meg peered over her shoulder at Harvey. "Would you please make me a cup of coffee?"

"You never drink coffee."

"I know, but it's time to start. I never saw anything like what happened today. I didn't think it was possible."

"Their holding hands or the glove episode?"

"Kyoko and Emiko holding hands. "You made it all

happen and saved the day when you lectured Emiko."

"You started it all with your drunken sailor story."

Harvey added coffee grounds and water to a two-cup coffee maker and sat at the table with Meg. She put a hand under her chin and reached the other out to Harvey. "You look beat." She stared a him, and they sat without talking while the coffee brewed. She picked up the pot and poured a cup of coffee for each of them, then sniffed hers. He just stared at his.

The phone rang. She held the phone out so Harvey could hear Finn's voice. "It won't work. Doctor Clark called. She was as angry as if we had pulled a trick on her. She said, 'Those two are animals. Their blood would kill recipients.'"

Harvey shook his head. "We should have had them take your blood instead." He studied the bedroom door for a moment. "I'm going to lie down a while." He went into the bedroom. Meg followed and watched, as he lay on top of the covers, folded his arms over his chest, and closed his eyes. She placed one hand over his while she stroked his brow with the other. She kissed him on the forehead and left the room.

Minutes later she returned, sat next to Harvey, and held his hand. He opened his eyes and saw she was crying. He wanted to ask why but couldn't talk. He wanted to sit up and hold her but didn't have the energy. He remained on his back and tried to speak. His lips moved, but sound didn't come. She repeated the movement he made with his lips. "I love you, too." She sat on the edge of the bed and cried.

Through fading eyesight Harvey saw a form enter the room. "Megumi Sakuma," Yoshi yelled, "get off your ass and quit your blubbering. We have work to do."

CHAPTER 31

Harvey was lifted and placed on a moving platform that jiggled and wobbled as it was wheeled into an open field that reeked of antiseptic. The platform moved down a road lined with white trees while people threw white flowers at him. An angel in white drifted down next to him and sang, "Today's the day to set the date." The angel reached out to hold his hand.

Harvey awoke with Meg's hand on his. "I must have slept for quite a while. I feel better now." He reached up and brushed tears from her cheeks. "I was just thinking we were supposed to set a wedding date today."

"That was four days ago, Harvey."

"No it wasn't."

She caressed his forehead. "That was Monday. This is Friday." She laid her head next to his and her arm on his chest.

Looking beyond her head, Harvey saw he wasn't in his bedroom but in a white room with two men in light blue scrubs standing next to the bed. "I'm Doc Ferguson," one of them said. "Glad to have you back with us. You're the first." He picked up one of Harvey's hands and checked his pulse.

"Where am I?" Harvey said.

"University Hospital."

"How long did she say I've been out?"

Ferguson set Harvey's hand on his chest. "Four days. If it wasn't for her, you never would've awakened again."

"You said I'm the first."

"Some of the others have improved vital signs, but they haven't regained consciousness. You're number one."

Harvey's voice was subdued. "Jason?"

Meg raised her head. "He's going to be all right."

Doc Ferguson touched Harvey's arm. "He's in another room with Larry Weggard. If they equal your progress, they'll both be coming around in a day or two."

Harvey's eyes filled with tears that ran off the side of his face onto the pillow. "Why are they taking longer? Because I only got a half-dose?"

"You mean because she's only half Kitsune? No. We tried the serum on you to see if your vital signs changed for the better. As soon as we saw your blood pressure headed in the right direction, we received permission to inject the other men."

"They all responded?"

"The two men in Kalamazoo are coming around slower, probably because of their age." Ferguson waved. "Get some rest and we'll see you later."

"Don't you feel he's had enough rest?" Meg said. "I want to be close to him."

"Being close to you is the best rest he can get."

After Doc Ferguson and the other man left the room, Meg closed the door and hurried back to the bed. "I know what you want," Harvey said. "and it's not rest."

"The doctor said my being close to you is the best rest you can get."

"His interpretation of close is different than yours."

"I just want to lie down next to you."

"That reminds me of an old joke about the three biggest lies. Want to hear the other two?"

"What's the problem if I just lie down next to you? You already have my antibodies in you."

"Someone may walk in on us."

She turned to leave his side. "I'll lock the door."

Harvey grabbed her hand. "Later. Right now, tell me what you did that the doctor said was so special."

She folded her arms. "Okay, if you really think that's more important than making your fiancée happy. . . . You may not remember, but before you went to sleep, you told me CDC should have used my blood. Barry drove me there. Doctor Clark wasn't going to draw my blood, even after I told her I'm human and have the right type of antibodies, but after some gentle persuasion, she consented to test it. You want to hear how I did it?"

"No thank you. I have a pretty good idea what you choose to call gentle persuasion."

"Anyway, Mark drew my blood, and Doctor Clark sent me to a waiting room while they ran tests on it. Then she called me back to the lab where he drew a bunch more. Then I came here. One would think that after all I've done for you, I could lie down next to you for just a little bit."

He grinned. "A little bit of what?"

She placed her palm on her chest and gave him a pleading look. "I've stayed here all of the time, alone on the edge of your bed. . . . I take that back." She removed the hand and the look and became serious. "Rosie came in for a while every day and every night to relieve me, and we've both spent time with Jason."

He reached for her hand. "You haven't had much sleep then. You must be tired."

"I slept on a chair in a lounge next to the nurses' station. They said they'd wake me if your condition changed."

"You ought to get some sleep."

She put her arms around him. "Then move over a bit, sweetie."

"Finish telling me the story of what happened."

She remained sitting on the edge of the bed. "That's about it."

"What about the cousins? Are they alone in the house?"

"I didn't tell you, did I? They've gone back to Japan, and Mama too."

"How'd you accomplish that?"

"You did it when you chewed out Emiko for playing instead of doing what she could to save Larry. That led to Kyoko crying for the first time ever. She must have realized shedding tears was a step on the way to developing human characteristics, so she made the decision to return to Japan and the Kitsune life. Emiko wanted to remain here, but she knew if she stayed around Larry, eventually she'd kill him."

"What about your mama?"

"She volunteered to join them when Barry told her, if she didn't leave, he'd blow up her den some night."

Harvey raised a hand to his ear as if it were a phone. "Did you call the college to tell them I wouldn't be able to teach my classes?"

"Yes. I told them you hooked up with a witch and had a baby."

Harvey's jaw sagged. "Did you really say that?"

"No, I told them the truth. I said you caught a disease from the student you've been sleeping with and went to the hospital to get cured."

"You're so bad."

"I'm so good," she said as she slipped her skirt off.

He put his hands up. "Can't do that here."

"Slide over, snake." She lifted the covers and slid in next to him, then tucked her skirt and undies under the covers. "I'll keep the blouse on, and it'll look like I'm dressed. No one will ever know what we're doing. . . . Uuuhh!

CHAPTER 32

The morning of the wedding, two crates, heavy as boxes of rocks, were delivered to the house. After Harvey carried them to the foyer, Meg leaned over and read the shipping tag. "They're from Japan, but I don't recognize the return address."

"Let's open them," Harvey said.

"Not right now. It's bad luck to open them before we're married." She peeked through openings in the crates and inspected the cardboard boxes inside.

"We slept together before we got married. Does that give us bad luck?"

She peered up at him. "We were practicing."

He checked the shipping tag. "They must have come from your mother."

"Uh, uh. They came UPS. She wouldn't pay to have them shipped." She poked a finger through an opening between the slats. "Look, the box inside has air holes in it."

He slid the crates into the closet next to the door. "Probably to prevent condensation due to the difference in humidity between Japan and here."

After the wedding, Harvey carried Meg across the threshold to their house. He kissed her, put her down, and opened the closet door.

She slid out of her shoes. "First things first." She

kicked the closet door shut, and hurried toward the bedroom.

He didn't move to follow her. "Don't you want to see what's in these boxes?"

She stopped. "When their time comes, but first let's consummate this marriage." She waved at him to follow her.

"Hold it. Don't you ever get tired?"

"Not of doing that. Do you?"

He grinned. "Occasionally, but we can do it after we find out what's in these crates."

She sauntered back to the foyer. "Okay, old man, where's a hammer?"

He opened the closet door, reached to the top shelf, and brought down a hammer. He grunted as he carried the crates one at a time into the living room, then used the hammer to remove the lid from one. He lifted the cardboard container out and eased it onto the floor. He put the hammer claw into an air hole, pulled a wedge back, and yanked the top off. Meg jumped up and down, dancing with excitement. "I know what they are. Oh, he's so beautiful."

Harvey peered into the box and saw what appeared to be a brown, glazed, ceramic bulldog with a handlebar mustache and goatee. "It's a he all right. Look at the facial hair."

"No, that's not it." She put her finger to its mouth. "See, his mouth is open. That signifies he's in command. The other will have her mouth closed to show the subservience of females."

"That's the way it's supposed to be."

"Not in this house, Boneyard."

"Where'd you pick up that name?"

"I told you before. One of your students."

He started to pry boards off the second crate, but Meg grabbed his hand. "She looks the same except for her mouth."

Harvey put the hammer down. "Why'd we get them?

270

Do they have some significance for newlyweds other than the guy discovering he only thinks he's boss?"

"They're shi-shis, Japanese lions. It's bad luck to have a door on the southwest side of the house. We have one here. If there is a door in that location, it's necessary to put shi-shis on the roof above it. The female, with her mouth closed, keeps the evil spirits out while the male, with his mouth open, invites the good spirits in."

"If I put them on the roof right now, then we'll be safe from your cousins. Right."

She placed her hand on the head of the shi-shi in the open box and combed his ceramic hair with her fingers. "We're safe anyway. Those horny witches are gone for good. I'll help you put these up after we consummate this marriage."

"Isn't that what our honeymoon's for? Plus that, I seem to remember we've done a lot of consummating these past few weeks."

"Then we'll do it again."

She bent down to the box and blew a kiss to the shi shi. Then she searched the room for Harvey, but he wasn't there. "Harvey," she yelled, but he didn't answer. She looked in the bedroom. He was in bed.

"I'm waiting for my lovely wife to join me. Come on-- hurry."